be my reason

Samantha Christy

For my husband, Bruce, who will always be my reason.

'Be My Reason'

Something inside me
Can't rest until I find
The way to make it up to you
The way to make you mine

I know I messed up good
And that you should walk away
I have no right to ask
But I'm begging you to stay

[chorus]
Be my reason…
My cause, my light
Be my reason…
My purpose, my life
'Cause baby it was always you
You're my reason
You've pulled me through

I don't have the words
I just can't understand
How everything about you
Makes me a better man

Something inside me
Just can't let you go
If you could let me in
You could help me grow

Grow into the man
I know that I could be
Because everything in you
Unfolds something about me

[chorus]

[chorus]

Prologue

I've been in love with Nate Riley since the seventh grade. Maybe I was in love with him even before that, but it was during gym class when I was twelve, when he looked straight at me with those gorgeous deep blue eyes and proceeded to hit me with the dodge ball. Hard. That was when I knew I had lost my heart. It was like he had strapped a piece of his own heart right to the red rubber ball and when it hit me, his heart collided with mine. From that day on, there was no one else for me.

Now, four years later, as my best friend Emma and I pull up to the address that Nate had scribbled on the back of his algebra homework for me—a piece of paper I vow never to destroy—I look up and see people funneling into the large house.

"I feel sick," I say, as I press my face against the passenger window trying to cool off my forehead on the glass.

"I don't know what you are worried about, Lyn," Emma says. "Nate is the one who asked you to the party. He already likes you."

"He didn't ask me, Emma, he *told* me about the party. Big difference." I sigh.

"Whatever." She rolls her eyes. "Telling you about a party is code for him wanting you to go so he can hang out with you. Don't worry, he likes you. You'll see."

Emma is always so sure of herself. Maybe I would be too if I had a face that belonged on the cover of a fashion magazine. If I didn't love her so much, I would hate her. But she is the sole reason I have made it this far in high school without jumping off a bridge. I think that if we didn't live next door to each other and hadn't become blood sisters—actual slicing of skin and rubbing hands together blood sisters—when we were eight years old, then we wouldn't even be friends. After all, I'm in the band and the science club and she, well let's just say she hasn't ever had to carry her own books around school. Since kindergarten.

My heart skips a beat when I spot him by the front door as we pass the driveway in search of a place to park. He is standing with some friends, Jake and Brian I think, from the baseball team. He is looking around at the faces that are passing him by as newcomers enter the party. He keeps shifting from one foot to the other like he has to pee. His right hand comes up to run his fingers through his dirty-blonde hair that curls up slightly at his collar and looks like he just rolled out of bed, but at the same time, perfect. *Sigh*. If I didn't know better, I would think he is nervous. Then again, the guy is a gorgeous baseball player and a senior on the varsity team with tons of colleges scouting him, so what could he possibly have to be nervous about?

Emma finds a spot to park a few houses down. "Ready?" She shuts off the engine and looks over at me.

"No . . . yes . . . no," I vacillate.

"Maybe this will help." She grins a Cheshire Cat smile as I see her hand reach under the seat and come up with a couple of those tiny bottles of liquor you see people drink on airplanes in the movies.

"What is that?" My eyes go wide and the surprised look on my face makes her crack up.

"Hmmm." She looks them over ceremoniously. "Whiskey, scotch, vodka . . . does it really matter? They will all taste like crap but will get the job done."

"Uh, what job is that?" I raise my eyebrows at her.

"The one that gets you to loosen up so you can talk to that sexy hunk of a baseball player without tripping all over yourself." This girl knows me all too well.

She hands me one and says, "Together, on the count of three?" Like we are about to grasp hands and leap off a bridge or something. Well, maybe we are. We've never done this before in all of our seventeen years.

I nod my head at her. "One . . . two . . . three . . . " I hold my nose and drink back the liquid that I can only describe as tasting like gasoline—on fire.

After what seems like minutes of making faces that I pray no boy will ever see me make, I cry, "Ewww!" I look over at Emma to see her self-satisfied grin. *What? Why isn't she making hideous faces, too?*

"You don't really think I'm stupid enough to drink when I'm driving tonight, do you?"

"So, all of this was just for me?" I narrow my eyes at her, wanting to be mad but kind of in love with her a little more for being so damn responsible.

"Here." She shoves the other bottle in my face. "Have this one, too. Just don't drink much more at the party or you could end up throwing up all over Nate instead of sucking his face."

I roll my eyes at her and reluctantly drink the second tiny bottle, which seems to taste even nastier than the first since I knew what to expect this time. "At least give me a mint or something so I don't smell like an alcoholic after that." She reaches into her bag and tosses one over to me. I stick my tongue out at her as I exit the car. Then we head back down the sidewalk towards the party.

A minute later, I feel all warm and tingly inside and I wonder if it is the alcohol or my nerves. I glance around as we approach the house and see that everyone has gone inside with the exception of two girls that are sitting on railroad ties by the front porch, both holding a cigarette. At least I hope that's what they are holding. I wouldn't want to be at *that* kind of party.

Going through the front door, it doesn't take us long to locate Nate and his friends as most people have gathered around the large, open kitchen where there is a keg of beer.

You know how they say that when you get into an accident you see your life flash before your eyes? Well, the second my eyes find his and he smiles at me, I am walking up a flower-lined aisle, then holding a strong hand while beautiful dirty-blonde-haired children run around a meadow, then rocking in chairs on a porch, gliding gently while wrinkled fingers intertwine. *Wow, what just happened?*

I take a peek at Emma next to me who is, graciously, pretending she doesn't notice me blatantly staring and quite possibly drooling over the most perfect person ever placed on Earth. She shrugs with a smug little expression on her face and nudges me forward with such force that I practically fall into Nate's arms.

Correction, I fall directly into Nate's arms.

"Oh my gosh, I'm so sorry," I say to him. I can only assume a blood-red blush is creeping up my face as I send a nasty glance back at Emma, who is faking a whistle while looking anywhere but at me.

"It's quite all right, Brooklyn," he says in a strong, raspy voice that is far too sexy for a seventeen-year-old. Then he does a fist bump with his friend who walks away shaking his head and smiling, leaving me alone with Nate.

"Call me Lyn." I try to gather my composure like I didn't literally just fall at his feet.

"But Brooklyn is such a cool name. It's so original. There are tons of Lyn's but I've never known a Brooklyn before." And right then, I love my given name that has always sounded nothing but pretentious to me and that only gets used by my mother.

"So, *Brooklyn*," he says, "can I get you a drink and maybe we could hang out and talk?" He raises his eyebrows awaiting my answer.

"Uh, I guess I'll have a beer." I eye his red cup half-filled with his own. "Let me tell my friend Emma where I will be." Looking around the room I catch her watching my every move, and she mouths, "*I'll be right over here if you need me,*" pointing over to where the rest of the baseball team has congregated. How can she do that, just walk up and become part of a conversation without even trying? I nod my head at her and look back at Nate.

"I'll be right back." He winks, *actually winks*. I think I just melted a little. "You can make yourself comfortable on the couch if you want to." He walks the short distance over to the keg.

I watch a couple of girls come up to him while he is getting my beer. They try to engage him in conversation but he looks back at me, smiles sweetly and gives me a slight raise of the chin. *Damn it, he caught me looking. Again.* I can't help myself.

I look around to see who is at the party. I'm not surprised to find that, although there are familiar faces everywhere, Emma is my one-and-only actual friend here. I've always been what most people call a band geek. I play the flute, which is not easy to do with braces by the way. I love to bake, which is about as un-sexy as it gets, and I run alone almost every day. I run to work off all those calories I eat when I bake and also, it clears my head. Nate and I don't exactly

5

hang around in the same circle of friends which is why I'm probably so nervous being here. I am totally out of my element.

"Here you go." He pulls me back from my thoughts. "Don't drink it too fast. And don't take a drink from anyone but me or your friend, Emma, okay?" Oh, he's trying to protect me, that's nice. But what if *he* put something in my drink? Not that he would have to go to such extremes to be with me. I'm his for the taking.

Uh . . . where did that come from? Would I really be with him, I mean, do it, like, for real? I think if he calls me Brooklyn with that sexy voice of his one more time, I would do just about anything with him.

Over the next hour or so, he tells me about baseball and his dream to play in the major leagues. He tells me a little about his dad who is an architect and his mom who owns a small boutique and spa on the other side of Savannah. But mostly, he asks about me and what I like to do and where I see myself going in life. I don't know if it is the alcohol or the fact that we seem to really be hitting it off but I feel compelled to tell him about my dream.

"I know it's silly, but one day I see myself opening a small bakery right here in Savannah." I look over at him with trepidation and see that he not only doesn't laugh at me but his mouth is hanging open slightly as he contemplates something.

"You are kidding, right?" he questions. "Or are you just messing with me?"

Huh? Now he's lost me. "Messing with you how?"

He studies my face. "You really don't know that before every home game I have to stop by that bakery on Fifth Street to get a red velvet cupcake?" He scrunches his nose just a bit which is freaking adorable, then bites his lower lip while awaiting my response.

"Umm . . . no. How would I possibly know that?" I ask.

"Yeah, I guess you wouldn't," he acquiesces, then goes on to explain how lots of baseball players are superstitious and that two years ago he pitched a no-hitter after eating one of those red velvet cupcakes. So now, he has to do it every time. Every. Single. Time. Or he will lose his edge. "Now who's the silly one?" He sighs.

He's waiting for me to laugh. Or say something. "No, it's not silly. I do the same thing when I have a solo." I shake my head. "Well, not eat a cupcake, but I have this thing I do. It's stupid I know, but I twist my hair like this." I show him how I get a thick chunk of hair by my right ear and twist it until it looks like a wrung towel. Then I add, "I have to do it five times. I think it's the counting and doing something with my fingers that relieves the tension or some psycho-babble like that."

"Wow! We're two of a kind then." He smiles a gorgeous smile that is all teeth as he reaches out to touch my arm gently and I could swear sparks ignite on my skin at the very place that he is touching me. "And I've heard you play a few times when the team walked by the auditorium. You are really good. Great, in fact," he says with . . . pride?

He's heard me play?

Somehow we have managed to inch a little closer to each other over the course of our conversation and now his thigh is touching mine. I can feel the heat from his skin right through our clothes, and it is making me feel even more tingly than the stuff Emma made me drink earlier.

Since I don't pull away, he leans into me a little more and places his hand on my leg, a little above my knee, over my skirt, but not too far up on my thigh. I can't pull my eyes away from his hand on my leg. Nate Riley has his hand on my leg. Nate, hot-and-sexy-senior-baseball-hero, is rubbing little circles on my leg with his thumb sending twinges of electricity right to my core. "Is this okay?" he questions when he finds me so obviously staring at that large, calloused, tan hand of his.

Is this okay? Don't move that hand. Ever!

"Okay, but when I kiss you later, I might have to move it around to your back or something." He smirks.

Holy crap, did I say that out loud? I could die from embarrassment.

Uh, hello? Did he just say he is going to kiss me later?

"Brooklyn . . . ," he whispers, all hot and breathy into my ear, and that's it, I'm dead. I'll do anything for this boy. I hold my breath and wait to see what he says next.

"Lyn!" I practically jump off the couch when I hear Emma call my name right behind me. Wait, what was he going to whisper in my ear? *Damn, Emma!* If she would have waited two seconds . . .

"Huh?" I look up at her with my what-the-hell-could-possibly-be-so-important-that-you-interrupted-me-while-Nate-was-whispering-in-my-ear look.

"I'm so sorry to do this to you but I have to go pick up my mom. Her car broke down and she can't reach my dad on his cell. I would bring you but with my two-seater it would be really cramped and kind of illegal." She looks at Nate but continues talking to me. "I guess I could come back by and pick you up after I go get her and take her home. But I would hate for you to miss curfew because of me."

"Um . . . ," Nate interjects, "why don't I just drive you home later, Brooklyn? I've only had one beer all night and it would be kind of a waste of gas for Emma to drive all over town and then come back and get you."

I look up at Emma and see her visibly exhale the breath she was holding in. "That would be so nice of you, Nate." She smiles. "Lyn, you okay with that?" She stares me down and I know better than to argue with that look. I begin to question whether or not her mom really has a situation.

"I guess." I look at Nate. "Only if you're sure. I mean, I don't mind waiting around for Emma." I immediately curse myself for giving him an out. Why would I want to do anything to jeopardize alone time with Nate Riley? *Please say you're sure, please say you're sure.*

"Yes, I'm sure, Brooklyn." He smiles sincerely and now I'm both nervous and excited to spend another few hours with him.

I hug Emma goodbye and whisper in her ear, "I will so get you back for this." But what I really mean is, 'Thank you.'

Shortly after Emma leaves, the party starts to get out of hand. Someone falls over and breaks a table. A few girls are getting really drunk and suggesting strip poker. I am so uncomfortable here. Why did I agree to stay without the one person who can handle all of this? I'm about to get up and use the phone to try and get Emma back here when Nate leans over and says, "Brooklyn, this is getting kind of crazy, do you want to leave and go for a drive?"

Thank you.

We drive around town and talk for a while. I'm surprised at how much we have to talk about given we are so different. Turns out, we have the same taste in music; we both like scary movies; we both must dip our fries in a chocolate milkshake; but most importantly, we both hate Mr. Goodwin, the advanced biology teacher who never looks at you when he talks and who apparently doesn't believe in wearing deodorant. We laugh telling stories about him and some of the other teachers that he had last year and I have this year.

He takes me for ice cream and pays. *Is this a date?* Then he asks if it is okay if we head down towards The Bend. The Bend is a secluded place where kids sometimes hang out late at night. It is along the Little Black River, just this side of the South Carolina border. There is a place where the river curves around like a hairpin, thus it earned the name The Bend. I'm not even sure it is officially named that or if some kids just made it up. All I know is that legendary things have happened there and I'm about to go there with none other than the gorgeous captain of the baseball team.

We pull into the small makeshift gravel lot to see the place devoid of other cars. He looks around at the empty lot. "We can leave if you aren't comfortable being out here alone."

What, is he crazy? That's why I want to stay! "No, it's okay, we can stay."

"Good." He smiles. "Because I've been dying to kiss you all night." He slides closer to me on the bench seat of his pickup truck. He puts a hand behind my neck and another on my knee. He slowly closes the gap between us, eyes locked onto mine and I'm certain that even in the relative darkness I can see those deep blue eyes of his burning into mine. He shifts his eyes down to see my tongue come out, wetting my lips in an invitation. I can smell him as he inches closer. He smells of clean, fresh laundry and something else that is pure Nate. My heart is pounding out of my chest and I swear I can hear the blood flowing in my ears. His hot breath mingles with mine as he draws even closer, with a slight hesitation, asking me with his eyes if he can continue on this journey.

Oh, yes, please.

I'm not sure what to do with my hands so I just let them fall onto his legs. As our lips touch for the first time, it is like magic the way they connect—like they are two parts of a puzzle finally put into place. His lips gently caress mine in a seemingly never-ending dance of soft touches before I feel his tongue glide across my bottom lip asking for me to give him more. I part my lips for him and his tongue enters my mouth, mingling with my own as heat rises through me along with a wanting that I never knew existed. He tastes of mint chocolate chip ice cream and I silently vow to never again eat any other flavor.

This, right here, is the best moment of my life. We kiss for . . . seconds? Minutes? My lips feel swollen and I struggle to get my breathing under control. I need to know what is going on in his head. I need to know what is going on in *my* head. I pull away slightly and ask, "Why haven't you ever asked me out before?" Then I feel my face heat up. "I mean, not that this is a date." *Oh my God, now he thinks that I think this is a date.*

"I've wanted to all year but baseball takes up so much time and energy. I couldn't blow my chances of getting recruited by a top school," he explains. "But now that the season is over, I have more time to do other things and get to know other people." He smiles down at me. "And, yes, Brooklyn, I'd say this qualifies as a date." He squeezes my knee. "Our first date." He looks at me sweetly.

I'm still stuck on *I've wanted to all year* . . . and then I realize he's said we are on a date. *Holy crap.* A date, a first date, that implies there will be more. I want to twirl around, scream with delight and high-five someone. I catch myself looking around to see if anyone else is witness to me, Brooklyn Vaughn, ordinary band girl and baker wanna-be, on a date with *the* Nathan Riley.

I remember that we are alone and that I've just experienced what I can only describe as the best, most unbelievable, earth-shattering kiss of all time. "Okay then," I say with a small voice because I can't believe what I'm about to tell him. "I guess I wouldn't mind if you did that some more."

He smiles down at me, takes my face in his hands and kisses me again and again until I not only can't feel my lips, but I'm pretty much sure I don't care about anything except his hands on me and what I want those hands to do to me. I think back to the few kisses and over-the-clothes encounters I had with Chris Wright, the lead alto sax player in the band. Those experiences did nothing to prepare me for what I feel when Nate's hands are on me. He pushes up my shirt a little and as he touches my side at my ribs and starts to run his hands upwards, I think I'm going to melt into a pool of hot lava if he continues what he is doing.

Please . . . please continue what you are doing.

He reaches my nothing special, didn't-know-anyone-was-going-to-see-it, bra and breaks our kiss long enough to ask if he can undo it. I don't think I can speak so I simply nod my head and reach down to help him maneuver the clip at the front.

Thank goodness it is so dark outside because I can only picture what I must look like with my top disheveled, my bra hanging off my arms and what I can only imagine must be a look of shock on my face that he wants to do such things with me. Grateful that he leaves my top in place, because I really don't want to look naked if someone pulls up next to us, I lean in and kiss his neck under his ear in a bold move that surprises me but feels so right. "Ah, Brooklyn, that feels so good." I feel him shift around in the seat, trying to arrange himself in his jeans. I'm silently exploding with joy over the fact that I'm affecting him the same way he is affecting me.

His hands caress my meager breasts. The sensation is incredible, sending waves of electricity straight to that bundle of nerves between my legs. I let out an involuntary moan of pleasure which only makes him take in a sharp breath and mutter, "Oh, God."

He takes my hand and places it on his jeans and slowly moves it up his thigh. I can't believe I'm doing this. I'm scared to death but relieved that he is helping me along because I'm not sure I would know what to do. In a leap of faith and certain I may die of embarrassment, I look away shyly and tell him, "Um, Nate, I haven't done this before."

Oh, gods of all virgins that don't know what they are doing, strike me dead now.

He keeps his hand on top of mine and runs his other hand quickly through his hair before placing it under my chin, turning my head so that we are eye to eye. "Would it surprise you to know that I haven't done this before either?" he says. Even through the darkness he notices the shock displayed on my face and he laughs nervously. "Well, I've done *this* before." He squeezes my hand that still rests very close to his hardness. "But I haven't done what I think we are about to do."

I shut my gaping mouth and try to form another coherent sentence. "Are you sure?" I ask. *Yeah, not what I was going for. God, I'm stupid.*

"Am I sure I'm still a virgin, Brooklyn?" he asks with raised eyebrows. "Yes, I'm sure."

All of a sudden the question in the back of my mind—will I or won't I—is answered. Although I'm still nervous as hell, the fear is gone. Hearing that we could do this together, something unknown to both of us, somehow seems even more intimate and exciting.

I start to think about what we are going to do. Will it hurt? I wonder what I will feel like after. Will I have an orgasm and will it feel different than the ones I've had by myself? *Oh, God, will he watch me?* Will I bleed? I wish Emma had prepared me for this.

He thankfully interrupts my silent freak out. "I mean, if you were thinking of doing the same thing, that is."

"Um, Nate . . ." I think carefully about how to ask him this. "If we do this, does it mean, uh . . ." I'm so flustered. "Are we, um—"

"Brooklyn," he cuts me off, "will you go out with me? Like—walk you to class, eat lunch with you and drive you home—out with me?" He grins over at me and I'm still so fully aware of where he has kept my hand during this entire conversation. I'm even more aware of what is lurking underneath it.

If I wasn't completely sure a minute ago, I am now. This boy already owns my heart. He might as well own my body, too. "Yes, I would like that," I say. That makes him smile a smile I've never seen before—one that reaches his eyes. I thought I knew all of them. This one, I think, is reserved just for me.

He moves my hand up to the buttons on his jeans and the intention is clear, he wants me to unbutton them. I do so with trembling fingers but then I'm not sure what should happen next.

Do I reach inside and grab him? Does he take off his pants? How am I supposed to touch him?

He saves me from my dilemma by taking my hands in his, and then using his mouth he trails kisses from my lips down to my neck. Then he follows a path along my jaw up to my ear making me shiver and producing goose bumps up and down my arms. I feel his smile against my skin before he gently sucks on a place behind my ear that has me practically panting. He pulls back, breathing heavily, locks his eyes with mine and puts a hand on my knee, sliding it up my leg and under my skirt, all the way up to the apex of my thighs. I think I am about to combust and then, because I know he is silently asking my permission, I let out the breath I was holding and nod my head slightly.

I can already feel the wetness in my panties and when he touches me there I let out a moan. "Shit, Brooklyn," he murmurs. "If you keep doing that this will be over before we get started."

Really? Note to self: throaty noises drive Nate wild.

He moves my panties aside and slips a finger inside me. I'm so wet now that it just glides in and out easily. He puts a second finger in and I start to feel a burning down deep inside. He again trails feather-like kisses up my neck and around my ears, blowing on the places he just kissed. His hot breath, heavy breathing and soft kisses are only sending me higher and higher. Then he starts circling his thumb around my sensitive nub while keeping up the movement with his fingers still inside me. Soon my thighs tighten and my insides start to quiver.

Oh my God, I'm going to come. "Oh, Nate. Oh, God," I say breathlessly.

"Oh baby, that's it," he whispers. Hearing his voice along with the endearment he uses pushes me over the edge and I'm floating then falling as rapid waves are slithering down my body and I dig my nails into Nate's arm. As I come down from the high, my throat is dry, my lip aches from biting it and even my fingers are tingling.

Before I fully enter reality again, he has pulled down his jeans past his thighs and is pulling me on top of him so that I'm facing him, straddling him and sitting on his knees. He stops to get something from his wallet. It's a condom. *Oh my God, I completely forgot. What if—*

"Brooklyn, are you sure about this?" He pulls me from the thought. "I'll stop right now if this isn't what you want." He looks up at me and I know for certain that he would stop if I asked. I also know for certain that I don't want him to.

"No, Nate. Please don't stop. I'm ready," I beg.

With my panties still pushed to the side, he grabs my hips and oh, so slowly, eases me down onto him. "Jesus, Brooklyn! That feels . . ." His eyes close and his breathing speeds up as he fills me like nothing and no one ever has before.

"Oh, God," I hear myself mutter as I get used to this foreign feeling of being stretched from the inside. It doesn't hurt like I thought it would, a little uncomfortable maybe, but it isn't painful. He starts to move and I feel the fullness and the friction and think that, yes, I could get used to this.

He opens his eyes and watches me as he moves faster and faster. In the moonlight, I can see his mouth open, his eyes glaze over, and his brows scrunch together. Then he shuts his eyes tight and shouts, "Brooke . . . aaaah!" He grabs my hips, holding me still as he finds his release.

We stay together for just a minute and then he helps me climb off him. I wrinkle my nose and wince as we come apart.

"Are you okay? Was that okay?" he asks with concern.

"Yes, I'm okay," I say shyly, not really knowing how to act or what to do at this moment. I pull my skirt down and adjust my panties but it's too dark to see anything clearly. *Oh, please, gods of recently deflowered virgins, let there not be blood all over my skirt.*

He gets rid of the condom and fixes his jeans then reaches over to grab my hand. We sit like this for a little while listening to Nickelback sing *'Someday'*. I wonder if the radio has been on this entire time.

Headlights blind me as a car pulls into the lot. The incredible timing of this is not lost on me. I check my watch and see that I've got only twenty minutes until curfew. "I need to be home by eleven," I remind him.

"Right. We better get going then." He leans over, still holding my hand and places a chaste kiss on my lips before briefly letting go of my hand to start the engine and back out of the lot. He turns the truck around and drives out of the one place that I will remember for as long as I walk this Earth.

We make the short drive to my house in comfortable silence while holding hands and listening to the radio. I smile when he turns into my neighborhood and asks, "Which way?" Then he shrugs because he knows that I know that he knows what neighborhood I live in and that is pretty cool. I direct him to my house and when he pulls up to the curb the first thing I notice is Emma's face peeking out from behind the curtain of her second floor window. I roll my eyes, but smile, knowing I'm in for the Spanish Inquisition.

Nate turns off the engine. "Wait here," he says. He quickly hops out and runs around the front of the truck over to my door and opens it.

Sigh. I could totally get used to this. I get out and he walks me up to the door.

"I have to spend the entire day helping my dad tomorrow, but can I meet you at your locker Monday before school?" he asks me.

Hmm, let me think . . . YES, YES, YES!

"Okay, sure."

"Good. Tonight was really great, Brooklyn." He smiles, leans in and kisses me lightly on the lips and then turns to walk away, looking back at me. "I'll see you Monday then." I watch him walk down the sidewalk to his car, get in and drive away waving a hand out the window as he does.

As I sit on the bus to school, courtesy of Emma's early morning dentist appointment, I think about spending yesterday holed up with Emma, re-living the entire night I spent with Nate down to every minute little detail. Nothing less would satisfy her curiosity. We both cried a little, laughed a lot and there may have even been a high five or two mixed in.

As I glance around, I wonder if I look different because I seem to be getting some strange stares. *Can they tell I'm not a virgin anymore?* Maybe it is just this huge smile I'm wearing this morning.

I hear bits and pieces of conversation through the regular commotion that ensues on the very loud bus. ". . . they just up and left?", ". . . mom was arrested . . .", ". . . my dad said it was prostitution . . .", ". . . Nate say anything?" *Nate?* This gets my attention and I stretch in vain to try and hear more as we pull up to my school.

When I get off the bus, my friend and fellow flautist, Abby, grabs me by the elbow and practically runs me to the nearest bathroom, shooing out everyone that was in there. "What happened with you and Nate this weekend and have you heard anything yet?" she asks, with a worried look on her face that more than concerns me.

I give her the abbreviated version of my Saturday night. Then I ask, "What do you mean have I heard anything yet?"

"Oh, Lyn." She closes her eyes and sighs big. *I mean big.* "I don't know how to tell you this."

"Oh my God, did something happen? Did he get in an accident? Is he dead?" I'm seriously freaking out right now. My hands are getting shaky and she had better start talking or I'm going to beat it out of her.

"Um, his dad took off yesterday with him and his sister. They just up and left. Apparently his mom and some other women were arrested Saturday night. Something to do with running a prostitution ring out of her spa." She looks like she is about to cry as she says, "Nobody seems to know where they went but my friend who lives down the street from Nate said a moving truck showed up late yesterday and totally cleaned out their house."

"What?" I'm trying to process this information. He said he had to help his dad all day yesterday but he didn't say anything about moving. I'm so confused. "He said he would meet me at my locker today." I look up at her like she will have all the answers.

"I'm so sorry, Lyn." She looks at me with a helpless look on her face. "He's gone. Not even his teammates know where he is. I don't think he is coming back." Her voice cracks a little.

My shirt feels wet and I look down at it when it dawns on me that I am crying. I'm crying and I can't breathe. I drop my books, spilling loose papers over the dirty linoleum. I lean over and put my hands on my knees and try to take in a breath, but all I'm getting are short little puffs in and out.

"Lyn, are you okay?" I shake my head at her, unable to talk, barely able to breathe. "I think you are hyperventilating. I'm going to get the nurse." She runs out of the bathroom and I'm alone. Alone, just like he has left me. I back up until I hit the cold, hard concrete wall and I sink slowly down to the floor, struggling to breathe, trying to figure out if my heart is still beating. I know it's not, because it is no longer within me. He took it with him.

Chapter One

Eight years later . . .

"Again, Michael?" I ask through the wave of exhaustion that has taken over my body. "You know I love you, but aren't you worn out yet?"

"Well, you know what they say. If at first you don't succeed—" *Swat!* I hit him playfully on the chest.

"What?" he says. "I really want to get you there and if we keep going, I think I can."

I think men are brainwashed by the movies. I mean, in real life, we don't always come. And we definitely don't always come at the exact same time. In fact, I think I could knock on wood and cross my fingers while hopping on one foot at the precise moment that all the stars align and that still wouldn't happen. But, hey, I guess all this trying doesn't exactly hurt my chances.

"I wish you would understand that it's good for me even when I don't always come." *Besides, I can always get myself off later.*

"Lyn," he whines, when he notices the scowl on my face, "I just want to send you off with a bang. I'm going to miss you so much."

He's so cute when he pouts. I smile up at him. "It's only for a week. Plus, you'll be at the hospital so much that you won't even know I'm gone."

"Sweetheart, one day without you is too long." He kisses my cheek as he springs out of bed. Who springs out of bed at five o'clock in the morning? Oh, right, third-year residents who are used to living on four hours of sleep. "I'd better get going anyway. I've got rounds in thirty," he says. I smile as I watch his perfectly sculpted ass head towards the bathroom. I bring my knees up to my chest and cover myself with the bed sheet as I thoughtfully watch him through the open bathroom door.

Michael's toned abs tighten and relax as he bends over to brush his teeth. His reddish-blonde hair is cut short to fit under his scrub cap. I wonder if someday he'll grow it out a little so I could run my fingers through it. As he gets into the shower, I pad into the bathroom and grab his toothbrush—a habit of mine ever since I first stayed the night at his place. It feels so intimate, like I'm part of him somehow. I stand and stare at myself, toothbrush in mouth, and ponder what I see in the mirror. My skin—far too pale for my wavy dark-as-night hair—stands out even more now that I've lost that summer glow. The nose I got from my dad is too pointy, but I make up for it with Mom's green eyes. I lean over to spit in the sink and jump when I rise back up. "Ahhh, Michael!" I scream half-heartedly as he reaches around to grab my breasts.

"Mmmm," he murmurs. "They fit perfectly in my hands." He smiles at me in the mirror, eyeing his toothbrush hanging from my mouth. "You know, now that we're engaged, don't you think you should at least have your own toothbrush at my place?" I shrug my shoulders, watching him run his hands down my hips as I reach for a towel.

"Lyn, you don't need to cover up in front of me. You are so beautiful," he says so sweetly that I know he thinks it's true, even if it's not. It's not that I think I'm fat, just curvy. But I think women are conditioned to believe that if anything jiggles, except our boobs, it is a bad thing. So that is why I run. And with all of the running I do to keep the pounds off, my legs and butt have become my best features.

He slips a t-shirt over his head and quickly dresses in the requisite light-blue resident scrubs. "Everything covered at the shop?" he questions. "Is Kaitlyn good running the show all week alone? I could swing by and help her out," he says, with not so much as a thought to his own killer schedule. I can't help but love this man for all of his self-sacrificing qualities.

"Got it covered," I assure him, as I gather my hair into a messy bun and throw on last night's clothes. "But it is so sweet of you to ask." I give him a quick peck on the cheek and head out to the kitchen to wait in a trance for the automatic coffee maker to finish brewing my sanity.

I sit at the bar, tracing my finger over the shiny, smooth scar on the back of my right hand as I think back to when I met Michael. Although it was almost two years ago, it seems like just yesterday. I was twenty-three and starting out with the bakery when I suffered a pretty bad burn to my hand that landed me in the hospital. He was a first-year resident doing his ER rotation.

"Miss Vaughn?" he said, entering the room while looking down at the paperwork so that I could only see the top of his head. "It says here that you burned your right hand. Can you tell me what happened?" He fumbled a bit with the paperwork and snuck a look behind him. Then he looked up at me all nervous-like, but obviously trying to look like he knew what he was doing.

Oh, this doctor is seriously good looking, I thought. I had all but forgotten about my hand that, merely a moment before, felt like it was searing over hot coals lit on fire from the depths of hell. Thank God that I didn't have to remove any clothing or get into a compromising position in front of Doctor Adonis. I shook my head at the horrid thought.

"B-Brooklyn," I said quietly. *Dang it!* I thought. *Did I just stutter? What am I, twelve?*

"Brooklyn? Is that where you sustained the burn?" he questioned, with a little furrow between his eyes like he was trying to figure something out. "Is that an area of Savannah? I'm pretty new here . . . uh, to Savannah, not the hospital. Well, I'm a first-year so I am new to the hospital, but what I meant to say was that I don't know much about the area. I haven't been exploring yet but I hope to very soon if I can find a local to show me around." He looked at me long and deep like I hadn't just burned the crap out of my hand and wasn't in need of medical attention.

"Ahem," I heard. I looked behind him to find the source of the interruption. There was another doctor standing in the doorway staring him down. That seemed to get him to regain his composure rather quickly.

Red crept up his face which brought out the auburn in his light hair, making him appear sexier, if at all possible. "So, you were saying about Brooklyn?" He was flustered just like I was.

Was he flirting with me? Why would he be? He was a doctor for heaven's sake and I'm me. I couldn't pull my eyes away and was probably beginning to look a little stupid staring up at him like that.

"Yes. Uh, no. I mean, yes I got burned at Brooklyn's. It's my bakery and I was so stupid wearing a bracelet while getting my trays from the oven. It got caught and I couldn't pull it loose and my hand started burning and it smelled awful and there was screaming and maybe a little crying, and finally it came out but I broke my bracelet so Emma is going to freak because she gave it to me for my birthday . . ." *Oh, God kill me now! Just stop talking,* I thought. He probably assumed I was crazy, going on and on like that.

Then I added, "But, it's also my name." I looked up into those grey-as-steel eyes and tried to get myself together. Was my mascara running? Why didn't I look in the mirror before arriving? Of course it's running, you dimwit, I thought. You were crying which also means your eyes are puffy and you look like hell in general.

"Your name?" he said, still looking confused from my rambling.

"Brooklyn. It's my name. You called me Miss Vaughn. Please call me Brooklyn, well . . . Lyn," I squeaked out, thankful that I could complete a sentence.

He smirked. Did that mean he thought I liked him? Well, okay maybe I did but that didn't mean he should smirk at me. "Okay, Brooklyn or Lyn, the girl and the bakery, call me Doctor Michael. Let's have a look at this." Back in full doc mode then because, well I was hurt and, well, I could only guess that was his boss still standing behind him with that stern look on his face. But don't think I didn't see him look up at me repeatedly with a gorgeous grin only to catch me staring right back at him. Damn that guy in the doorway, I thought. Leave hot Doctor Michael and me alone!

I smile to myself when I remember that Michael referred to his boss as a 'cockblocker'.

Let's just say I was completely bummed that Dr. Cockblocker never left that doorway and a follow up visit with Michael was not going to be required. On the way home that day, I had even started considering other 'accidents' I could have to send me back to the ER.

To think that this same man, my Doctor Michael, will be mine for the rest of my life. Well, as soon as we can get around to setting a wedding date that is. With his rigorous schedule, we may never get around to it. His specialty, pediatric cardiology, is especially strenuous since it is in fact, two specialties. After this year he will have to get a fellowship somewhere which presents a whole new set of problems. Although he works at Memorial Health here in Savannah now, he will need a children's hospital for his fellowship and he will have to go where the offers are. Right now, the closest option is still more than three hours away at Egleston Children's Hospital in Atlanta. *Three hours.* Can we survive a long-distance marriage?

I don't think I could bring myself to close Brooklyn's. I put blood, sweat and tears into my bakery. It is the one thing I've accomplished in my twenty-five years that is all mine. Okay, so maybe I'm just barely breaking even after paying my expenses. I can't even begin to think of relocating the shop, I could never get as good a deal on rent as I have now. My best friend and roommate, Emma, owns the space where my bakery is along with our two-bedroom apartment directly upstairs in a trendy little area of Savannah. I know the going rate for retail space and she more than cut it in half for me. Plus, I couldn't leave her high and dry. What am I thinking? I can't live without Emma. I can't leave Savannah, can I? But I can't live without Michael either.

". . . coffee?"

What?

"Sweetheart, did you hear me?" Michael says, ripping me from my nightmare of having to choose between my best friend—my female soul mate, my surrogate sister—and my fiancé.

"Do you have time for a quick coffee?" he asks again, looking at me so sweetly.

"Of course I do." I smile weakly, happy to be torn from my depressing thoughts of tough choices ahead. "I have a few minutes before swinging by the shop to make sure Kaitlyn is all set up and then I'll meet Emma at my apartment."

"Are you excited to go to Raleigh?" he asks, pouring my coffee.

"Mmm hmm," I mumble.

"I'm sorry that I can't be the one to experience it with you for the first time." He frowns. "I'll make it up to you. I promise that when I make Attending, I'll have more time for vacations and then you and I will have lots of firsts together."

"We already have lots of firsts," I assure him. "First fiancé, first ER injury, first Christmas as a couple—"

"But not *the* first," he interrupts, looking sad. "I wish we would have had our first time together. I hate the idea that some horny little shmuck who couldn't keep his dick in his pants had you before me."

I sputter my coffee onto the counter. "Oh my God, Michael, I can't believe you just said 'dick'! You are always so clinical. And why would you make me think of that loser anyway?"

"Okay, penis," he acquiesces. "You know, he may have been a horny little shmuck, but he most definitely was not a loser if he set his sights on you." *Could he get any sweeter?* "What was his name, Nick, Norman, Neil?"

"Michael, he did not have his sights set on me. His name was Nate. I had a high school crush on him. He used me for one night and then I never saw him again." *See, loser.*

Dang, now I'm in a bad mood when I'm about to leave and not see Michael for a whole week. Wanting to leave on a happy note, I look up at him through my lashes. "Um, so let's get back to all the things you are going to do to make it up to me."

"Oh, I plan to make it up to you all right, in all kinds of ways and in all kinds of positions." He raises an eyebrow. "That all right with you, future Mrs. Brooklyn Bridges?"

"Hmmpf. I don't know what kind of sick joke fate is trying to play on us." I can't help rolling my eyes. "But for the millionth time, I will *not* be taking your name," I assert.

"I know, *Ms.* Vaughn, and I understand. But it is still fun as hell to tease you about it."

I smile at my perfect guy as he gets up from the bar with our mugs, takes them over to the sink and rinses them before placing them in the dishwasher. "Now get your pretty little butt over here and give me a proper good-bye."

His eyes darken and watch my every move as I deliberately and slowly lick my lips when I saunter around the counter towards him. He is focused on my mouth when I reach out and place my hand on his chest. "I'll miss you so much," I whisper. I kiss him slowly at first; then I want him to know what he'll be missing so I work my tongue into his mouth and tangle it with his before I suck gently on his tongue until he makes little moaning noises. Then he grabs my head, deepens the kiss and presses the length of his body, hardness and all, against mine, grinding ever so slowly. *Damn, he gives as good as he gets.*

I can feel him smile against my lips. He knows what he is doing to me. Well, at least I'm not the one who has to adjust myself while heading out the door. He pulls away still gripping me tightly. "Time to go, sweetheart. Don't forget to text me and don't be upset if it takes me awhile to get back to you. You know how busy it gets at the hospital."

He holds my hand as we walk downstairs to the parking lot. He opens the door to my less-than-impressive car and plants a kiss on my cheek. "Be safe and have fun. But not too much fun, I know how Emma can get."

"I love you, Lyn," he says, staring down at me with so much meaning in his eyes.

"You too, Michael." I look up at the face that I will miss so terribly for the next few days. "And don't worry about Emma, she'll be all work and no play in Raleigh."

He closes my door and watches as I back out and drive away.

~ ~ ~

It never gets old turning onto my street and seeing my name—*my name*—emblazoned in hot pink over the outline of a light-blue cupcake twenty feet up over the entrance of my shop. After earning my Certified Pastry Culinarian designation from Savannah Tech, and saving almost every cent I made babysitting, waitressing and temping, and okay, I'll admit a lot of help from Emma, I was able to start a small bakery. It still feels like a dream to have my own shop. My mom and I used to bake together when I was little. I can remember being seven years old and realizing what I wanted to be when I grew up.

Mom smiled down at the confectionary creation I had attempted with the admiration only a mother can have for something that looked so hideous. "Brooklyn, you can be whatever you want when you grow up as long as it is something you are passionate about. There are no limits to what you can do. You could be a teacher, like Daddy, or a Mommy like me, or a doctor or scientist. You could even be a baker and make wonderful cakes like this one."

My eyes widened and my smile about split my face in two when I realized one could actually bake. For a job. And make money. That was it for me. From that day on, if I wasn't at school, I was making a mess in Mom's kitchen. God love her, she never complained about cleaning up after me.

A flash of pink catches my eye and I look over to see Kaitlyn, my one and only employee, as she pops her pink-streaked head of hair out the door to put up the daily special board. I quickly drive around back, park by Emma's Beemer and Kaitlyn's Beetle, which is—surprise—pink, and make my way in through the back door.

I'm immediately struck once again by the powerful and intoxicating smell of fresh muffins and cinnamon rolls baking to perfection. I hope I never get tired of this. I don't want running the shop to ever become just another day at the office. Bakery air is just too good to take for granted.

I know Emma is waiting for me upstairs and I am running a few minutes late but I need to hit the shop for a second. I pass by the doorway that has stairs leading up to our apartment and I head on through the kitchen to the front of the bakery that smells of fresh coffee.

I see Kaitlyn setting up the pastry cases for the fresh stock. I look around the shop which is really too large for its purpose. The morning light streaks through the front windows that a local artist has adorned with etchings of baked goods. The mixture of low and high-top tables, along with the few booths that I added, give it an eclectic, yet quaint feel.

I head over to the coffee station behind the counter to grab some to-go cups for myself and Emma. "Hey, boss. You ready for your road trip?" Kaitlyn looks up as she sips from one of the oversized Brooklyn's Bakery mugs Michael had made for my last birthday.

"I don't know." I sigh, looking around at my shop thinking about how I will miss it this week. "Maybe I should stay. I mean, five whole days on your own here is an awful lot for me to ask of you," I say, knowing full well that is not why I'm reluctant to leave.

"Lyn, are you crazy?" she practically shouts. "I live for this. You know I need this to see if one day I can maybe open my own place. Plus, you know your mom will probably stop by every day to help out."

I know she is right. My mom and biggest cheerleader, second to Emma, stops by almost daily. She also insists on working one morning a week to give me time off. She conveniently schedules that morning to coincide with Michael's day off. She refuses to let me pay her, saying that this is what you do for family and just wait until I have a daughter one day and I'll understand. That is just one of the perks of living in the same city as my parents. Also another reason not to leave Savannah.

"Okay, if you're sure." I start to go into the kitchen. "I'll do a quick check in the back to make sure you have everything you need."

She watches me walk past her and through the large swinging door; the kind of door that you see in restaurants with a giant round window at face level. I know exactly what she's thinking because she knows that I checked everything just yesterday. Twice. "I know you are rolling your eyes at me Kay," I say without turning around.

"Hmmpf," I hear. "Don't let that back door hit you in the ass on the way out," she says. "You know I love you, Lyn. Don't worry about a thing."

In the large kitchen that has become my second home, I run my hand along the shiny stainless handle of the large baking oven that I will probably never pay off in my lifetime. I hold up my right hand and thoughtfully regard my scar. I don't hold a grudge; it was my own fault for wearing that chunky charm bracelet. I learned my lesson. I will never wear a bracelet again. To the left of the oven are the cooling racks that already hold dozens of heavenly breakfast treats for the morning crowd. Taking in a long, slow breath through my nose, I again drown in the almost sickly-sweet smell that has become the favorite part of my morning. *Other than waking up next to Michael.* My mom had the brilliant idea to place the cooling racks by the only window in the kitchen so that when weather allows, we can open it which practically guarantees that anyone within a quarter-mile will follow the mouth-watering smell to find the source.

I pluck a low-fat blueberry muffin from the rack for myself and a cinnamon roll for Emma, thinking how totally unfair it is that she never has to count calories like I do. And then I add more gooey fat-filled cream cheese topping to hers just for good measure. Then I head to the back of the kitchen and up the stairs to where Emma is undoubtedly tapping her foot on the ground waiting for my arrival.

Chapter Two

"Hey, Thelma," I hear as I walk through the door to our upstairs apartment.

"Thelma?"

"Oh, come on," Emma whines, as I round the corner into the small but impeccably designed living room that separates our bedrooms. "I know you don't watch a lot of TV, but you have to know who Thelma is."

"Flintstone?" I raise my eyebrows at her in question.

"Really, Lyn, you must get your head out of those business books and hang out on the couch watching old movies once in a while," she admonishes me. "Thelma. As in Thelma and Louise. As in we are BFFs going on a road trip. Sound familiar?"

"Whatever." I roll my eyes as I place her breakfast on the coffee table and head over to my bedroom. "I'm taking a quick shower and then we can leave. I've already got my suitcase packed and ready to go so I won't take long." I shut my bedroom door as I hear her mumble something about Brad Pitt in a cowboy hat.

In the shower I mentally go through the list of things I must not forget to take. My books and my notes top the list as I'll be studying for finals in our hotel room when Emma is at the convention. Although I hate to admit it, being away from the bakery this week will be kind of a blessing. It will allow me to concentrate on studying for the last three finals I have in my on-line business classes before I graduate in a few weeks. I smile at myself. I will soon be a college graduate and although it took me twice as long as most people, I'm finally going to earn my degree in small business management.

I quickly dry my hair, letting it stay in long, loose waves. I put on some mascara and lip gloss and dress in something semi-professional because I will have to accompany Emma to the convention today since our hotel room won't be ready until after three o'clock.

After we struggle to get our bags down the stairs, I can't help but poke my head around the corner into the bakery kitchen and look longingly through the window to the front at the morning crowd that has started to trickle in. "Don't even think about it, Lyn." She grabs the strap of my bag and pulls me along. "We have to leave now if we want to make it in time for the keynote speaker."

I reluctantly follow her out the back door. "Tell me again why I'm going to a design and build convention with you when I own a bakery?"

"Because you love me and you want to support your BFF who happens to be the best corporate interior designer in Savannah." She smiles brightly with her chin up.

"Oh, you mean there is more than one?" I tease.

"Bitch." She slaps my arm playfully. "Plus you know I won't know a single person there so I need you for moral support and after-hours fun so I don't sit and stare at the walls of the hotel room."

As we pack our bags into the trunk of her car and head out, I think about what she said. She doesn't need moral support. My best friend does not know any strangers and with her looks, she would not be at a loss for people wanting to hang out with her. I think it is just an excuse to get me away from work for a while and 'let loose' as she says. I guess I'm okay with this, as long as she doesn't expect me to 'let loose' the way that she does. Emma doesn't date men. She sleeps with them and then moves on. She never seems to develop feelings for any of them and she seems completely okay with that. I, on the other hand, am quite the opposite. I couldn't imagine going from one guy to the next and never having a connection with them. I've slept with two guys in my life and that's one too many if you ask me.

As we head toward the Interstate, we inevitably pass the dirt road the leads to The Bend, a place I haven't visited in eight years and never plan to set foot on again.

Emma looks over at me sympathetically. "What?" I snap at her.

"Nothing. I was just wondering if it still bothers you to drive by this place."

Maybe I do drive out of my way sometimes to avoid it. Okay, if I'm being honest, I take the beltway in the opposite direction, twenty minutes out of the way, to the only other road that gets me to my parents' house. "Not in the slightest," I lie and take a few silent deep breaths.

"Mmm hmm," she mumbles. "That's why you won't open your eyes right now or look over in that direction. Oh, and your fingers are turning white from the way you are squeezing the seat."

"Hmmpf," is all the response she gets from me. "I think I'm going to crash for a little bit." I close my eyes and drift off, trying not to think of a certain dirty-blonde-haired boy who loved to play baseball.

We make the four-hour drive to Raleigh in record time, only stopping once for gas and a drive-thru burger that will add two miles to my run tomorrow. We switch drivers at the gas station so that Emma can freshen up before reaching our destination. We arrive just in time for her to see the speaker she was talking about. But only if I drop her off at the front so she can run in while I navigate the massive parking lot to find a spot.

"This thing lasts about two hours. Go to the main hall to browse the exhibits and I'll text you after my session so we can meet up." She hops out of the car and hurries into the huge convention hall.

I drive down row after long row of cars to finally find a spot about a half-mile from the building. "Are there really this many designers and architects?" I say out loud to myself.

After pulling into the spot, making sure to leave plenty of room on either side, lest Emma kill me about getting a ding in her 'baby', I pull out my phone and send a text to Michael.

Me: **Made it to Raleigh. Miss you already.**

I'm about halfway to the convention hall when my phone chirps at me.

Michael: **Glad you are safe. Miss you too. Bed will feel lonely tonight.**

Me: **Only four nights. We'll make up properly on Friday.**

Michael: **Looking forward to it. On call, have to go. Call me later tonight. Love you.**

Inside the huge convention hall, I follow the signs to the conference wondering what I will do to keep myself busy for a few hours. I settle on people-watching. It is always good to help pass the time. Many of the people here are dressed professionally, which is why I'm wearing my black pencil skirt and light-pink fitted blouse to try and look like I belong. Emma once told me that interior designers are very big on appearances because if they don't look like a million bucks, how would a client think they could design something that does? Who can argue with that logic? I have no trouble distinguishing the architects from the designers—it seems the architects didn't get the memo on the dress code. They are mostly on the casual side, some even donning t-shirts and jeans.

One such guy I see over by the hallway to the restrooms. I can only see the back of him, and what a nice back side he has. He is leaning in and kissing a beautiful redheaded woman, who herself is impeccably dressed. I look around to see if anyone else notices this inappropriate behavior but apparently I am the only people-watcher at the moment.

I move across the massive hall, far away from Mr. Inappropriate-nice-ass and spot a table of baked goods. Oh, this I can handle. It is a small but tastefully done banquet table with displays of hundreds of bite-sized goodies such as cupcakes, petit fours and miniature cookies. I reach for a red velvet cupcake and roll my eyes at the fleeting memory of the night it became my favorite confection. I brace myself for the sweet vanilla taste with that hint of chocolate and gooey cream cheese frosting, then I silently curse when I pop a piece in my mouth and it doesn't fulfill my expectations. Ick, this is bad. I should know. It took years for me to perfect my own recipe so I know a good red velvet cake when I taste one. And this is not it.

Inspiration strikes me as I look at the sumptuous display. I should start catering. There are plenty of places like this in Savannah. Well, maybe not this big, but on a smaller scale. I have already planned on trying to find investors to help me expand my business as soon as I graduate. I would love to hire another person and perhaps get another location. Maybe catering could fit into this plan as well.

I pitch the rest of the unfinished cupcake into the nearest bin and go in search of a bottle of water to wash the taste from my mouth. I see a drink station across the main hall and make my way over there, taking time to peruse some of the design displays set up in booths. Along the way, I once again see the back of Mr. Nice-ass as he is rubbing his hands up and down the arms of that bimbo. Uh, wait, no . . . new bimbo. This one is blonde. Damn, he is really working this place. I must get a look at his face and maybe introduce him to Emma. He is definitely her type.

Mr. Playboy and Blondie disappear to God knows where, I really don't want to know, and I decide to kill some time listening to my iPod and reading one of my textbooks. I get lost in the music and my studies for a while and am startled when Emma kicks at my toe, pulling me from my academic trance. I look up at her and she is all giddy. *Emma, giddy*? And she is standing next to a really cute guy.

"Lyn," she says, as I pull the buds from my ears, "meet Graham. He is a junior partner at an architectural firm here in Raleigh and he has agreed to show us around while we are in town." Her eyes widen as she stares me down and I know she is silently willing me to go along with this. "He said there is this great place to eat called the Angus Barn."

"Nice to meet you, Lyn," he says. "Emma tells me you aren't in the business but that you own a bakery. That's cool. And she said you are engaged. Congratulations."

He shakes my hand with a firm but gentle shake that doesn't linger too long. Okay, points for that. He is cute, but not one of those gorgeous, model-types Emma usually goes for. He is tall, of course, since she prefers guys much taller than her five-eight frame, but still I would be surprised if he were over six feet tall. He's fit looking but not too buff, has dark hair and a nice, round face with a good amount of stubble. Kind of looks like a big teddy bear to me, like someone you can cuddle up with and tell all your secrets to.

"Um . . . thanks. Nice to meet you, too. So you two got a lot out of that keynote speech I see," I say, smiling and shaking my head at my friend and her new boy toy.

Graham laughs and says, "People mainly come to these things to make business connections. We could care less about the speakers and workshops, but we go because our employers expect us to."

"Graham and his partner have a lot of connections on the East Coast so I think it would be great for me to hang out with them some while we are here," she says, looking down at me with puppy-dog eyes. *Who is this creature and what has she done with my best friend?*

"Them?" I raise my eyebrows.

"Yeah. Graham is going to bring his partner to dinner." She holds her hand up to stop my next words. "Don't worry, it's not a date or anything, it's just work stuff."

"Lyn," Graham adds, "it's nothing to worry about. This is purely platonic."

I'm not worried. First, I'm engaged. Second, I know Emma would never try to hook me up simply so *she* could. It's just that I'm not exactly comfortable with strangers and what could I possibly have in common with a junior partner in architecture?

"Anyway, he doesn't, um . . . date." He blushes slightly.

"Oh, he's married?" I question. I guess we could talk about our significant others.

He shakes his head.

"Gay?" I ask, my eyes widening. Maybe we could talk clothes and shoes and who won best dressed at the Oscars?

He shakes his head again. "Uh . . . he's kind of a player. But you have nothing to worry about being that you're engaged and unavailable. He will probably grab a quick bite with us and then head out to see whoever he picked up today." He says looking embarrassed for his friend.

"Sounds like a winner." *And a perfect guy for Emma.* Maybe she should dump Mr. Polite-teddy-bear and go after his friend.

"He really is great. Just misguided I'd say." He shrugs. "Well, I have to get on to my next workshop. It was nice meeting you, Lyn and I'll see you two later tonight." He walks away and winks at Emma as she shamelessly watches every step he takes across the expansive room.

I wave my hand in front of her face to get her attention. "What has gotten into you, Emma? I'm not sure I've ever seen you drool over a man before. I may have to get a mop over here to clean up this puddle you've made."

She swats my arm and says, "He is seriously hot. And smart . . . really smart. He has great ideas about how design and architecture work together. He's running a class on it later this week. That reminds me, I have to go change my schedule." She sighs. "Shit, Lyn, I may be in love," she teases.

"Yeah, that'll be the day. You've never even given a guy your phone number, let alone a second date." I shake my head at the thought. I love Emma to death and she is seriously smart—as in she tested at the genius level in tenth grade—but she is the queen of love 'em and leave 'em.

She looks at me like the cat that ate the canary.

"What?" I ask her.

"I may have already given him my number," she says. Then she tucks her lips into her mouth and scrunches her eyebrows.

She did not. "You did not!"

"Yup," she says.

"Wow!" I'm dumbstruck. I nod my head and say, "I'm so proud of you Emma Crawford. What a big step for womankind." I look around almost sad for all of the guys at this conference that won't get to brag to their friends about the things they did with my BFF this week.

"Ha. We'll see. Right now I have to get to my next session. This one only lasts forty-five minutes and then I'm done for today." She starts to walk away before she adds, "I'll meet you right here after, okay?" I nod and open up my book again when my phone chirps.

A text from Kaitlyn. I smile. I wasn't going to check in with her for another—I check my watch—fifteen minutes.

Kaitlyn: **Just letting u know b4 u bombard me with ur worried texts and calls that everything is going great. Good morning crowd today. Delivery went well. No need to call, I got this!!!**

Me: **K you are my absolute favorite employee. Remind me to take you to dinner when I get back. Hugs**

Kaitlyn: **Lyn, I'm your ONLY employee so that doesn't hold a lot of weight. U know I love u and I'll take u up on that dinner. Later.**

Thirty minutes and two chapters later, eye fatigue sets in and I check my watch. It's almost time to meet Emma. I get up to find the nearest bathroom. A few minutes later, after I wash up, I'm walking out to look for Emma. There are a lot of people standing around now and I realize the conference must be over for the day.

I'm wandering through the people, slowly making my way over to where Emma left me before, when my eyes catch those of a guy who is looking at me from across the room. He looks familiar. What is it about him? He is totally checking me out. Yes, my athletic legs look good in this pencil skirt. *Mental high five.* His eyes travel further north. *Oh, crap.* I realize who he is. He is Mr. Playboy from earlier. The nerve of him, is two not enough? His eyes reach my face and he stares at me for a long moment and then his face pales—actually loses all color—and his mouth drops open as he runs his right hand through a mess of dirty-blonde hair.

Oh God, no, no, no. My heart sinks. I try to catch my breath and my hand comes up to cover my mouth to muffle the shocking cry coming out of it. I turn in the opposite direction and walk as fast as my three-inch heels will allow. I hear him call from far behind me, "Brooklyn, wait!"

Oh God, that voice. That voice that has haunted my dreams for eight years. I walk even faster. I'm almost at a full-on run when I see Emma appear in a doorway.

Her smile drops immediately when she lays eyes on me. "What's wrong, Lyn?"

"I have to get out of here," I say, flying past her. I look over my shoulder and see that nobody is following me, but that doesn't slow down my exit. I have to get out of the building. Now. The walls are closing in on me and I start to feel sick. I can't breathe. I can't think. So I run.

"Lyn, wait!" Emma yells behind me. Her plea does nothing to slow me down.

I reach the exit, plow through the glass door and am temporarily blinded by the bright light of the setting sun but I keep going, unsure if I'm even headed in the direction of Emma's car. I don't really care as long as I'm leaving behind the one person who had wrecked me, scarred me and left me gutted unlike any other.

I'm not sure how long I've been running when it dawns on me that my feet hurt. I look around and don't know where I am. I glance back to see what is now a small building behind me in the distance and what appears to be Emma, still trying to catch up with me, her stilettos no match for my more practical wedges. I slip in between two large SUVs and crouch down to try to catch my breath and absorb what has just happened. Did I even see him? Did that really happen? Am I sure it was him?

"Lyn!" Emma is frantic when she finds me cowering among the vehicles. "What the hell is happening? Talk to me," she demands.

I'm bent at the waist still trying to catch my breath. I can feel a bead of sweat trickle down between my breasts. I hold up a finger asking her to wait while I compose myself. I close my eyes and hope that what just happened was a hallucination or some weird phenomenon due to being in a strange city with unfamiliar people.

Breathe, Lyn. I grab a chunk of hair on the right side of my head and twist it. One . . . two . . . three . . . four . . . five. I'm starting to calm down. I do the ritual two more times.

Emma is patiently waiting and I can tell she doesn't know what to do. She looks ready to cry. I need to tell her what I think just happened. I'm not sure I can even say the words. I look up at her and feel wetness roll down my cheeks. I whisper the two words I never thought I would say again. "Nate Riley." And then I spectacularly lose my lunch all over the shiny wheels of some poor guy's new Tahoe.

Chapter Three

After checking in at the hotel that is right around the corner from the convention hall, we go up to our two-bedroom suite that Emma has graciously paid for. I am silently grateful that she has her own room in case she decides to have any late-night company. The suite is tastefully decorated with contemporary art and large but comfortable looking furniture. It smells like lilies, thanks to the large flower arrangement adorning the coffee table.

I thank the concierge for bringing in my bag and then immediately head into the bathroom to clean up my vomit-spattered shoes. They are my favorite wedges or I would simply throw them in the trash.

Once I'm sure they are perfectly clean, I glance up into the mirror to see my pale mascara-streaked face complete with puffy eyes. *God, Lyn, you are pathetic.* Did I really just throw up, in a public place no less, over a guy? I guy I haven't seen in eight years? That is plain stupid. I think it must have been food poisoning from that greasy drive-thru cheeseburger I had for lunch. I clean up my face and brush my teeth and then take off my clothes, swapping them for the hotel robe I see hanging on the back of the bathroom door.

When I make it out to the living room, Emma is already on the couch with two drinks sitting on the coffee table in front of her. "Sit." She pats the cushion next to her.

"Cosmos?" I eye the pale-red liquid in the martini glasses as a smile tries to creep up my face.

"Thought you could use one."

"I love you, Emma. You know that, right?" I sit next to her and give her a hug.

"I love you, too, girl. More than anyone in this lifetime." She pulls back but still keeps her hands on my arms. "What do you want to do? If you want to go home, we can leave right now." I know she means it.

"What? Of course I don't want to go home. We just got here and you have much more schmoozing to do and many more connections to make. Plus, it's not like I'm going to see him again since I'll be staying at the hotel studying while you are at the conference." I pick up my glass, take a drink and savor the sweet burn of my favorite cocktail.

"Yes, but just knowing you are in the same city as that slime ball—won't it drive you crazy?"

Well, I hadn't considered that, but now that she's brought it up . . . *yes*.

"Slime ball," I roll the words over my tongue. "Emma, you have no idea. I saw him a few times earlier in the day when you were in your sessions, but I didn't see his face so I didn't know it was him. He was all over these women, *different* women. He was kissing them and caressing them and disappearing down the hall with them." I sigh. "It's like it wasn't even him. He was never like that in high school. Then again, that was a long time ago. Today he was . . . well he seemed . . . well, like the male you." I shrug.

"So, maybe it wasn't really him, but someone who looks a lot like him. His, what do you call it . . . doppelganger? Anyway, what does it matter what he is like or if it was really him? He is a low-down dickhead slime ball who isn't worth getting upset over."

I smile weakly at her choice of colorful words. "I know. It's just that I never expected to see him ever again. Early on, after he left, I thought he might come back, but then after graduation, I kind of gave up hope." I take another drink. "And, yes, I'm sure it was Nate. When he realized it was me, he turned white as a ghost. He even called my name." I close my eyes remembering the sound of his voice today after so many years of hearing it only in my head.

"Lyn, maybe we should cancel tonight. We can hang out here, get toasted on Cosmos and order up 'Thelma and Louise' on the TV."

"Are you crazy? And waste an opportunity to see *the* Emma Crawford fall all over herself because of a guy? No way. We are going out and I won't give that bastard another thought."

"Oh, thank you, thank you, thank you." She hugs me hard. "I really like Graham. And I'm not talking about just wanting to get in his pants and see how big his dick is. I want to find out about his job and his family and crap like that," she rambles. "How weird is that?"

"Precisely why we need to go to dinner and see where this thing with him is going. What time are we supposed to be there?"

She checks her diamond encrusted watch. "About an hour, you good with that?"

~ ~ ~

Emma scoots to the inside of a booth and I sit down next to her. She gives me a look so I say, "What? I'm not about to sit by Graham's friend. You two will just have to rub knees under the table or something."

We order our usual Diet Cokes and talk about some of the interesting design exhibits that I saw earlier today. I tell her about my catering idea and she says she will talk to her dad, who is a corporate banker, about ways to find investors after we get back. She is telling me about her last session of the day on lighting in design when a big smile creeps up her face. "They are here. Do I look okay?" She quickly pats down her stick-straight hair then takes a drink of her soda. The very same soda that a second later spews all over me.

"What the hell, Emma?" I grab my napkin and start to wipe down my shirt as beads of Diet Coke run onto my jeans. I look up at her and follow her wide eyes over to the door Graham has just walked through and see none other than Nathan Riley trailing in behind him.

He looks at me and pales again, as he did earlier. I'm quite sure the blood has drained from my face as well. How is this happening to me?

"You have got to be freaking kidding me," Emma says, loudly I might add, staring at him in disbelief as I hit my ankle on the corner of the booth making my quick exit towards the ladies room. *Ouch! Damn that hurts.*

Emma follows me and I keep my head down, not making eye contact as I hobble by them on the way to the bathroom. I hear Graham say, "What is going on?"

"Ask your dickhead friend why don't you," Emma huffs as she walks by them.

She ushers me into the ladies room and sticks her head back out the door to say, "Graham, just give us a minute, will you please?" Then she closes the door and grabs onto my arm. "Oh my God, Lyn. Nate Riley is the player that is Graham's partner? I guess you really did see him earlier. Wow, what are the odds of—"

"Give us a minute?" I interrupt her rambling. "Give us a minute, Emma? What the hell does that mean? I know you don't expect me to go back out there and actually eat a meal with that snake." I rub my ankle and try to keep it together, doing only a slightly better job of it than earlier today.

She stares pointedly at me and I can almost see the cogs spinning in her brain. "Lyn, calm down. Think about this for a minute. If you leave now and go off crying back to the hotel, he sees you all weak and broken. But if you hold your head up and go out there and show him what a beautiful strong woman he missed out on, then you win, not him. Be the bigger person."

Damn it, she has a point.

"Please, Lyn. You can do this. One hour, that's it."

She takes her bag and places it on the counter, retrieves some makeup and proceeds to touch-up my splotchy face. "Good as new and gorgeous as ever," she says a minute later, nodding at me in the mirror.

I take a deep breath and nod back at her. "Okay. I'm doing this for you. Because I love you more than life and I believe you really like this Graham . . . and maybe because I want to show Nate he didn't break me." *He didn't break me, did he?*

I'm shaking and my throat goes dry as we head back to the table. Grateful beyond words, I see Graham rise from his side of the booth and move over to where Nate is sitting. He looks at me sympathetically and says, "We don't have to do this tonight if you are uncomfortable."

Obviously the snake has filled him in.

Emma pokes me in the back urging me to say something. "No it's okay, we can stay for dinner. It's fine." I put on a fake smile and look anywhere but at Nate.

Funny thing about the word *fine*, it can mean just about anything, but it almost always means the opposite of fine. You can be sick as a dog but when someone asks how you are you don't say 'I'm sick as a dog', you say 'I'm fine', even when what you really mean is that you just prayed to the porcelain god for hours on end and you can't believe that much vomit can ever come out of one body.

We sit and order more drinks since Emma's first one is now gloriously displayed down the front of my white blouse. I try to ignore the fact that Nate is staring at me. I fail miserably. I can't keep looking away all night. I probably look stupid looking everywhere but at him.

Just do it already. I slowly shift my eyes until they meet with his. My heart skips a beat when I take him in. He looks the same, but with more defined features. Those deep blue eyes pop out on his tanned, chiseled face. He has broad shoulders and I can see his biceps bulging out from his too-tight navy blue t-shirt that only brings out more of the blue in his eyes. *Man, he's hot.* Subconsciously I had hoped he had peaked in high school and that he ended up with a crooked nose, ears too big for his head and really bad teeth.

He is smiling at me, probably assessing me the way I am him. "Brooklyn, you look beautiful. I knew you would."

Knew I would?

"Um . . . thanks. You look nice, too." *What else was I supposed to say?* "And my name is *Lyn*." I look away and try to feign interest in the other conversation going on at the table. I am willing Emma to include me in it so that I can start breathing again.

She doesn't let me down when she looks over and finds me staring a hole into the side of her beauty-queen head. "So, Lyn opened her own bakery a few years ago and it is doing really great. She is also about to earn her business degree," she says with the pride of a true best friend.

Thankfully, Graham seems genuinely interested in my business and I am in my element talking about my one true passion. I glance over and notice that Nate seems ticked off about being left out of the conversation. *Ha!*

The waitress comes over and asks for our orders. I pray that nobody orders something that takes a long time to make. The quicker we get out of here, the better.

Graham and Emma are engaged in a discussion about the conference. Nate is fiddling with his phone. Why is he acting like nothing happened? Like he didn't take my virginity and throw it on the ground and stomp all over it. I still can't believe I'm sitting across from him after eight years. I want to yell at him. I want to reach into his chest and rip out his heart so that he can understand what it feels like to have someone dangle love at you like a carrot and then whisk it away without so much as a word of explanation. I want to tell him what it was like to be a young girl in love with a legend at school, only to become the butt of jokes when he left suddenly, leaving me a heap of melted mess on the floor of the school bathroom.

But I don't. I remain quiet about all of it. I don't want him to know how he ruined me. How he crushed my heart, rendering it incapable of feeling until years later. Until I found Michael.

Oh, God. What'll I tell Michael? He will freak out, won't he? I mean, he's not really the jealous type but he knows how much Nate hurt me so he will be pissed. He will probably want me to come home. I shouldn't tell him. Yes, I should. I don't want to keep anything from him. I'll tell him when we talk tonight, by then this will be over and I will never have to see Nate again. So, it's settled. I'll tell him. *Maybe.*

I become less comfortable with the next topic of conversation. Graham smiles over at me. "So, Lyn, when is the big day?"

Nate perks up and breaks his silence. "What big day would that be?"

"Oh, didn't Graham tell you that Lyn is getting married?" She has a huge bitchy smile on her face like she just told him the ending of a movie he hadn't seen yet.

Nate takes in a sharp breath. "No." He gives Graham a what-the-hell look. "No, he didn't mention that. Who is the lucky bastard?" he asks while staring me down.

Oh, so now he wants to talk. "His name is Michael," I say.

"Michael?" He snorts. "Michael? Sounds like he changes toner cartridges and wears a pocket protector." Now *I'm* the one giving *him* a what-the-hell-look.

"Dude!" Graham elbows him and gives him a disapproving look.

"Actually," Emma pipes in, "Michael is a doctor doing his residency in pediatric cardiology down in Savannah." She squeezes my leg under the table. I could high five her right now. I've never used Michael's job to make him or me look better, and I had no intention of bringing it up tonight, but damn, to see the look on Nate's face—so worth it. He looks like he just ate a lemon. Or maybe a little crow.

"So, Nathan Riley," she says to him, spitting out his name like it tastes bad coming out of her mouth, "I thought you were going to be a big baseball player or something, yet here you are at an architectural convention." *Oh, boy, Emma is unleashed.*

If looks could kill, Emma would be dead. His phone chirps and thankfully, he ignores her attack and his temper is now directed towards whoever was on the other end of that text. He slams it back on the table muttering something about a bitch and then he runs his hand through his hair. Wow, I may be engaged to be married but I'm not dead. It is still flat-out sexy when he does that.

"Claudia?" Graham asks Nate.

"None other. The bitch won't leave me alone," he responds.

"Girlfriend?" I raise my eyebrows at him in question. I know it's been eight years and all, but the thought of someone you once loved, or thought you loved, with another person, even if you hate that someone right now, is not a pleasant thought.

"Ex-wife," he says, and now *I'm* the one with my mouth hanging open and blood draining from my face.

Emma coughs up her Diet Coke for the second time tonight. Thankfully it was in the other direction this time. "You were married?" she asks in utter disbelief.

"Briefly," he says, his left hand coming up to rub on his right bicep. I think I see the hint of a tattoo peeking out from under his t-shirt. It looks like some kind of script. He rubs it absentmindedly and stares out the window of the restaurant.

He was married? I shouldn't care about this. I am about to be married myself. Then why does it feel like a sledge hammer just hit my heart?

Our food arrives and interrupts what was bound to be a thorough Q & A session from Emma about his failed marriage. I study the clock on the wall thinking that I just need to get through this dinner and show him that I have a good life, and then get on with my life. I mean, I have a great guy and my dream job. He doesn't seem to have anything that he wanted at age seventeen. Divorced at twenty-five? Well, of course he is. He is a playboy. I saw it myself. Why would anyone get married to a guy like that? He called that . . . Claudia, a bitch. *Hmmpf* . . . I bet she's nice and beautiful and in a world of hurt dealing with his philandering ways. Maybe we could start a club.

I'm pulled from the thought when I hear a high-pitched, "Hi Nate," coming in tandem from two tall gorgeous women passing by our table. He lifts his chin and winks at them and they giggle as they walk out of the restaurant. *Did they really just giggle?*

Nate and I struggle to make idle conversation while Graham and Emma are hitting if off big time. "So," Nate says, "what are you going to do all day at the hotel when Emma is at the conference?"

"Study for my finals." I'm deliberately being short because I have no desire to have a heart-to-heart with him. "And run."

"Your hotel has a great running trail." He stops talking and scrunches his eyebrows together while stroking his chin with his thumb and forefinger. "Um . . . so what are you studying?"

"Small business management."

"Not big on words tonight, are you Brooklyn?"

"It's Lyn. L-Y-N," I spell it out for him.

"Well, *Brooklyn* . . ."

I roll my eyes at him.

"It looks like you've gotten everything you wanted." He frowns and looks down at his wrist which he is moving around in circles. I notice some small scars on it but don't ask about them. The less we talk the better.

"You're really getting married, huh? Why would you do that?" he asks.

"It is usually the progression of events after meeting, dating and falling in love," I quip.

He looks pissed. "Marriage is a bunch of crap, you know. Expecting two people to stay together forever is unrealistic."

Whoa, hello Mr. Personal. I really don't want to talk about love and marriage and forever with the guy, who I thought, eight years ago, was going to be all of that for me. I know. Deep down, I know it was just one night and that it obviously meant so much more to me than to him. But for a minute, actually for thirty-three hours and twenty minutes, I really thought that he was it for me. I was finished. Done. At seventeen I had found my prince and he came in with his silver pickup truck and swept me off my feet.

"Just because your marriage failed doesn't mean everyone else's will," I say, twisting my engagement ring.

He shakes his head. "No, it's not natural. Most people end up divorced anyway so why bother to go through all the trouble of dating, flowers, meeting the parents and garbage like that?"

"The trouble of dating?" I snap at him, raising my voice because he has really hit a nerve. "Oh, yes, how could I forget? It *is* too much trouble for *you*. You would rather just sleep with everyone and then leave." There, I've said it.

He takes in a sharp breath and looks like I've just punched him in the stomach. Is that . . . *regret*, I see? He shakes his head and recovers quickly. "Whatever," he says in clear frustration. "It won't work out. You'll see." He rubs his tattoo again.

I see out of the corner of my eye that Emma and Graham have been following our conversation like watching a tennis match. Emma is turning red. *This is not good.*

"What the hell is your problem, Nate?" she yells at him. "You have no right to say that to her, especially since you are the man-whore of the East Coast. What could you possibly know about having a good relationship?"

I look at my best friend in awe of her brashness, the hypocrisy of what she has said is not lost on me, but I have to smile as she defends my honor.

"You don't know shit, Emma!" He slams his drink down. I'm getting pretty tired of being splashed with drinks tonight.

"Hold on there." Graham puts a hand on his friend's chest to hold him back. "I think now might be a good time to call it a night." He looks at me apologetically as he motions for the waitress to come over.

Graham settles the check and we all stand up and go out the door quietly and in single file. I thank Graham for dinner and head over in the direction of Emma's car to give her and Graham some privacy. Nate follows me.

"Hey, I'm sorry about that. A lot of things have happened since back then, Brooklyn." He holds out his hand to me and I stare at it as if it might burn me. "Come on, friends?" He looks at me with that smile I haven't seen since that night. The one that reaches his eyes. The one I thought was just for me.

Since this will be the last I ever see of Nate Riley, I put my hand out to shake his. He takes it as he looks into my eyes. When our hands touch there is a familiar spark of electricity shooting through me and I'm seventeen again. He stares into me for a long minute while he rubs his thumb on the back of my hand. He must feel my scar and he brings my hand up into the light. "You got injured," he says, tracing the scar carefully. He meets my eyes again. "We all have scars, Brooklyn. Some are simply easier to see." He leans in and pecks me quickly on the cheek and then walks away.

Confused as hell, I wave to Graham and quickly climb into the passenger seat of Emma's car to await her. What just happened? He was a jerk the entire night until just now. Maybe he is bi-polar or something. All these years of wondering what happened to him and here he is, whoring all over North Carolina. Then he is talking to me about scars. What scars, the ones on his wrist? His tattoo? I'm not sure how to process this information.

Emma slides into the driver's seat and looks over at me. "I am so sorry. We should have left when he walked through that door. He is such an asshole." She leans over the stick shift to hug me.

"I love you Emma, but I will not be doing that again. Ever. If you want to see Graham, you can go on your own and I'll stay at the hotel." *Maybe I can book a plane ticket home.*

"I will do no such thing. I dragged you here. We are going to go out and have fun. I'm not leaving you. I can just eat lunch with Graham at the conference." She looks sad and I'm not sure if it's because I am hurt from seeing Nate or because she won't be seeing Graham as much as she wanted to. Probably both.

"I don't want to ruin this for you. I can see you really like hi—"

"No way, Lyn. I'm not leaving you alone. We are Thelma and Louise, remember? Well, except for killing someone and robbing a store and driving off a cliff." She laughs. "Although, I came awfully close to killing someone tonight."

"Okay, you've piqued my curiosity. Let's go order up some drinks and watch us a movie."

$\sim$ $\sim$ $\sim$

Back in our suite, Emma orders bar service and I head into my room to call Michael at the hospital.

"Hey sweetheart." He picks up on the first ring. It is so good to hear his voice. I admonish myself at how I could possibly let another man get to me. Michael is my life, he is my future.

I start to choke up a little. "Hey Michael, can you talk for a minute?"

"Lyn, what's wrong? You sound sad."

"Nothing, I just really miss you, that's all." *Nothing*—there's another word that, just like *fine*, can mean the exact opposite. The problem here is that men tend to take women so literally. When we say nothing is wrong, they move on, when we say we're fine, they are freaking dandy.

"I miss you, too. Did you have a good time today?" I can hear the smile in his voice.

Did I have a good time today? Uh, let's see, today was probably the worst day of my life since junior year of high school. And that includes the day my six-year-old cat, Wiggles, got run over by a car. "It was fine." I mentally smack my forehead. "The conference was huge and there were a lot of cool design displays. I can't believe Emma knows how to do all that stuff." *Why am I not telling him?* I tell him my plans for tomorrow when she is at the conference and he reminds me to be safe when I'm running in new surroundings.

"Lyn, I have to go, there is a new kid being admitted right now. I'm sorry."

"No, it's okay, I know. Just text me later if you can." I learned pretty early on with Michael being a doctor that sometimes, a lot of times, he has to go and go quickly and that for the time being, I get put on the back burner. That is fine with me. I think. I mean, he is saving lives and all. It's not like he is cutting me off to go draw a stupid sketch of a building or something.

"I will. I love you, Lyn. Have a good night."

"Love you, too."

He hangs up and I hold onto the silent phone a little longer, wondering why I didn't say anything.

I hear some voices in the living room and go out to see Emma thanking someone for our drinks, all four of them. I think I heard her ask him to bring more in an hour. *Geez, drink much?*

"How's Michael?" she turns to me, handing me one of the Cosmos.

"Huh?" I squeak about an octave too high.

"Michael. You called him, right? What did he say about you seeing Nate? Did he freak out? I bet he asked you to come home, didn't he?"

"What?" I don't meet her eyes while I slurp my drink and move over to the couch.

"Oh my God, you didn't tell him, did you?" Her eyes widen. "Why didn't you say anything?"

"Uh, I guess I just didn't want him to worry about me. I don't see the need to upset him when I'm going to be gone all week. He needs to concentrate on his work. I'll tell him when I get home and he can see that I'm okay." *I'll be okay by then, right?* "Plus, I'm never going to see Nate again so it really is no big deal."

She narrows her eyes at me and takes a drink. "I guess that makes sense. You know we can talk about it if you want to, right?"

"I know, and thanks, but I'm done talking about Nate Riley. Let's just please watch this movie so I can figure out who the hell Thelma is."

Chapter Four

My eyelids flutter and struggle to open against the early morning light dancing through the heavy curtains in my room. I think I'll sleep a little longer; after all I don't have to get up at the crack of dawn and start baking today.

Why am I so warm? Then I smile as I feel Michael run his hands over my stomach and up to cup my breasts. He has his leg draped over both of mine, holding them captive and is moving his hands in a sensual way I've not felt before. He is paying special attention to my nipples. Pinching, tugging, running his thumb around each stiff peak, sending little shock waves down to my core and turning me on in a way I've never experienced. *Mmmm, that feels good.* A moan escapes my throat.

"Oh, baby, let me hear you," he says.

Wait . . . that's not Michael's voice! I stiffen and in a millisecond, my mind goes over the events of last night and the five . . . no, six Cosmos I had with Emma. *Oh God, Oh God, Oh God, what did I do?* I look down to see the top of a dirty-blonde mess of hair just as my nipple is being sucked into his hot, wet mouth. I try to ignore the incredible sensation rippling through my body as I attempt to process what is going on and what the ramifications might be.

He looks up at me with those deep blue eyes and that magnificent smile, the one that is only for me, and he says, "Brooklyn, I'm leaving you."

I blink down at him. *Leaving me?*

"Lyn . . . Lyn . . . Brooklyn, I'm leaving now." I snap awake and frantically look around the bed, under the sheets and behind Emma who is now looming over me with a very confused look on her face.

"Lyn, are you okay?" she asks. "We got a little carried away last night with all the drinks." She puts a bottle of water on the nightstand. "I thought you could use this."

Still coming out of my haze I'm not sure if I'm relieved that it was a dream or disappointed that it was.

What? No. Of course I'm relieved it was a dream. I would never cheat on Michael, especially not with someone who thinks he is God's gift and goes through girls as quickly as most people go through a pack of gum.

Then I discover the horrid taste in my mouth. It is bad. Like something actually crawled in there and died. I silently thank God that there really is nobody in bed with to me to breathe in the nasty smell that must be coming from me right now. Then there is the slight pounding at my temples to top it off. I swear off drinking. Yes, yes, I know I'm fooling myself but I do it anyway.

I pull the sheet up over my mouth and tell Emma, "Thanks for the water. I'll be fine. Go have fun at your conference and I'll see you later."

"I ordered breakfast if you can stomach it. Some toast and cereal, I figured you couldn't do much more than that." She twirls around in her floaty skirt that may be a few inches too short of professional and says, "How do I look?"

One thing I know about Emma is that she never asks anyone, not even her best friend, if she looks okay. I always thought it was because she was so confident, or maybe because she simply didn't care what other people thought. Now I wonder if it was because she just didn't have anyone interesting enough to care about looking good for. I'm not sure how to deal with this new side of Emma. I wonder if I should call her out on it or merely go with it and see what happens. I decide on the latter and say, "Emma, you look gorgeous and he will want to eat you for lunch."

Her eyes widen and she doubles over in laughter.

I blush and say, "I didn't mean. Um . . . I didn't say that—"

"I know what you meant. God, you are adorable sometimes." She turns to leave my room and shouts back on her way out, "Text me if you need anything. Bye!"

I practically chug the bottle of water she left for me and then I lie back on the lavender-scented hotel pillow and contemplate the dream I just had. It makes sense. I did just see Nate yesterday after all these years. I was bound to have some kind of subconscious reaction to him. The thing is, I swear I could feel him. I could feel the heat coming off him. I could feel his hands on me. It was so real.

I need to go for a run. Yes, that will help clear my head. I get out of bed and pad over to the en-suite bathroom. Looking in the mirror, I look like I feel. Death warmed over. I put my dark hair in a messy bun, splash water on my face and wash off last night's mascara that now makes me look like the walking dead. I have two more glasses of water, brush my teeth and then head out to the living room for a light breakfast.

Feeling a little better after some toast, I throw on my running clothes, grab my pack and go downstairs. I head out the back door of the hotel where there is supposed to be a nice running trail. It looks to be a beautiful day with a bit of a morning chill that will make for a good run. I sit down on a patch of grass to stretch out before heading off. I'm not always that great at remembering to stretch before my runs, but I figure with the damage I did to my body last night, I'd better not push my luck today.

After a few minutes I get up and strap my pack around my waist. It is a pack that Michael insists I wear whenever I go for a run. He personally put it together for me. It consists of a bandage, antiseptic wipes, an emergency contact card, a small bottle of water and of course my phone which also has my music. I can almost hear him say, *'Don't turn it up too loud or you won't hear your surroundings. You can never be too safe'.* That's my Michael, always the caretaker.

I push the pack around to my backside and pick up the pace as I think back to the first care package Michael ever gave me. It was two days after I met him in the ER.

"Delivery for a Miss Vaughn?" a teenage boy said, walking through the front door of the shop. He was carrying a gift bag with a Mylar balloon attached to it. The balloon had a picture of a large Band-Aid across it.

"That's me," I said, all excited to get a delivery that looked like it didn't have anything to do with the bakery. I thanked the kid, letting him pick out a cupcake to take with him and sat down to remove the contents of the bag.

"What is it?" Kaitlyn came over to see what I had laid out on the table before me.

It was a care package complete with sanitizing wipes, new sterilized bandages, anti-bacterial gel, latex gloves, cream for reducing the appearance of scars, and instructions on how to use all of the contents. But what really impressed me were the Band-Aids he included. They had pictures of little cupcakes on them. And when I turned over the paper with the instructions, on the back side was Doctor Michael's name and cell phone number with the handwritten words . . . 'House call included with care package. Please call to set up a time.'

I thought it was the most romantic thing anyone had ever done and I took the leap and called him that very afternoon.

I find my stride as I run through the lovely grounds of the hotel and adjoining park. I admire the beautiful oak trees that line the trail. They make it seem like I'm running down a tunnel with streaks of light peeking through the heavy branches. As I make my way through the trail that winds all the way around the back of the convention center, I start to wonder if *he* is in there. Is he pushing another tall, beautiful blonde or redhead up against the wall? How many of them has he handed his business card to? Most likely with his cell phone number and maybe even a hotel room number printed on the back. I wonder what he does with them. Is he gentle like he was with me or is he rough and dominant? Does he even take the time to get to know them like he did with me? Maybe that is his MO, he makes you think that you are the only girl for him and then once he has what he wants, he leaves you broken and tattered.

Snap out of it, Lyn. I reach around to my pack and turn up the music, hoping it will drown out these ridiculous thoughts. I pass by a few vendors selling coffee and pastries and the smell has me thinking about Brooklyn's and how I hope that Kaitlyn is managing okay. I must remember to call her as soon as I get back, after her morning rush.

I'm lost in my thoughts, mentally going through the inventory I need to order when I get back on Friday when I spot him. At first, I simply see a guy stretching out on the grass up ahead. Good looking, yes, but that body in those tight running shorts with a t-shirt slung over his shoulder makes me envy the grass he is sitting on just a little. Okay, a lot.

My heart is already beating quickly with the pace I'm keeping but I swear it increases to Mach Two when my eyes meet his and realization dawns that this is the very man that was in my dreams a short hour ago.

Oh God, d*on't trip, don't trip*. It takes all my strength to keep my eyes front and center on the pavement in front of me and to run right past him without so much as a wave or tip of the chin.

What is he doing here? It takes a boatload of willpower not to turn around and look to see if he is behind me. I know that he is. I can feel it. *Crap*. What do I do? Should I stop running and lay into him . . . do I keep going as if I didn't see him . . . do I act like it doesn't bother me that he is here? What if he runs here every morning? He did say that the hotel has a great running trail so maybe this is just his beat. This is purely coincidence, nothing at all to do with me being here.

Just as I've convinced myself to do nothing and pretend he isn't running behind me, looking at my ass jiggling all over kingdom come, I see out of the corner of my eye that he is coming up to run beside me. I can also see out of the corner of my eye that he has a huge smile on his smug little face.

This running trail is a pretty wide trail, about the size of a golf cart path, bigger than a regular sidewalk but smaller than a one lane road. And keeping with Running Etiquette 101, I must stay to the right side of the trail to allow oncoming runners their own space. I can't very well distance myself from him without breaking this rule and I'm nothing if not a rule follower.

I slow down and he slows down with me. I increase my pace in hopes that he will get the hint but there he is right alongside me, step for freaking step. I keep this up for about a mile, but at the pace I've set I am getting a serious side stitch and I can't keep going without the possibility of another public vomit session. I slow down to a walk and then head over to a large grassy area. I walk around in circles for a minute and then I succumb to my exhaustion and sit down on the damp grass. All the while he is just staring at me with a big grin.

"What?" I practically scream at him and he holds his hands up in defense. "Are you stalking me? Were you just going to wait here all day? Don't you have a conference to go to?"

He walks over and sits down a couple of feet from me. "Well, in no particular order, I'm not stalking you but I did want to talk to you today and I remembered that you like to run in the morning. And, yes, I'll probably hit the afternoon sessions but I hate these conferences. I only go because my dad wants me to try to drum up more business."

I vaguely remember he said his dad was an architect. He must work for him. I decide not to ask about his dad or his business as that might seem like I'm interested in conversation, which I'm not. I settle for, "How exactly do you know I like to run in the morning?"

"Back in high school, I would see you run the track every morning before school. The baseball team had some morning practices and you were always there. It didn't matter if it was freezing cold or raining, you always showed up. I was impressed." He takes off his shirt again, throws it over his shoulder and stretches his arms over his head.

Holy God, look away. He may attract every single lady within eye-shot but this isn't going to work on me. And there is that tattoo again, on his right bicep. I dare not stare at it but it looks like script that goes all the way around his arm. The script is printed over the outline of something on the underside of his arm but I can't make it out.

Well since he brought it up first, I say, "Speaking of high school—"

"That's not what I came here to talk about. I want to talk about Emma and Graham."

Geez. Deflect much? "What about them?"

"Well, I'm assuming Emma has talked to you about Graham, and Graham sure as hell won't shut up about Emma. You know I'm not for all that two-people-together-forever crap, but Graham had a pretty bad relationship end last year and this is the first I've seen him really interested in a woman. Hell, he's only known her for a day and he is already talking about what business he could do down in Savannah."

I throw my head back and sigh. It's worse than I thought. I know Emma is into Graham but I thought maybe she would just sleep with him and get over it like she always does. But then after dinner last night I realized she actually feels something for this guy. I know that because she didn't sleep with him last night. Why does this have to be happening with Nate's best friend and partner? How many other men are at this stupid convention that are gorgeous and available and don't have a man-slut for a friend?

"Okay, so they are into each other. So what about it?" I know I must sound like a bitch, but he pretty much did just blow me off when I started to talk about high school.

"Listen, I get that you hate me. I'm a dick. I don't like myself most of the time either." He closes his eyes and shakes his head. "But Graham is a great guy. He has been there for me through some pretty terrible things and I owe him."

Terrible things? I wonder what he means. Maybe it has to do with those scars that he mentioned last night. Or maybe his ex-wife.

"What does any of this have to do with me?" I'm getting irritated.

"Well, Graham really wants to spend time with Emma this week. However, he says that she won't socialize outside of the conference because you refuse to be a third wheel and that you won't go if I'm there."

Yes, that about sums it up. *Wait, how does he know this?*

"Um, how do you know this?" I ask.

"So, you didn't hear them talking on the phone until three in the morning last night?"

No, I was drunk and apparently dreaming of you. "No, I actually slept pretty hard last night. I wouldn't have heard a freight train."

Emma was on the phone until three in the morning. *With a guy.* I'm floored by this news.

"So, I was thinking that you could put your . . . dislike of me aside." He winks at me. "And suck it up and hang out with us for the next few nights. You know, for them?"

I would do anything for my best friend. Anything but this. She will understand. I'll talk to her again. I could always just leave and go back to Savannah. I could even fake an emergency at the bakery.

"Brooklyn, before you say anything, just think about it. Graham told me some stuff that Emma told him last night about how she never really dates and hasn't had a serious boyfriend. He told her about his past relationship. They talked for hours. They are really hitting it off. You need to do this for her. Wouldn't she support you if the tables were turned?"

Now he has hit a nerve. Talk about friends being there for support, Emma has been through some pretty awful things with me. The day *he* left . . . that was awful. She stayed up with me for nights when I was crying until the tears ran dry and my body would just convulse. She comforted me all those times I wished I had a boyfriend but was afraid to get too close to anyone again. She was my biggest cheerleader when I took the plunge and called Michael after that wonderful care package he sent me. She has helped me plan my wedding. She's given me a place to live. And, most of all, she helped me with my dream of opening Brooklyn's. I can never repay her for what she has done. *Damn it! Oh, curse the gods of doing the right thing.*

"Fine," I acquiesce. He releases his breath and looks just a little too happy. "With two ground rules." The smile drops from his face and he raises his eyebrows at me. "One, this is not, I repeat not, a double date. I am engaged to be married and I am in love with Michael. I will do this to support Emma and that is the only reason I will do this."

"Okay, not a date. What's your second condition?"

"No touching. You will not touch me, hug me, dance with me or even catch me if I trip and fall. Understood?" As those last words tumble from my mouth I can't help but remember a time when he did catch me when I fell into him at the age of seventeen. I fell into him and then I fell hard for him.

"What if you are crossing the street and a car is about to hit you and I have to run out and pull you out of the way? What if you are trapped in a burning building and I have to carry you out to safety, can I touch you then?" He laughs.

"Not even then. Let the car drag me along the road. Let me burn in the fire. Got it?" I stand up and turn away to finish my run back to the hotel.

"You hate me that much?" are the last words I hear come from him before I turn the corner.

No, I loved you that much. And I'm not willing to risk everything I have with Michael to re-live what would surely be a repeat of the nightmare that still haunts me after all this time.

Chapter Five

"Lyn, you are a saint," I hear as Emma comes dancing into the room. "Are you sure you want to do this?"

No, no, I don't want to do this, but she is my best friend, my partner in crime and the other half of my female soul. And, if she asked me to, I would drive off a cliff with her.

"For the tenth time, yes, I am sure about this." I roll my eyes.

"Okay then, Graham promised to keep it casual."

Thank goodness for small favors. I'm beginning to really like Graham, in a he-is-perfect-for-my-best-friend kind of way. He is a nice person who seems to truly care about others. I really couldn't be happier for Emma. It's about time she found a man with staying power. I do wonder what she will do when we head back on Friday. Surely this is more than a week-long affair. I mean they haven't slept together. Twenty-four hours of knowing a new, cute guy and no sex . . . that is a record for her. I wonder what he will think about her pre-Graham sexcapades.

I put on a pair of jeans and a cropped sweater. I do not wear heels, they suggest wanting to impress, and they make my hips wiggle a lot and the last thing I want is for Nate to be looking at my hips, or any other body part. I throw my hair into a low ponytail and dab on a little gloss and mascara.

Emma, on the other hand, goddess that she is, looks totally hot in her tight black jeans, strappy heels and fitted cap sleeve blouse. She has left her hair loose and straight. We are so completely different. I am the handmaiden to her princess, the Phoebe to her Rachel.

The guys are waiting for us in the lobby. I take a deep breath as they head over towards us. I can do this. For Emma. As if she reads my mind she pulls me into a quick hug and whispers, "I love you, Lyn. You are the best."

Damn it. I was about to tell her no way in hell will I sit in the back seat with him, but I keep my mouth shut and vow to take one for the team.

As I suspected, Graham and Emma sit in the front with Nate and I in the back. I'm just glad Graham drives a large SUV. Mainly so I can stick to the no touching rule. I already had to walk around the car and let myself in as I wasn't about to get in the door that Nate opened for me. I have to remember that he is still the snake who broke my seventeen-year-old heart. Don't think I haven't noticed that he ignores any reference to that night and to high school in general. I look at my watch, only three or four more hours to go . . . tonight. *Ugh.*

We end up at a local pizza hot spot. Dinner is quite uneventful with Emma and Graham once again hitting it off. I think I even saw some hand holding under the table, which was, thankfully, a square table with a chair on each side. Nate and I stay with safe topics like the weather, running and my bakery, which I am always happy to talk about.

"So, we thought we'd take you girls out for a little goofy golf after dinner," Graham says.

"Um, what is that?" Emma looks confused and then adds, "You aren't going to get us drunk and take us to a country club are you?"

Graham and Nate share a look and start cracking up. "No. But that could be arranged." He winks at her. "Goofy golf. You know, miniature golf, putt-putt—whatever you southerners call it."

"Oooo . . . that sounds like fun." She looks at me. "Doesn't that sound like fun, Lyn?"

"Loads," I deadpan.

The golf place is right down the street. I've got to hand it to Graham, he is doing his best to accommodate me. This night just screams platonic. I've actually never played mini-golf before. Michael and I never have time for such things. I'm sure once he is an Attending, we will get to have all kinds of fun adventures. Until then, I'm happy simply running the shop and working towards my degree.

Graham gives us a rundown of the rules. *There are rules?* Then we each take our fluorescent-colored golf balls and putters over to a number-one marker. I tell them all to go first since I've never played. I watch them and think that it looks simple enough. Then I set down my bright-green ball and proceed to swing, leaving said ball exactly where I placed it.

Graham and Emma grab each other and try to muffle their laughter. Not very well I might add. I am, of course, turning three shades of red. How could I miss the ball? It looked so easy. I'm thinking about my next move when strong arms come around me, enveloping me as his hands grab the club over my hands. Together, we hit the ball—right into the little hole at the end of the green. Everyone cheers.

Everyone but me, that is. I turn around and swing my club at him like a bat. He barely has time to reach up and slow the momentum before it strikes his right arm.

"Ouch!" He says, too loudly. Give me a break, I didn't even hit him as hard as I would have liked. "What the hell was that for?"

"For breaking rule number two," I hiss through my teeth.

Emma walks over to where he is rubbing his arm and she pushes up his sleeve. "Nate, what kind of tattoo is that?" Now she has my full attention. I've wanted to know this since last night. Well, purely from a curiosity standpoint. I couldn't see what it was yesterday or even today when he had his shirt off. I sigh.

Oh God, did I just sigh at the thought of him with his shirt off?

"Don't bother, Emma." Graham snaps his head in Nate's direction. "He won't even let *me* get a good look at it and he sure as hell won't talk about it."

Nate looks irritated. "Mind your own goddamn business, Graham."

"Buddy, I'll never understand why you would get a tattoo when you know people will want to see it and ask why you got it." Graham shakes his head.

"Just because I got stupid drunk one night and did this,"— he motions to his arm, saying 'this' like it tastes bitter coming out of his mouth— "doesn't make it any less personal. Let it go already."

Personal. And he doesn't want to talk about it. Just like he doesn't want to talk about high school. Now it really is going to bother me. What the hell is that tattoo? It obviously says something but, not in English. Not German either. I should know. I took four years of it in high school.

We finish our eighteen holes without any more touching from Nate or club-swinging assaults from me. I'm pretty quiet, just watching the Graham-Emma dynamic. They, on the other hand are touching about as much as two people can without someone telling them to get a room.

I catch Nate watching them as well. Actually he is more than watching. He is staring, studying them as Graham runs his hand up and down Emma's arm. He blinks rapidly, shakes his head and looks over at me with a sad face. He looks at me appraisingly from head to toe, then closes his eyes and takes a deep breath while his hand rakes through his hair. When his eyes open and he looks at me, he smiles and then gestures over at the bar and says, "How about a beer to end the night?"

All things considered, this night has been almost completely benign. Nate has been practically a perfect gentleman and there haven't been many awkward moments. In fact, I hesitate to say it was almost fun.

We sit and nurse our beers for another hour, falling into comfortable conversation. Graham and Emma are now openly holding hands and are clearly lusting after each other. Nate has been surprisingly nice tonight. He is a totally different person than he was yesterday. Now that I think of it, I haven't even seen him ogle any woman here.

Back at the hotel, I say goodnight to Nate and Graham at the car. Nate holds his hand out for me to shake but pulls it back almost immediately and wrinkles his nose. "Sorry," he mumbles.

"No, it's okay." I smile and offer him my hand. After all, he was a good boy, for the most part.

He gives me that smile again. I hadn't seen it all night and it stirs something inside me. He takes my hand in his. I feel his calloused fingers against my soft skin as once again, sparks shoot up my arm from the point of contact.

I pull my hand away as he leans in close to my hair and whispers, "I feel it, too." Then he turns and gets back into the car and I head upstairs alone. But not before I go into the hotel bar and order a Cosmo to take up with me.

~ ~ ~

As I run through the beautiful oak-tree-lined trails again, I can't help but smile at the way Emma floated into my room last night. She kicked off her shoes, got on the bed with me and proceeded to tell me all about the panty-melting kiss Graham planted on her at the door to our suite. I felt like we were teenagers at a sleepover, because the way she was describing it was like a very first kiss. What surprises me is that she didn't sleep with him and they stopped at a kiss. This is serious. Big-time serious.

I'm trying to figure out if I should be supportive or try to break them up so I won't have to see Nate again when none other than the man himself appears by my side and is matching me stride-for-stride. I decide to keep on running and see what happens. Like yesterday, I slow down a fraction and then speed up a little and since he seems dead set on keeping pace next to me, I resolve just to keep my natural time and go with it. Every so often I glance over and see him smiling at me. I roll my eyes. That only makes him smile harder. Sometimes he speeds up, running out in front of me, and I think it is so that I can admire his ass. I'll admit it's a nice one and, because I'm right behind him and there really isn't any other place to look, I'm pretty much forced to watch it.

He is keeping to my right which means I don't get a good look at the tattoo on his right arm. I've never been one to find tattoos very sexy. I would never get one myself. But, on him, with that bulging bicep, it works. And God help me if I don't want to run my fingers all the way around it.

Michael. I need to think about Michael. Michael doesn't have a tattoo. *Okay, not that.* Something else about Michael. When we talked last night, I was reminded of all the wonderful qualities that make him perfect. It is not his fault that he can't take trips like this with me. He is a doctor for goodness sake. We talked about our wedding and we even picked out a date for next spring, March nineteenth to be exact. I was supposed to go out looking for wedding dresses while I'm here but I just can't find the time between running, studying and being Emma's wingman. Michael told me that he stopped by the bakery yesterday only to find my mother already there helping out. I'm glad for that, he is stretched thin enough already.

Thinking about Michael, the bakery and my mother almost makes me forget who is running next to me. Maybe if it weren't for the hairs standing up on my sweaty skin, I *would* forget. He has not uttered a word this entire time.

Twenty minutes later we reach the entrance to the hotel and slow down to a stop. We both remove our ear buds and he says, "Thanks for the run." Then he turns around and starts running in the other direction.

That has got to be the strangest half-hour of my life.

Chapter Six

Emma gets back a short time after I stop studying for the day. She tells me that Graham is treating us to The Raleigh Experience tonight—a night of must-do things starting with dinner at The Angus Barn. I guess that sounds okay with me. Last night was fine and if Nate behaves himself again tonight, there shouldn't be any issues.

I flat iron my hair and wear it straight down my back. Then I put on a pair of white jeans with my cleaned-up wedges and top it off with my favorite blue and white off-the-shoulder sweater. If we're going to the hip places, I might as well look the part.

The guys meet us in the lobby again and we have the same seating arrangements in Graham's car which isn't as weird tonight. I even let Nate hold the door for me. As long as he is being gentlemanly I should let him. It's better than him being the ass he was that first night. But don't think I didn't catch his smirk as I got into the car through the door he was holding open.

We get to the restaurant and I laugh because it really does look like a barn and I wonder if we are going to have some kind of barbeque or something. However, once we are seated, it becomes quite clear to me that this is not just a run-of-the-mill barn restaurant. This is a nice place. High-end food, high-end drinks, great service. Basically all the things that I am not accustomed to.

Graham and Emma slide into a booth as she looks nervously behind her shoulder at me like I might take her head off. I roll my eyes at her. Sometimes I wonder if my mother was right and my eyes might actually get stuck at the top of their sockets if I roll them too much. I am so testing that theory this week.

I slide into the booth first and place my purse down next to me, giving me a buffer as Nate sits down by me. He eyes my placement of the purse as he grins and shakes his head. *Yes, buddy, that's right, no touching.*

The conversation is light, just like last night and it really is getting easier to be around Nate without hating him so much. He is such a different person from that first night that it almost seems like he *is* someone different, merely another friend of Graham's along for the ride so that I'm not a third wheel. If it weren't for that smell of fresh laundry and pure Nate that permeates even the smell of cooked meat, I would think it was someone else entirely.

We are halfway through dinner when an attractive and curvy woman stops suddenly as she walks by the table. *Oh, here we go, enter Mr. Playboy.* She has long blond curly hair, and I mean silky spiral curls from root to tip, the kind those of us with frizzy curls envy. She puts her hands on the table in front of Nate and leans over so that her cleavage is gloriously on display for him . . . and me.

She starts talking to him but is looking at me. If she could shoot daggers from her eyes, I would be shish-ka-bobbed to the booth behind me. "Hey, baby, I didn't realize you were feeding them before fucking them these days," she says with a hint of a French accent.

My eyes go wide and my chin falls to the table in front of me. Nate pales as his fists ball up under the table. Graham closes his eyes and shakes his head and Emma is about ready to jump out of the booth and grab Miss Curly-hair-boobs and rip her head off.

Nate quips back with hardly a hesitation, "Isn't this a little far from the corner you are working, Claudia?"

Oh, God. Claudia. The ex-wife.

Now the color drains from *my* face. I'm looking eye-to-eye with the woman who snagged the one that got away from me. She doesn't look at all like I imagined her. Okay, so maybe I have been imagining what she looks like even though I know I shouldn't care about it. I thought she would look angelic, like a wounded little girl who had been crushed when the love of her life wronged her. I realize that I was probably projecting what I looked like at seventeen onto the image of her. But, this I didn't expect. She looks . . . well she looks like a total bitch. She is dressed like a slut and although she is very beautiful, she also seems kind of skanky.

I can't decide which emotion to go with. Jealousy? Hatred? Anger? Sympathy? After all, she was wronged and probably deserves my sympathy, but she is the one who got him, even if only for a while when I only had him for one night. I decide on hatred, it is the easiest for me to express.

"Honey, don't bother asking for a second date," she says to me with a big smirk on her face.

There is nothing worse than being called honey by another woman, especially one your own age. It drips with condescension. I stare at her right back in the eyes-slash-boobs and without thinking too much about it I grab Nate's hand, entwine his fingers with mine, place our clasped hands on the table just under her breasts and say, "Don't count on it, honey. He must like this milk so much that he decided to buy it." Then I flash my large engagement ring at her.

I think it will take a crane to lift her jaw off the floor. She looks back and forth between Nate and me for what seems like forever. Then she huffs, turns on her mile-high Jimmy Choo's and walks away.

It takes about two seconds for the other three people at the table to laugh, sputter, and scream in excitement at my decidedly out-of-character outburst.

"Girl, I think I'm in love with you," Graham says with a wink to Emma. "That was epic! I've never seen someone put her in her place like that."

The guys bump fists and go on and on about how great that was when I realize that Nate is still holding my hand. Or maybe I'm still holding his. I pull it away quickly, shrugging my shoulders when I say, "I just hate it when people call me honey."

"Duly noted." Nate leans close so only I can hear him whisper, "Baby it is then."

I'm about to kick him in the shin when the smile is instantly wiped off his face and he freezes like a deer caught in headlights. Everyone at the table follows his gaze to where we see Claudia across the room being helped into her coat by a very attractive and muscular guy.

"Who is that guy she is with?" Emma asks Graham.

Graham looks sympathetically over at Nate. "That is Jonathon Cassidy. He's a pitcher for the Braves." Then he tries to lighten the mood. "What do you say we kill this bottle of wine?"

I'm not sure why Nate looks so crushed over seeing her with another man. Didn't he call her a bitch that wouldn't leave him alone after she sent him a text the other night? He brings a hand up to rub his bicep over his shirt where his tattoo hides underneath and realization dawns.

Claudia. *Claudia with the French accent.* The writing on his tattoo, it must be French. He got it for her, or because of her. But if he cheated on her, why is he so reluctant to talk about the tattoo?

Then he starts that thing again that he did before with his right wrist, moving it in circles. The wrist with all of the small scars. I don't think he's even aware of what he is doing. He is kind of spacing out, looking into his wine glass. Then he runs his hand through is hair, takes a breath and downs the entire glass in one drink.

We get through the rest of dinner but Nate is very quiet and reserved. Graham tells us that we are heading out to Fayetteville Street after dinner. It is a popular nightlife area with shops, restaurants and clubs. I can see Emma squirming in her seat; this is definitely her cup of tea.

Graham pays the check. I don't even want to know what it amounts to, but I wouldn't be surprised if it were a few hundred dollars based on what I saw on my menu. Thankfully, Claudia and Mr. Baseball are long gone by the time we hit the parking lot. I find myself actually feeling bad for Nate and I don't even know why.

On the way to our next destination, my phone chirps and I look to see that Michael has sent me a text.

Michael: **Hey sweetheart, have little break, wanted to say I miss you.**

I close my eyes and picture his face.

Me: **Hey to you too. Miss you more. Heading to trendy nightlife spot right now. Just had the world's best steak. You would like it here.**

Michael: **Be safe, Lyn. Don't drink too much and don't take a drink from anyone but the bartender. Steak? You? I don't believe it!**

Yeah, I'm not much into red meat. But I thought it was one of those 'when in Rome' moments.

Me: **Well, when you eat in a place called the barn, you go with the flow!**

Michael: **Haha. Got to run. I love you. Call me when you get home.**

Me: **Love u too. Will do. Bye.**

I put my phone away as we park the car in a huge lot. I hope someone will remember where we parked. We walk by all kinds of unique shops and restaurants and I wonder if there are any bakeries here. We head slightly off the main drag and arrive at the club. It is aptly named 'The Architect'. I stare at the awning wondering about this coincidence as Graham and Nate share a look. I have a feeling this is not their first time here.

Nate snags one of the few tables close to the dance floor. Graham orders a bottle of champagne and when the waitress brings it out and pours it into our four glasses, Graham raises his in a toast. "To new friends." He winks at Emma and they clink their glasses together before turning to clink ours as well.

Nate leans into me and whispers, "And old ones." He smiles brightly and then sips his champagne while eyeing me over the top of his glass.

We finish the bottle, order some waters and we head out to dance to the latest top-forty hits. This is okay. I can do this. Group dancing is not very personal and as long as we don't split up as couples, I can hang in there. I give Emma the stare and she nods her head. I love that we can have an entire conversation with only a look or a movement.

We dance in kind of a square with equal distance between us. This continues pretty effectively for a while and we all have a thin layer of sweat somewhere on our bodies at this point. What is it about sweat that makes guys look more attractive? Someone once told me that when a guy sweats, his body puts out some kind of smell that is genetically proven to attract females. Well, if looking around this club is evidence, I'd say that theory is dead on. Bodies are coming together, grinding and moving as one. Girls are stripping off their outer layers to the excitement of the males around them. Even Graham and Emma are inching closer together and seem lost in their own little dance world.

Dancing can be like a drug. It releases endorphins and makes you feel better even if you are in a bad mood. It must be those endorphins kicking in when I look at Nate. Watching him dance is like seeing a recipe perfectly come together. It builds up with each ingredient and then you stir it all together and all of the flavors mix, and you are then rewarded with the aroma of the scrumptious pastry as it bakes. But, just like most of the confections I make, I cannot have, nor do I want him. Okay, in all honesty I do want everything that I bake. But I don't want Nate. Nope. Don't want him or his sweaty, dirty-blonde hair that he sometimes runs his hands through. Not his broad shoulders or even that strip of skin between his low hung jeans and his shirt that rides up when he raises his hands over his head.

I'll admit, however, that he is eye-candy for women. Case in point. There is a curvy, attractive woman behind him. She starts grinding into him from behind. *Hello? Am I not even here?* I mean we aren't dancing closely but it should be kind of obvious that we are dancing together. He is sporting a huge smile as he moves against her. *Of course he is.* Then he opens his eyes and sees me in front of him and a look of shock crosses his face. He quickly reaches out and takes my hand, turning us around so that I'm the one who is now standing with my back to sweaty-grind girl. He releases my hand the instant we change positions. Sweaty girl pouts behind me and walks away and Nate is smiling once again.

A slow song comes on so I head over to the table and down my water. Nate follows me but Graham and Emma stay on the dance floor, glued together, hands roaming every which way. We go ahead and order another round of drinks for everyone. I try to pay the waitress but Nate won't let me. We are enjoying our drinks and are watching the dance floor when another woman comes up to Nate and asks him to dance. *Seriously, am I invisible?* He tells her no thank you and shrugs an apology at me.

"You know, it's okay if you want to dance with someone. It's not like I'm your date." I blush. "I mean, we're not together. Well, not together-together." I roll my eyes at myself.

"Brooklyn, I'm not going to leave you sitting here all by yourself." He smiles at me and lifts his chin to the dance floor. "But if *you* want to dance with me, that would be great."

Dance with him. Touch that sweaty body. Grind up close to him. No, I don't think that would be a good idea. I don't want to give him the wrong impression. I'm no longer that little girl who will fall for some romantic lines and then fall into bed with him. No, I'm perfectly fine sitting right here where it's safe. Just a few more hours tonight and tomorrow will be the last I see of Nathan Riley.

Emma and Graham come back to the table for a drink. I finish my second Cosmo in no time and grab Emma's hand and drag her to the dance floor. "Girls' dance," I say, as I point to the guys to stay put.

Out on the dance floor Emma can't stop gushing about Graham and how good a dancer he is and how great he is and how good he smells and on and on. In between my eye rolls, I notice Nate and Graham intermittently talking and staring at us. I know they are talking about us; hopefully they are talking about Emma because there really isn't any point in talking about me. My story is already written, there are no alternative endings, no chances of turning the tables, no way am I going to cave to the playboy of the modern world. I see the way he is looking at me when I dance, like he wants to eat me alive. It should make me feel uncomfortable but I don't let it. After all, I'm probably the one woman here he can't have. So, look all you want, Nate, this book is shut. Done. Finished. Period.

Emma and I dance our asses off until I think my feet will become disconnected from my body. I am so in need of water right now. We go over to the table where the guys have fresh water and another round of drinks waiting.

"Damn, you two look hot." Graham smiles at Emma. "And I'm not talking about your temperature. You guys looked great. I think every guy in this club is wishing they were us right now." He points his finger between himself and Nate.

A slow songs starts. "Later you two," Emma says, pulling Graham up from the table.

Surprisingly, a few guys come by and ask me to dance. The second guy doesn't take no for an answer until I show him my ring. Then he turns to Nate and says, "You are one lucky guy, man."

Nate simply says, "You have no idea." The other guy walks away and Nate looks upset.

"Listen," he says, while gesturing to my ring, "if you dance with me, I promise I'll respect the ring."

I don't know if I believe those words or if the alcohol is kicking in, but for some reason, against the better judgment of womankind and the Jiminy-freaking-Cricket on my shoulder, I say, "Fine, but you'd better be good." I blush. "I mean, you better behave yourself."

He chuckles. "I know what you mean, Brooklyn. And I *am* good."

I ignore his words and head out to the dance floor. He stands in front of me, holding out his hands while raising an eyebrow to ask permission to put them on me. I give him a slight nod and hold my breath. As soon as his hands touch my sides, my eyes close spontaneously and my breath hitches. My flesh is burning under those large hands and electricity is working its way through my veins. I wonder if I keep my eyes shut and imagine I'm dancing with Michael, if it will make this more tolerable. Only, I can't do that because what I'm smelling, now that he is so close to me—that fresh laundry and Nate smell that is now mixed with a heady dose of man-sweat—*that smell* is most definitely not Michael.

"Um, Brooklyn, usually the way it works is that you put your hands somewhere on me as well." He smirks as my eyes pop open.

I'm glad the dance floor is dark because I'm sure I'm blushing again. "Oh, right," I say, putting my hands up on his shoulders and then around the back of his neck, but I don't grip them together. I still want to maintain a little buffer no matter how hard that is to do while slow dancing.

I try not to move my fingers much but I can feel the sheen of sweat along with the rigid muscles of his neck. Ordinarily this would gross me out. I'm not like Michael. I'm not used to other people's bodily fluids getting on me. But instead of pulling away, my body betrays my mind and plants itself right up against him.

I hear him take in a long breath through his nose. *Is he smelling my hair?* There are still little sparks that are igniting under my skin whenever he rubs his thumb in a circle where he has placed his hand on my lower back.

This is harder than I thought it would be. I think I'm a little drunk and should probably not be doing this. This feels too good for someone who is happily engaged. As my conscience argues with my goddess within, I decide to give him one more song. But that's it. I smile at myself for having such resolve.

Karma is a funny thing. I never really believed in it before. The whole, do the right thing and good things will happen to you theory,

I don't buy it. I think you should do the right thing because the right thing feels right, not because you fear some wave of cosmic badness will follow your soul.

Well, apparently tonight, I am Karma's bitch. Because the song that starts playing through the speakers of this very loud, very trendy club is the same song that played about five seconds after I lost my virginity to the very guy whose hands are burning a hole in the fabric of my favorite sweater. Nickelback is singing 'Someday', and I am transformed back into a seventeen-year-old girl, sitting in the front seat of Nate's pick-up truck, thinking that it was the best day of my life and that my future had just been decided for me and it was exactly what I had dreamed. I am frozen in time. My body stiffens. And just because Karma wants her brownies with ice cream, fudge topping and a freaking cherry on top, a tear rolls down my cheek.

Nate pulls away from me and looks at my face, which I know must be horribly streaked with mascara. His brows furrow together. "Brooklyn, I—"

"I—I'm sorry," I interrupt. "I need to hit the ladies room." I peel myself out of his grip and try not to embarrass myself by running to the bathroom.

I hear quick steps behind me. *Don't follow me. Please don't follow me.* I keep going, quickening my pace until I realize the sound of the clicking behind me couldn't possibly be Nate. I turn to see Emma following me into the bathroom.

"What happened?" She wets some paper towels and runs them under my eyes.

I explain the best I can through my heavy breathing, feeling foolish the entire time that this song would affect me. I have avoided listening to this song—okay every song by Nickelback—for the past eight years. But tonight, between the alcohol, the fun night we've had and the fact that I'm out of my element, the lines are blurring and clearly I'm not in the correct frame of mind.

Once I'm calmed down and cleaned up, we head back to the table where I gulp down another glass of water. No more alcohol for me tonight.

"Everything okay?" Nate asks, looking genuinely concerned.

"It's fine. Just some sawdust from the dance floor in my eye. I'm good now," I lie.

He stares at me, runs his hand through his hair and then opens his mouth to speak but then apparently decides to let it go. I hope he doesn't know why I really freaked out. Surely he doesn't remember the song. Of course he doesn't, guys never remember things like that.

Emma and I dance to a few more songs so I can shake it off. Dancing with Emma is great therapy for anything. It is practically a sport. She gets me laughing and back to myself in no time.

We decide to call it a night and head back to the car. We have a long walk since we parked all the way at one end of Fayetteville Street and ended up at the opposite end. Nate is keeping pace with me while Emma and Graham stroll slowly and lag way behind us swinging their entwined hands between them like a couple of little kids. We are not talking but it is a comfortable silence. I feel like I might just be able to let go of this anger I've harbored against him all of these years.

We are at least a half-mile from the car when it starts to sprinkle and our steps quicken. Then it starts raining lightly and we share a 'what-now' look. Realizing we are nowhere near the car and that all of the shops are closed, there is no place to go but forward so we walk faster. When the rain really starts to come down, Nate removes his jacket and covers our heads as we forge on. We are practically at a full-on run. Well, as much as we can be, considering my heels and the fact that we are practically stuck together like Siamese twins by the coat that is covering our heads. By the time we get to the car we are laughing, smiling and soaking wet.

Almost simultaneously, we look at the car and realize that Graham has the keys and that he is not right behind us. Our eyes grow big and we look at each other for a second before breaking out in hysterics. Thankfully, I hit the bathroom before leaving because I swear I would pee my pants. I think I may have even snorted a few times, but I don't care because Nate is making some pretty freaky sounds himself. My stomach muscles hurt and my face is about to crack open from smiling so hard.

The rain eases up and both of us are trying to catch our breath. He looks at me with his wet, messy hair and glistening face and reaches over to pull a piece of wet hair from my mouth. His fingers touch my face, sending tingles down to my chest. His hand cups my chin and my heart starts beating a thousand miles an hour. I feel like I'm out of my body watching this play out for some other girl.

Kiss her.

Wait, what? That's not what I want. Then why am I letting him trail his thumb along my lower lip? I'm staring at his mouth. He is staring into my eyes. Oh God, this is really going to happen. He leans in slightly, probably to see if I will pull away.

Pull away.

He grabs my hip with his other hand and draws me to him. With his thumb, he pulls my lower lip out from between my teeth while he smiles and comes closer. I can smell the mint and beer on his hot breath and then I can't think of anything else except how I want his lips to touch mine. And then—

"Oh my God, you guys are soaked," Emma squeals and I'm instantly jerked back into my body.

I step away from him and shake my head. I hear the beep-beep of the car unlocking so I run around the back of the car, let myself in and slam the door shut. Emma and Graham get in and don't seem any worse for wear. They also don't seem to have any clue of what they interrupted.

Oh, thank the gods of all stupid girls that almost cheated on their perfect fiancés that they interrupted us.

Nate takes a minute to shake the water off and get himself into the car. He is staring a hole into the side of my head but I cannot look at him. I realize I am twisting my hair and counting to five over and over. *Calm down, Lyn. Breathe.* I don't know what came over me. Was I actually going to let him kiss me? Am I losing my mind? Of course I wasn't going to kiss him; he is a philandering man-whore. I'm engaged. I love Michael.

A wave of nausea washes over me.

"I don't feel very good," I say, as Graham pulls up to the hotel curb. "I'm going to head on up. Thanks for a great night and I'll see you guys later." I quickly exit the car and go into the hotel, leaving Graham and Emma looking at each other in confusion.

"I'll be right up!" Emma shouts out the window.

"No." I turn around briefly. "Take your time. I'm going to shower off and go to bed." I don't want her to come after me, yet again, so I can explain what a weak person I am when it comes to Nate Riley. What I need is to get a good night's sleep and forget about the last fifteen minutes of my life. Chalk it up to alcohol and adrenaline, that's it.

After my shower I remember I was supposed to call Michael. I can't call him. I don't know what I would say. I need time to get some distance from tonight. I type out a quick text to him that says I think I may have gotten food poisoning from dinner so I can't call. He, of course, immediately texts me back instructions on how to manage the food poisoning and to call him if I can't keep any water down after eight hours. I type out another message to thank him and tell him I'll call him tomorrow.

I lie in bed and try to sleep. Then I lie in bed and fake sleep when Emma cracks my door a half an hour later. Then I lie in bed and eventually watch the sun rise through the heavy curtains.

In the morning, I tell Emma that I don't feel well, feigning food poisoning. I tell her that she shouldn't count on me for tonight. She says she will send my apologies to the guys and check on me later.

I finally manage to get a few hours of sleep. It clears my head and I decide that I shouldn't see Nate again. It is a disaster waiting to happen and I will only end up hurt. Why risk ruining what Michael and I have together? It's the right thing to do. But I don't want Emma to miss out on seeing Graham the last night she is here so I've got to keep up this whole sickness charade.

I spend the morning studying. Then after a quick nap and a light lunch I head down to the hotel gym to hit the treadmill. No way am I going to risk the running trail and Nate.

When I return to the suite, there is a new bouquet of flowers on the coffee table with a note sticking out of the vase. I'm nosey so I peek at the card. Oh, not for Emma. For me. My heart beats a little faster. I open the card.

Brooklyn, I missed you this morning. I hope you are feeling better. Nate

He sent me flowers? I throw away the card so I don't have to explain anything to Emma. After all, we are in a suite and they have provided fresh flowers every day, what is another bunch?

The rest of my afternoon is spent returning texts from Kaitlyn, my mom and Emma. Thankfully when I call Michael, I get his voice mail so I leave a nice message for him telling him how I can't wait to see him tomorrow and that I'm feeling much better.

Before Emma gets back, I hide the evidence of lunch and my run and climb into bed hoping she'll leave me alone and go out with Graham. I must be a better actress than I thought because she buys it without so much as an 'are you sure?' That or she is glad to finally be alone with him without us tagging along.

I'm studying again when there is a knock on the door and I hear a muffled, "room service." I didn't order anything, but I look at the clock and it is close to dinner time. I open the door and direct the waiter to put whatever it is on the table while I fish around for a tip. When he is gone I look at the tray that is donning a chocolate milkshake and when I lift the silver dome covering the food I see a plate of french fries. There is a note but I don't have to look at it to see who sent this. Of course I read the note anyway.

Brooklyn, I hope you can eat something tonight. I'm sorry you don't feel well. Get better soon. Nate.

I am starving. I shouldn't eat this. Is it like cheating if I eat this? Nobody is here to see if I eat it or not. I could have even ordered it myself. Except that I haven't eaten this combination since that night in high school. How did he remember? It was one short conversation we had eight years ago. No, it doesn't mean anything if I eat it. I'm being stupid. It's food, just eat it.

I pick up a french fry and dip it into the shake then bring it to my lips. God, this is so good. Why did I go so long without eating this? I finish the entire tray.

I make sure I'm in bed before Emma gets back. I leave her a note to tell her that I'm feeling better and that I can't wait to get back to Savannah tomorrow.

~ ~ ~

On the drive back home, I get the play-by-play of her date last night. Apparently Graham has already made plans to come for a visit in a few weeks. She won't stop smiling and I'm glad that she is so wrapped up in Graham that she doesn't grill me about my own feelings. I make sure to keep the conversation focused on wedding planning so that she understands that nothing has or will ever change.

I am truly excited to get back and see Michael. He is my life, he is my future. I fall asleep in the car hoping I dream of him and only him.

Chapter Seven

The past few days have been spent trying to get back into the swing of things at the bakery. Now that I know the place will run smoothly and won't literally burn down in my absence, I can feel comfortable moving forward after graduation to find ways to branch out.

My first night back with Michael was great. *He* is great. I got to his apartment before he did and when I used the bathroom, I noticed that he had purchased me my own toothbrush and there it sat on the bathroom counter, still in the packaging. I proceeded to open a drawer in the vanity and place the un-opened toothbrush in the back, behind some other toiletries. I liked the gesture, but being a guy, he just wouldn't understand the sentimental bond I've created by using the one he does. Maybe once we are married, I'll stop using his.

The next morning when he noticed me still using his toothbrush, he smiled, shook his head and continued on into the shower without saying a word. I think maybe he got the picture.

Today, I'm in the back after the morning rush when my phone chirps. I look at it to see a number that I don't recognize. I open the text.

Nate: **Brooklyn, I hope you are feeling better. It was so nice to see you again. N**

If the 'N' didn't give it away, the 'Brooklyn' did. He is the only person who calls me by my proper name other than my mom.

Damn Emma. She must have given him my number. Why would she do that? So I ask her.

Me: **Why did you give Nate my number? He is texting me.**

Almost immediately she responds.

Emma: **Lyn, I swear I didn't give him your number and I didn't give it to Graham either.**

She had to have given it to him. It's not associated with the bakery so there is no way he could have gotten it.

Nate: **Before you get pissed at Emma, I lifted your number from her phone when you were both in the bathroom. N**

At least he is honest, but I'm still not sure I want him texting me. We are not friends and I'm with Michael. I decide not to text him back and I leave my phone in the office when I go out front.

I try my hardest not to go back to the office to check my phone. It's not like I *want* to get more texts from him, but it is compelling all the same. Like when you see a car accident. You know it can't be good and you don't want to look. You tell yourself that when you pass it, you will just keep going and not turn your head like every other rubbernecker out there. But when it comes right down to it, you can't not look. You have to look. You have to look or it will kill you. So I look. *Damn it.*

Nate: **Brooklyn, I'm sorry if you were uncomfortable at the club. And then again in the rain. But at least admit to yourself that you felt something. I know I wasn't the only one. N**

What does that have anything to do with anything? Even if I did feel something, and that is a big freaking if, I would never do anything about it. He was my first crush, my first love. It's understandable that I might have some residual feelings. Plus, he's hot. However, I'm not about to become a Nathan Riley statistic. So I tell him.

Me: **I would never dream of becoming another notch in your bedpost, even IF I had feelings for you. Which I don't. B**

I sign my text the same way he signed his. Belatedly, I realize that I used a 'B', not an 'L'.

A few seconds later, he texts me back. *Doesn't he have anything better to do?*

Nate: **So you've told what's-his-name all about our week together? N**

Okay, now I'm getting mad.

Me: **First of all, his name is Michael. And it wasn't OUR week together—it was Emma's and my week together. B**

Nate: **Purely semantics. I take it you didn't tell him then. It was great to see you. I have thought about you a lot and I wish things could have been different. I want to say I'm sorry for so many things. Things that happened a long time ago. Things I can't talk about. Just know that I am sorry. N**

Why couldn't he have said this last week? What is it about guys and their inability to communicate?

Me: **I appreciate you saying that. Doesn't change things though. B**

Nate: **Wish it could. Wish you would give me the opportunity to try. I'll throw away my old bed post and you could be the ONLY notch in the new one. N**

Words. Just words. I'm not sure why he would want to waste his time on someone who is so far away when he clearly has many willing candidates all around him. I decide not to acknowledge his last text and start to clean up for the day. Thankfully, he does not text me back. But that doesn't keep me from checking my phone every few minutes.

A few days have passed since Nate texted me. I guess he has lost interest since I didn't show any. Emma grilled me on the whole texting scene with him and she thinks I handled it appropriately which is good because if she knows anything, it's how to handle men.

I am out to dinner with Emma when my phone chirps.

Nate: **You know, it is customary in this country to thank the giver of gifts. I assume you got them? N**

Well, this is just great. Now I have to show Emma the text because she won't let it go, and then she will want to know all about the flowers and food he sent that I never told her about. So I confess everything. Then the conversation takes a turn that I didn't expect. "Well, why haven't you told Michael?" she asks.

Shoot. Why haven't I told him? Because of that Karma bitch? Because I feel guilty even looking in another man's direction? Because if I admit deep down inside, I do still harbor those feelings even if common sense tells me it's only because he was my first?

"Because I don't want to cause problems where there aren't any, Emma. Nate is not an issue. I love Michael. End of story. There is no reason to upset Michael." I'm not sure if I'm trying to convince Emma or myself.

She doesn't push the subject and I don't respond to Nate's text.

~ ~ ~

It's Friday night. Emma is on a date with Graham. Okay, not a real date as she is, in fact, in the next room and he is still in Raleigh. It's a Skype date, but she thinks it is real so I'll go along. So here I am, alone. Alone because Michael is at the hospital. Again. So I'm sitting at home trying to figure out what slasher movie to watch. Emma is more a romantic-comedy type of girl. Not me, give me the blood, guts and gore every time. I will never get tired of yelling at the television because someone in the movie is stupid enough to go somewhere alone. My phone chirps.

Nate: **Most people say that Friday the 13th is better than Nightmare on Elm Street because it is just too unbelievable that people can die in their dreams. Your thoughts? N**

What? How in the hell? I look over my shoulder and around the room. My phone chirps again before I can respond.

Nate: **If I assume correctly, Emma is in the next room to you, as Graham is to me, leaving us high and dry for the evening. Are you still into scary movies? N**

Oh, he is good. What, did he tape record our entire high school encounter?

Me: **First, how do you know I'm not sitting here with Michael? Second, why are you not gallivanting around looking for your next conquest? B**

Nate: **Gallivanting? You're quite the wordsmith. I heard Emma talking about you being home *alone*. And I don't . . . gallivant . . . anymore. I bought a new bedpost. N**

Whoa! I decide not to touch that with a ten-foot pole but, instead, play nice and since I'm so bored, we put in the same movie and occasionally text about how stupid the characters are.

When the movie is over and I'm ready for bed I text him one last time.

Me: Off to bed. Plz don't comment on that. P.S. Thanks for the flowers . . . and stuff. B

Nate: **You are most welcome for the flowers . . . and stuff. Sleep well, beautiful. N**

Well, crap. I read his text again. That text right there—that is why I have to end this . . . thing. Whatever this is. He can't call me beautiful. He can't make references to his bed and me. I have to tell Michael.

Sitting in the shop after Monday morning's rush I think back on the weekend I spent with Michael. The rare weekend that he actually got forty-eight hours in a row away from the hospital. The perfect weekend with the perfect guy. I really didn't think it was going to turn out that way. I had decided to lay it all out there. Well, almost all. There may have been a few minor details I left out. But, for the most part, I was completely honest, telling him about how uncomfortable I was with Nate and how he is a womanizer and that yes, we slow danced once but only because everyone else was and that no, we did not kiss.

Technically, it's the truth. I even said that he had somehow gotten my number and had texted me and that I would show him the texts if he wanted. Of course, he said he didn't need to see the texts. He said that he trusts me completely and that if I wanted someone else, I would be with someone else and that he knows I would never leave him for someone like Nate, a cheater who abandoned a young girl and ruined a marriage. Once a cheater, always a cheater, he said.

When I think about it, I realize that everything Michael said is true. If I wanted to be with Nate, I could go be with Nate. But what would that accomplish? He would just hurt me again. Even if I did have feelings for him—which I don't—he would cheat on me and move on to his next conquest.

I knew all this but somehow it took Michael telling me to really make me understand. It took Michael accepting my flaws and trusting me completely to free myself from Nate. I know what I have to do. If he contacts me again, I will beg him to leave me alone. I will ask Graham to do whatever it takes to keep him away from me. I need to focus on Michael. My life is with him, with the perfect man who I know will be true to me. A sense of relief washes over me. The weight has been lifted from my shoulders. I am at peace.

$$\sim \ \sim \ \sim$$

It has been almost a week since Nate texted me last and I really thought he would simply go away so I wouldn't have to confront him. I'm bad at confrontation. But my phone chirps, and Karma, she just won't leave me alone.

Nate: **I've tried to stay away, do the right thing, but I can't. I know the reason you cried that night at the club. I remember the song, too. I remember everything about that night. Brooklyn, I always wanted it to be you. I wish I could explain things, please let me. N**

Damn him. I wish he would stop this. He is making this hard. I'm sticking to my guns. I have to tell him to go away if I want a chance at happiness. I take a deep breath and type out a text.

Me: **Nate, I told Michael everything and he was very understanding. He is the one I love. I don't want anyone else. I don't want you. I'm sorry about whatever happened back then that caused you to leave but this is my life now. I can't have you in it. I've made my choice. Don't contact me again. Please.**

I am shaking as I re-read the text and then I close my eyes and press 'send'.

I open a bottle of wine and drink a glass rather quickly. I'm proud of myself for my resolve. I did the right thing. I'm ready to move on.

My phone chirps.

Unbelievable!

Nate: **Brooklyn, I promise to respect your request not to contact you again. I just had to send you one final text. Please do something for me, for the old me you knew in high school before I left and screwed everything up. Listen to a song for me. 'Be My Reason'. It's my story. It's how I feel. It says everything I can't. It says everything I want to. It's always been you. Nate**

Just like the damn car wreck I can't not look at, it takes all of about a five-second battle between my conscience and goddess within before I pick up my phone and download the song. I listen closely to the chorus.

Be my reason . . .
My cause, my light
Be my reason . . .
My purpose, my life
'Cause baby it was always you

You're my reason
You've pulled me through

The song sounds familiar. It is about a man who had hurt a woman and is asking for her help, for her to be the reason for him to change and become a better person. By the end of the song, tears are running down my cheeks. It is a very romantic gesture, one that would have been nice about eight years ago. It might have even worked on me then. This emotion that I'm feeling right now . . . I fight it . . . it's not real. It is the emotion of that seventeen-year-old girl who I no longer am.

I pull up the texts he sent me and press 'delete all'.

Chapter Eight

Between studying for exams and all my time at the bakery, due to giving Kaitlyn a much-deserved vacation, the past few weeks have flown by. Life is good. Life is comfortable. Michael and I have been doing some wedding planning. We tasted cakes and listened to a few bands on his rare nights off. If anything, I feel a deeper connection to him than ever before.

Nate has stayed true to his word and has not contacted me at all. My heart has mostly healed and maybe it was even a good thing that I went to Raleigh with Emma and ran into him. I think I would have carried around that anger and resentment forever. I've let it go now. I can even take the shortcut to my parents' house again which means passing by the entrance to The Bend. I still don't think I'll ever actually *go* there . . . but baby steps are good. I even find myself ordering my favorite treat again—a chocolate shake and fries—whenever we go out. Shame on me for depriving myself of the deliciousness for so long.

One more night of studying and I'll never have to crack open a textbook again. For once, I'm glad Michael has a long shift including an overnight. If today were one of his days off I would feel the need to spend it with him since we get so few together. But, luckily, he is there and I'm taking advantage of his quiet apartment to study into the night. Tomorrow morning I will have to visit the campus on the other side of Savannah to take all three exams for my on-line courses. They won't let you graduate unless you show up in person for the exams. I'm not worried about the exams at all. I know I will pass them. But just like how I had to perfect my red velvet recipe even though my original was good, I can't go into an exam knowing I will simply pass. I have to know I will pass with flying colors. So I study all the material again and again.

I wake up in Michael's bed surrounded by still-open textbooks and notes scattered all over the bed. I smile knowing this is the last day of school. I've got this.

I punch out a text to Michael and Emma.

Me: **Wish me luck . . . here goes nothing!**

Emma texts me back right away despite the early hour.

Emma: **Lyn, you don't need luck. You rock!**

I don't get a response from Michael, but I don't expect one. When he is working it takes a while for him to get back with me. He will be home, probably sleeping, when I get done with my tests and I have special plans that involve how to wake him up.

Four hours later I emerge, zombiefied, from my three tests. How can one person regurgitate that much information in that amount of time? I look around at students walking around campus and smile a huge face-cracking smile because I'm no longer a student—well technically not until after they hand me my diploma next month—but I'm not counting that.

I reach into my purse and turn on my phone again. I smile when I see I have several voice mails, first from Michael and then from Emma and my mom.

I smile at Michael's voice. "Lyn, I know you probably won't get this until after your exams. I'm sure you did great. You are so smart and beautiful and I can't wait to share my entire life with you. I'm heading home now and I'll probably be sleeping but I want you to wake me up. We should celebrate . . . any way you want to." He laughs. "I'll see you later. I love you, sweetheart."

Any way I want to? Yeah, that's kind of what I was thinking, too. I'm practically skipping to my car as I listen to the next voice mail from Emma.

"Lyn . . . um . . . I need you to come to the hospital. There's been an accident and . . . ," she pauses and clears her throat, "just come to the ER and I'll be here." She sounded nervous, excited even.

I think I know what is going on here. I listen to the next one from Mom. "Honey, I don't want you to worry and we need you to drive safely, but you need to come to the hospital as soon as you get this message. We will see you soon."

I smile. Yup. Just as I suspected. Really, you think he could be a little more original. But I guess when you practically live at the hospital, you do what you have to do.

I check my watch to make sure I will arrive about the time I told him I might get done with my exams. I don't want to get there too early and ruin the surprise. As I'm making the twenty-minute drive to the hospital, I recall the last time there was an 'emergency'.

"Lyn, you have to come to the hospital right now!" Emma's shaky voice screamed over my voice mail as I was leaving the bakery for the day. *"Michael is okay, but he collapsed at work and he is asking for you."*

I tried to call her back but couldn't reach her which is unusual since she practically showers with her phone. I tried to call Michael but it went straight to voice mail. I couldn't even contact my parents. I was getting worried and made the drive in record time.

Upon arriving at the ER, I couldn't find Emma so I told a nurse who I was and she ushered me immediately into a large room and left without saying a word. Looking around the room, I realized it was the same room where I met Michael for the very first time eighteen months before. It was a very white, clinical room with one of those curtain things that separates all of the patients that are in the area.

I heard someone clear a throat and thought it must be Michael so I went over to the curtain, ripped it quickly to the side and was stunned by what I saw. Standing there with stupid grins on their faces was pretty much everyone I knew. My parents, Michael's parents, Michael's brother and sister, Emma, Kaitlyn, a few other close friends and some hospital staff that Michael called friends. Then I looked down to see Michael in front of me, on bended knee, still in his scrubs, holding out a small black velvet ring box.

"Lyn, I know this isn't the most romantic place for this, but I figured if you aren't used to this by now, you'd have run out that door long ago."

I already had tears streaming down my face.

"I think I fell in love with you the moment I saw you in this very room. You are the best thing that has ever happened to me and I want to spend the rest of my life with you." The tears started to run down his face as well. *"Lyn, will you marry me?"*

I wonder what he is going to do to top that one? I have to admit, planning something today did catch me off guard. I expected something after graduation next month, but not now. And especially not the day after one of his long thirty-six hour shifts. That is probably why he chose today, because I wouldn't expect it. He is such a sweetheart.

I arrive at the hospital and park in the ER lot. I know better now than to leave my car in the ambulance bay like last time. It almost got towed away. Not today.

When I enter the ER, there is a nurse waiting for me. They all pretty much know me by now. She is directing me to a private room. *Private room, nice touch.* Her eyes are red-rimmed and she is sniffing. *Geez, emotional much?* It's just a surprise party.

As I enter the room, I'm so excited to see everyone there and I skim their faces. Again, it's Michael's parents, his brother and sister and their kids. A bit overkill bringing the kids, but I'll take it. My parents are there. I see Emma, but none of my other friends. Maybe they will jump out and surprise me in a minute.

Emma plows through everyone to get to me when she sees me enter the room. She has tears running down her face. She almost tackles me into a hug and I can feel her body heave as she squishes me.

What is going on? Where are the balloons and the cake?

It's then when I really examine the faces of everyone in the room. Most are crying. My father is sitting down with his head in his hands. Michael's older sister, Janie is in the corner with her ten-year-old daughter, Amanda, trying to console the child who is practically in hysterics. Michael's mother and father are in an embrace and she is shaking and crying.

Where's Michael? I frantically look around the room again, sure that I've missed him. But he isn't here. I look behind me into the hallway and don't find him there but I do see several staff hanging around all crying and hugging.

"Lyn, I'm so sorry," Emma hiccups the words. "I'm so, so sorry."

What is she sorry for? What has happened? I reach up to stop the tickle on my face and realize that I have tears streaming down my cheeks. "Someone tell me what is going on. Where is Michael?"

They all look at each other for a second before my father stands up and walks over to take my hands in his. "Brookie," he says, calling me by a nickname he hasn't used since I was a small child, "Michael was in an accident on the way home after work this morning. They think he might have fallen asleep. His car went off the highway and hit a retaining wall." He takes a deep breath that looks like it hurts. "Brookie—"

No, no, no, no, no, no, no, no. "No, don't say it," I beg him.

"Brookie, I'm sorry. It doesn't look like he's going to make it." He pulls me into a hug with Emma.

"No!" I shout. "Stop right there. Stop talking. He will be fine. Michael is fine. Take me to him. He just needs to see me. Everything will be okay when he sees me. We are in the middle of planning our wedding so he wouldn't leave me now. No. This isn't right. This isn't happening."

I try to rip myself away from Emma and my dad but they are holding onto me so tightly that I can't move. My dad leads me over to a chair and helps me sit down when a few doctors come in the room to talk to me.

I'm not even here. In this room. I'm not here. I'm out of my body, floating above, looking down on my friends and family as they fall apart. I feel numb. I can't move. Tears are rolling down my face, soaking the material on the front of my silk blouse. I hear words such as life support and brain death but I'm not really listening. I can't put together a thought let alone pay attention to these doctors and their technical terms when I know what they are telling me is that my life is over. My love. My Michael. He is leaving me. My stomach turns.

"I'm going to be sick." I bolt out of my chair and one of the nurses grabs my arm and runs me to the nearest bathroom just in time for me to lose my breakfast into the sink basin. Footsteps fall behind me and then my mother and Emma are both here rubbing my back and handing me some wet paper towels.

I sink down to the floor, staying put until I'm sure I won't throw up again. Emma hands me a stick of gum. She is always prepared. I look around the bathroom. It smells of bleach. I eye the floor and absentmindedly hope it is clean. It is so quiet in here. The hum of the heating system is the only thing I can hear and it is eerily calm. Everyone is waiting for me to do something. I don't want to leave this place. As soon as I do, nothing will be the same.

"Brooklyn?" Mom pulls me from my trance.

I look up at my mother and Emma. "I don't know what to do. What am I supposed to do? Tell me what to do."

My mother, designer dress and all, sits down on the emergency room bathroom floor next to me and grabs my hands. She looks into my eyes and says, "You go say goodbye to him."

This is when I start to lose it. I cry hard and loud. My heart hurts so much that I think I must be the only person in the world that has ever felt so much pain. I feel my mother's soft touch, her hand running down my long hair. She starts at the top of my head and smooths my hair down until she reaches the ends. This is something she did for me as a child when I would skin a knee, or when I didn't get chosen for the soccer team in middle school, or when my science fair project failed to work.

Or when your fiancé is dying.

Minutes later, or hours—I have lost track of time—she and Emma help me up and lead me out of the bathroom. I let them take me because I am a shell of a person. I am a lifeless puppet being led around by others. I can't feel my legs move, yet I can see that we are walking because we are passing by strangers in the ER.

I spot a little boy with a twisted arm who is being comforted by his mother while his little sister draws with her crayons on the table next to them. The mother makes eye contact with me and I can see in her eyes that she knows. She knows I will never have a little boy with auburn hair who will fall off his bike and need his mother to take him to the hospital so that his daddy can fix him up. She knows I will never have a grey-eyed girl that will grow up to love to bake just like her mommy.

As we walk down the hall I see an older lady pushing her husband in a wheelchair that is adorned with 'get well Grandpa' balloons and my step falters. Michael will never get to be a grandfather. He won't grow old with me. He won't grow old at all. I close my eyes and refuse to look at anyone or anything else.

We must get on an elevator because I have stopped walking but still feel movement. Just like my heart has stopped beating yet I am still alive.

"We're here," my mother whispers into my hair, still keeping a tight grip around my shoulders.

I open my eyes and see Michael's parents outside a closed door. The door that will lead me to my fiancé. The door to the tomb that encases him. I want to go in there with him and never come out.

I look at his parents, his mom in particular and realize she is just as broken as I am. I've never been very close to her, but in this moment we share a bond that nobody else can possibly imagine. We are part of a club that nobody wants to join. We love the man behind that door more than any other women in this world. We move simultaneously towards each other and embrace, both shaking and crying. It is strangely comforting knowing that someone else feels the extent of my pain.

She pulls away and looks at me. "Lyn, we thought you might like a moment to be alone with him before . . ." She can't say the words. I can't even think the words. I look at the door and can't help but think that as soon as I go through it and he sees me, hears me, smells me, he will wake up. Our love is so strong that I will be the one to pull him back from where he is. They will all see that the doctors were wrong. They are wrong sometimes. Michael always tells me stories of how people have these miraculous recoveries that are beyond what science can explain. I have no doubt that he will be one of these.

I find the words, "Yes, I would like that. Thank you." I give her one last hug.

I look back at Emma and my mom. My mother gives me a weak smile and says, "We will be right outside this door if you need us."

I turn to push through the door when a nurse grabs my elbow and proceeds to tell me that there are a lot of wires hooked up to him and a machine that is breathing for him so there is a tube coming out of his mouth. She tells me there is a bandage wrapping his head and a few others on his arms. All I can do is nod at her and stare blankly.

She lets me through the door and closes it gently behind me. I'm overwhelmed by the soft sounds in room. The whooshing and whirring of the ventilator and the beep-beep-beep of the heart monitor echo through the dark room. I try to match my own heartbeat to his but mine is beating too fast.

I take in his appearance starting with the bandages at the top of his head. I can still see his beautiful face but it is now marred by a gash over his brow and some scrapes on his cheek. He still looks like my Michael. He is wearing a white and blue hospital gown with his arms sticking out and resting by his side. One arm is bandaged almost entirely from shoulder to wrist while the other looks completely unscathed. I sit in the chair pulled close to the bed and take his hand into mine. His hand is much warmer than I thought it would be.

I bring it to my lips and kiss his unmarred skin. "Michael," I whisper. "I need you. Don't leave me." Tears drop down onto his hand and roll off onto the bed. I sit, rubbing his hand, being lulled by the rhythmic noise of the machines. It is oddly reassuring being enveloped in this sound. Maybe that is why he won't wake up.

"Michael!" I shout at him. "It is time to wake up. We have so many plans to make." I lower my voice again and say, "My exams are over and I can concentrate on our wedding now." I go on about our wedding and what I dream it will be like. Then I tell him about our kids; one boy, one girl—just like we planned. I talk and talk until my throat goes dry.

The door opens and his parents walk in.

"No. I'm not ready. He's not ready," I cry, refusing to let go of his hand.

"Lyn, sweetheart," Michael's dad says to me. "He's already gone. This is not Michael. It is time to let him go." He pulls me and his wife into a hug. "Nobody else wanted to be here when . . . ," his wife lets out a stifled cry as he continues, "well, if you want to stay, we will be here, too."

A few doctors and nurses come into the room.

Oh, God. This is happening. This is really happening.

I don't let go of his hand. A doctor says something to Michael's dad who nods his head. The doctor explains to all of us what will happen but I can't see him through my blurry tears and I can't hear him through the sound of my heart pounding in my ears.

His mom and dad walk around to the other side of the bed and his mom holds Michael's other hand. His dad nods to the doctors.

They turn the heart monitor off first and immediately I put my head on his chest so that I can still feel his heartbeat. *Don't go! Don't leave me!* I scream in my head.

I hear someone flip a switch and the whooshing and whirring sounds cease. The door opens and some people leave. The room is so quiet. Almost peaceful. The only sounds are muffled sobs and sniffles.

His chest rises and falls a few more times and then it goes still.

Breathe. I implore him.

His heart is still beating, although I can feel it slowing. It is lighter and lighter and as I feel him slipping away, I grip his hand harder. I put my other hand around him, under his back and mold myself to his chest. I want to become part of him, part of his body, part of his soul. I want to become one with him at this moment so that wherever he is going, whatever journey he is going on, he can take me with him.

Slower and slower now I hear the beating in my ear . . . then nothing.

Michael . . . take me with you.

Chapter Nine

Two years later . . .

"Emma, if you would have had a rehearsal, like every other bride, you wouldn't be so freaked out right now."

"I'm not freaked out, Lyn," she says, while the hairdresser takes the super-large curlers from the top of her head, "I'm just excited. You know that Graham couldn't take any more time off than the two weeks for our honeymoon. So we didn't have a rehearsal. How hard can it be to remember in what order to walk down the aisle?" She points at me in the mirror. "*You* are the one freaking out."

"Am not," I whine. Apparently I am a ten-year-old.

"Lyn, I understand. You haven't seen him in almost two years. I know you are nervous even though you won't admit it."

I roll my eyes. "Whatever. Anyway, did you see the seating chart? Apparently the name of his plus one is Candy. What kind of name is that? Sounds like she belongs in a 'Deep Throat' movie if you ask me. Or maybe she's a stripper."

Emma laughs at me and gives me a big smile while shaking her head. The large curls bounce over her shoulders. She is gorgeous. I mean, Emma is beautiful all of the time, but today . . . wow, she takes even my breath away. Graham is a dead man at the altar.

The altar. The place I'm going to see him again. Of all the places in all the world, it has to be at a freaking church altar that I see him.

I look at myself in the mirror. I love what the hairdresser has done with my hair. She has it up in a french twist with tendrils coming out all over. The make-up artist has transformed my face into something even I think is pretty. How does she use ten pounds of makeup but make it look like I don't even have any on?

"Girl . . . we are hot." Emma laughs. "The guys will have a full-on meltdown."

"Who cares what I look like? You are the one that is hot." I get a tear in my eye. "Emma, you are so beautiful and I'm so happy for you."

"God, Lyn, don't cry and ruin the makeup. And not *all* eyes will be on me." She winks in the mirror. "I doubt Nate will even notice me after you walk down the aisle looking like . . . that." She waves her hand up my body.

"Two years, Emma. It's been two years and we have both moved on. I'm not interested in another relationship. Especially not with him. Plus he's here with Cherry, Chicklet, or whatever her name is."

"It's Candy," she reminds me with an eye roll.

Twenty minutes later I'm standing at the sanctuary doors. I'm trying my best to be supportive of Emma. After all, this is her big day. I just can't help thinking about what will happen in about thirty seconds when I go through these doors.

"It will all be okay, Lyn. You'll see," she says, comforting me.

120

I'm the worst best-friend-slash-maid-of-honor ever. "I'm sorry, Emma. I'm the one who should be saying that to you." I frown. "Emma, you are the best friend anyone could ever ask for and you deserve all the happiness you have found with Graham." I pull her in for a hug, careful not to tug on her veil. "I'm going to miss you so much."

"I love you too, sweetie." She pulls away and pushes me towards the door. "Don't worry, Thelma, we will still be seeing a lot of each other, even after I move to Raleigh. Now, let's go get me married."

The doors open and we line up to file into the huge room with cathedral ceilings that has been adorned with purple and white flowers. Flowers that match the dress I am wearing. The dress that Emma picked specifically because she thought it went so well with my dark hair. It swishes along the ground with its mini-train. I hope I don't trip over my own feet trying to walk in it.

The ring bearer and flower girl start their walk, followed by two of Emma's sorority sisters and then Graham's sister. When it's my turn, I have to will my feet to move. This is Emma's day, I remind myself. Don't ruin it.

I start my procession down the aisle and vow not to look up to where Graham and his groomsmen are standing. I look at the guests sitting in the pews. I find my mom and dad and focus on them.

I have to close my eyes for a second to stop the tears that threaten, when it crosses my mind that this should have been my wedding. I should be walking down the aisle wearing white, not purple. And it should be Michael waiting at the altar.

I take a few deep breaths and open my eyes. Then I do it. Because, it's just like that accident you can't not look at. I slowly raise my eyes and move my glance from the carpet at my feet to the steps at the top of the altar. I see the matching shiny black shoes of many feet standing side by side. My eyes immediately find the pair of shoes just to the right of the first pair. I know they belong to Nate.

I take in the jet-black pants of the tuxedo and then the contrast of the white shirt, thin black tie and black jacket that hangs so gloriously on his broad shoulders. My heart is beating wildly and I'm sure those around me can hear it.

When my eyes meet his, my heart leaps out of my chest and slams into his. He is staring at me with his mouth open. I think I see him say, "Oh my God."

Graham elbows him and smiles.

He is so handsome in the tux that I can't look away. His hair is longer than it was a few years ago. It curls up at the ends, just like in high school. Those blue eyes jump out at me and I almost forget where I am.

The processional music changes to 'Here Comes the Bride'. Emma was nothing if not traditional in her wedding planning. I snap out of it, drag my eyes away from Nate's and finish my walk to the front.

I should be thinking of Emma right now as she walks down the aisle, locking her eyes with Graham's. But all I can think about is how I'm going to get through tonight with *him* in the same room. *Him* in the same room looking all delicious in that tailored tux. *Him* in the same room with Candy—the porn star.

I shouldn't care.

I silently vow not to care.

I am so screwed.

Thankfully, I'm able to pull off my maid of honor duties and I manage to get through the short ceremony without looking at Nate. However, when the minister pronounces them husband and wife and everyone claps, I can't help but look at him.

He has a proud smile on his face and is watching his best friend kiss my best friend. He shifts his eyes my way and gives me the smile. That smile. The one that haunts my dreams.

Graham and Emma start their walk together back up the aisle.

Oh, hell.

This is what happens when you don't have a rehearsal. I'm hit with the realization that I have to make the same walk with Nate. He walks to center stage and awaits me to join him.

My shaky legs are barely holding me up as I walk towards him. He, on the other hand, looks like confidence reincarnate and smirks at me. He holds his elbow out to me and I take it. After all, what choice do I have?

"Brooklyn," he says in a whispered breath. Then he places his other hand over mine where our arms are entwined. My skin is on fire where he is touching me. There are little shock waves going through my body and I think it must be static electricity from my long dress dragging along the carpet beneath me.

My heart is pounding in my ears. My palms are sweating. My dress that fit perfectly just this morning is suddenly too tight and I'm having trouble taking in a breath.

We make it up the aisle and out the large doors after what is the longest thirty seconds of my life.

I shed a few happy tears with Emma. Then we are whisked away for pictures.

At the reception, we get through our toasts with a lot of laughs and a few more tears.

When I see 'Candy' seated next to Nate at dinner I shoot daggers at Emma who is laughing at me along with Graham like they are sharing a private joke.

That bitch. Why didn't she tell me?

Sitting next to Nate is the most adorable blonde-haired, blue-eyed little girl I've ever seen. *Not a stripper.* She looks just like him. His niece perhaps.

When I look at Nate, he is shooting daggers of his own, right into the man sitting next to me.

I had to bring someone. I knew I would see Nate and I didn't want him to think I'm available. I'm not. Not to him. Not to anyone. Ryan was a safe bet. He and I have become close friends since I took him on as my business partner six months ago. He knows the boundaries. He knows my past. He has an incredible, understanding girlfriend. He is the perfect date for me.

I try not to watch Nate, but when I look over and see that he is away from his seat I find myself scanning the room to see where he is. I catch him dancing with his niece. Or rather I catch her standing on his feet while he is dancing. She smiles up at him like he is her hero. He makes her laugh and squeal little noises that only a six-year-old can make.

A good looking older man walks up, blocking my view of Nate. He says, "Ah, the illustrious Brooklyn. Finally we meet."

Finally?

He smiles at me and I instantly know who he is. There is only one other person in the world that is able to melt me with that smile. The smile that makes my heart go into overdrive and makes my palms get sweaty.

"Mr. Riley, I presume?" I take his proffered hand.

"Please, call me Nathan." He is assessing me in a way that doesn't quite make me uncomfortable, yet I know he is sizing me up. "I can see now why my son is drawn to you. You—"

"Pappy! Come dance wif me," a toothless Candy interrupts.

"How can I say no to that?" He swings her up and onto his hip. "Brooklyn, please excuse me, will you?"

"Of course. It was nice meeting you Mr . . . er . . . Nathan." I blush.

I'm sitting here left wondering what he was going to say. Nate is drawn to me . . . *still?* It's been so long. He's talked to his father about me? So many questions are running through my mind.

Ryan grabs my hand. "Looks like you need to dance, too. I'm just not sure I want you standing on my feet."

"Are you calling me fat?" I smile.

"Hell no, woman. What kind of death wish do you think I have?" he jokes.

We dance to some of my favorite songs. Emma let me help with the playlist. I made her swear no Nickelback. I still don't listen to them, especially not when Nate is going to be in the same room.

My head is resting on Ryan's shoulder while we slow dance when I catch Nate staring at us. He looks at me with the same eyes he had when I was walking down the aisle. Then he shifts his eyes to Ryan and his face goes through a transformation from pissed to hurt to frustrated as his hand runs through that messy-yet-incredible hair of his.

I turn away and finish the dance, determined that Nate will not spoil my evening. Who am I kidding? He has already spoiled it. Or I have. Because I can't stop thinking about him.

Stop thinking about him.

My feet are killing me so I lead Ryan off the dance floor. I lead him right off into the train wreck I see walking towards us.

Nate looks at me, takes a deep breath, and then turns to Ryan and extends his hand. "Michael, I just wanted to say you are a lucky guy."

Oh, shit.

Ryan shakes his hand and says, "I'll agree with you that I am a lucky guy to be escorting this beautiful woman, but I'm not Michael.

Ryan Thompson." He turns to me and says, "Michael, wasn't that your fiancé?"

Shit, shit, shit.

"Was your fiancé?" Nate says. "As in, not anymore?" He raises an eyebrow.

Ryan looks at Nate. Then he looks at me. Various scenarios simultaneously play out in my head as to how I should handle this. In the end, though, I stay silent.

Confused, Ryan looks back at Nate and says, "Uh, Michael died almost two years ago Mr . . . ?"

The blood drains from Nate's face and he struggles to remember his own name. "N-Nate. Riley," he chokes out.

"Oh, shit . . . Nate Riley!" Ryan raises his eyebrows at me. I can practically see the light bulb go off over his head. He looks at me like I might collapse right here on the edge of the dance floor. "Well, this couldn't have been any more awkward, could it?" He smiles. The bastard.

I haven't breathed a word yet. I don't know what to say.

Sorry, Nate, my fiancé died shortly after we had an almost-kiss and I told Emma and Graham to not tell you because I didn't want you in my life. In fact, I don't want you or any other man, ever again, so just leave me alone.

"Ryan," Nate addresses him, "would I be stepping on any toes if I asked to dance with Brooklyn?"

"I don't know, man. That is up to . . . *Brooklyn*, was it?" They both turn and look at me.

"Fine," I say, "one dance." I walk out ahead of him onto the dance floor as a slow song begins to play. He takes me in his arms without even asking, placing his hands around my lower back. I put my hands on his shoulders and instantly his smell washes over me. That smell of fresh laundry and Nate that invokes so many memories.

He pulls me closer and I have no choice but to wrap my arms around his neck. We dance like this for minutes without uttering a word. I don't think I'm capable of words right now. He is stroking my back through my thin silky dress. My entire world, my sole focus is on the small circles he is rubbing with those large hands and the heat that is generating from his touch.

I can feel his heart pounding on his chest wall. Or maybe that is my heart. He is matching my heavy breathing breath for breath. This is wrong. I can't do this. I squeeze my eyes shut and try to muster the courage to push away from him and walk away.

He blows out a breath. "Brooklyn, why didn't you tell me? Why didn't Graham or Emma tell me? I mean, I'm sorry, I know it must have been terrible for you. I can't imagine what you had to go through. But, what the hell, Brooklyn . . . why?"

"Why didn't I tell you?" I pull back and look at him like he is crazy. "Why didn't I tell you?" I repeat, as we stop dancing. "Because I knew you would try to lure me into your bed as soon as you found out. I was mourning the loss of the man I loved. The man who should have been my husband." I take a breath. "But then again, you apparently don't care about the sanctity of marriage since you threw your own down the toilet when you cheated on your wife."

He drops my hands like I just burned him.

"I'm not a cheater, Brooklyn. I've never cheated on anyone in my life. My wife was the one who cheated. She ruined my goddamn life and then she ruined my goddamn marriage."

He turns and walks away, leaving a small crowd staring at me. I smile at them as a blush creeps over my face and then I make my way back to my table and to the security of Ryan.

Chapter Ten

I don't want to release Emma from the big bear hug we've got going on. As soon as I do, she will leave me, and my life as I know it will change forever.

I've taken the morning off to see them on their way as they leave for Paris. I knew this day was coming. I've tried to prepare myself. I have to let her go live her life with Graham. But I don't have to be happy about it.

"Lyn, we'll be back in two weeks and we'll spend the whole weekend together before I have to move." She winks at Graham who gives her a knowing look. "Plus, we'll be back tons on weekends and holidays. You'll get sick of us."

"I know and I'm so happy for you guys. I'm just going to miss the heck out of you." I wipe the tears away—again. Emma and I are getting all blubbery and weepy. Then there is a knock at the door and Graham springs up to get it, probably happy to get out of this room so full of estrogen.

When we've pulled ourselves together and are putting another pot of coffee on, Graham walks back in the room. And Nate walks in right behind him.

"What is *he* doing here?" I blurt out, not very nicely. I'm still pissed at him for stomping away after that revelation he made to me last night. He didn't talk, or even look at me for the rest of the night.

I still haven't gotten the chance to ask Emma about it. I'm sure Emma knows everything about everything as she has practically lived in Raleigh at least part time over the past six months. All this time, I've told her not to talk to me about Nate. But after last night, I wonder why at the very least she didn't tell me that he wasn't the home wrecker I thought he was.

Nate turns around to walk out. "You said she would be at work," he huffs to Graham.

"Chill, man and sit on the freaking couch for a minute." Graham pushes his friend over to the sectional in our living room.

"Emma, can you and Lyn bring out some coffee please?" Graham sweetly asks his new wife.

"We're on it," she says, planting a kiss on his cheek. She turns to me. "Don't worry. We'll be out of here in a few minutes."

Emma pours some coffee into two cups and hands one to me. I shake my head at it. No way am I serving him. She rolls her eyes. "Follow me," she says.

In the living room, it doesn't escape me that Emma and Graham remain standing between the couch and the front door. Nate is sitting down looking pissed and I have no idea what to do or say.

"Sit." Emma points to the couch.

"What? Why?" I give her my 'what-the-hell' look.

"Lyn, sit your pretty ass down on the couch right now," she admonishes me.

Geez. So bossy. I walk the few steps over and sit at the opposite end of the sectional from Nate. I eye Emma and Graham nervously. What is this all about?

Graham looks from Nate to me and back to Nate. He points at both of us. "You two . . . you have to work your shit out. You,"—he points to Nate—"are my best friend. And you,"—he points to me—"are Emma's best friend. You have to learn to get along and play nice together."

"We are tired of being in the middle," Emma says. Then she looks at me. "Lyn, I love you and we have abided by your request not to say anything about you to Nate and about Nate to you. But it's exhausting. We have basically been lying to you guys by withholding the facts and we're tired of it."

She looks at Nate. "And you, we haven't said anything to Lyn about your situation because . . . well she wouldn't let us talk about you and because it's not our story to tell. But after your little outburst last night, you might as well get it all out there."

Graham adds, "Quit acting like adolescents and try to be friends. For our sake. For your sake. Work it out."

And with that, Emma grabs her purse and they turn around and walk out the door.

For their two-week honeymoon.

No goodbye or anything.

The door closes behind them, leaving Nate and me sitting on the couch, dumbfounded.

My eyes search the room for something look at. You could hear a pin drop. I have no idea what to do. Nate shifts on the couch and I know he is looking at me. I slowly turn my head in his direction and lock eyes with him. We stare at each other for about five seconds. Then we break out in hysterical laughter. My eyes are watering and my stomach hurts but I can't stop laughing. We both try to stop but then we look at each other and start up again.

"Why do I feel like our parents just gave us a lecture and then a time out to think about it?" Nate says, and then we laugh some more.

"Because that is pretty much what happened," I say.

Once our laughter subsides, it gets a little uncomfortable again.

I figure, what the hell, I'll start.

"Sorry—"

"I'm sorry—"

We both say at the same time and then smile awkwardly at each other.

"You go," he says.

I take a deep breath and try not to focus on the way his thumb is rubbing circles into the couch. Just like it was into my back last night. "Okay. Um, after Michael died I was a mess and of course I thought you were a philandering cheater, bedding every co-ed around so I didn't want them to tell you he was gone. I had a hard time getting over him. I still have bad days. I didn't need the added pressure of you . . ."—I wrinkle my nose—"pestering me." I look down at my hands.

And I never intend on getting into another relationship ever again.

"So, let me see if I understand this correctly." He clears his throat. "You told Graham and Emma not to tell me Michael died."

I nod.

"And you told them not to talk about me when they were around you."

I nod again.

"So, this whole time, you thought I not only slept around on my wife but was bedding everything in a skirt?"

"That pretty much sums it up." I bite my lip.

"God, Brooklyn. That couldn't be further from the truth." He closes his eyes and his head falls back against the cushions. "I hate that you thought that about me this entire time. Claudia . . . my wife . . ." he says, then takes a deep breath, "my *ex-wife*, she cheated on me so I ended the marriage."

I stay silent and wait for him to continue. I really want to hear the whole story as long as he's sharing.

"I kind of went a little wild after our divorce. I did sleep with a few too many women. But they all knew the score. I wasn't dishonest about my intentions. But I changed. When I saw you in Raleigh two years ago, I changed."

He shifts so that he is closer to me. "Brooklyn, this was all just one big misunderstanding. I'm sorry as hell that you lost Michael. Believe me, I am. But, I really think we could be great together. You can't deny the chemistry we have. We had. Even all those years ago."

He reaches out to take my hand.

I pull away. I pull away even though I want to feel his touch. I know what his hands feel like on mine. I know what they feel like on my body. I felt it again last night when we danced. I know that if I let him touch me, I might lose control. He is my kryptonite. He has been since I was seventeen. I will be fine as long as I stay away. Far away. I must stay focused. I can't let my emotions get in the way. Emotions lead to heartache. Every. Single. Time.

He looks hurt and is eyeing the hand that I pulled away. "Brooklyn—"

"Nate, I appreciate what you've told me. I'm glad that you are not the terrible person I thought you were."

I see him cringe. He runs his hand through his hair. "But?" he says.

"But that doesn't really change anything. I'm not looking for a relationship. With you. With anyone. Ever. It's not in the cards for me anymore. I'm sorry."

"What? That is crazy. How can you say you won't ever have another relationship? You are only twenty-seven years old. Besides, it looked like you were getting pretty cozy with that . . . Ryan was it? From last night." He pulls away from me.

"Ryan is a very good friend. He is my partner at Brooklyn's . . . remember, my bakery?"

"Partner?" he asks.

"Yes. An investor who is helping me to expand my business."

"Partner," he says again like he is trying out the word. "He didn't look like your partner last night. More like your boyfriend."

"He is not my boyfriend," I say.

"Does *he* know that?"

"Of course he does!" I bite back. "It's not like that. Besides, he has a girlfriend."

"She must be very understanding. I saw you dancing with him last night."

I roll my eyes at him. "Yes, she is. She is a nurse who works nights so Ryan and I hang out sometimes. As friends. She is cool with it."

"How convenient," he says. He looks pissed now.

"Whatever." I get up off the couch. "I don't have to justify anything to you, Nate. And as long as we are sharing, why don't you tell me what the hell happened in high school?"

He holds up his hands in surrender. "Okay, fine. I don't want to fight with you, Brooklyn." He sighs. "That is a long story. One I don't have time for right now. All I can say is that I was a young, stupid kid." He runs his hand through his hair and stands up. "I have to get going back to Raleigh. But I'm glad we had this talk." He smiles but it doesn't quite reach his eyes.

I stare at him. He looks conflicted. I want so much for him to tell me what happened back then. I hate that it matters to me. I hate that I think about it all the time and wonder how things might have turned out differently. How maybe I could have been his wife instead of that Claudia. How my life wouldn't be filled with guilt and shame if things had gone the way they were supposed to all those years ago.

"Yeah, I'm glad too. I'm sorry I thought so poorly of you and I'm sorry that your . . . wife . . . cheated on you. That must have been terrible." I almost choke on the word *wife*. I still can't believe he was married. It still hurts a little, down deep, knowing that he chose someone else over me. Even though I did the very same thing to him.

I see a hint of his tattoo as the sleeve of his shirt rides up when he puts on his jacket. The all too familiar jacket from a few years ago. It's the one he put over our heads in the rain that night. The night of the almost-kiss. I wonder what his lips would feel like on mine after all these years. Does he still taste of mint? Would he trail kisses up to that place behind my ear that drove me crazy at such a young age? Would it still burn like a hot trail of lava?

He reaches over and pulls my lip out from between my teeth, his eyes trained on my mouth. "Be careful what you wish for, Brooklyn," he whispers.

I snap out of it. "Um . . ." I try to recover, rather poorly.

"Friends?" He holds his hand out to me.

"I don't know about that." I eye his hand. "But we're getting there." I smile weakly.

I place my hand in his and brace for the jolt that runs straight from the point of his touch all the way up my arm and into my chest, like a bullet moving at warp speed. It makes my heart pound and my breath hitch.

"I'll see you, Brooklyn," he says, as he pulls his hand away slowly and turns to walk out the door.

The door I stare at for minutes after he is gone.

Chapter Eleven

I'll admit, it's hard without Emma here. She is the one person that keeps me grounded. She calls me on my crap, tells it like it is and has pretty much kept me going through the bad times.

Although he is no replacement for Emma, Ryan and I have been hanging out. A lot. We get along extremely well, but without the are-we-going-to-hookup pressure. He and I have established somewhat of a sibling relationship. Maybe it stems from the fact that we are both only children. Whatever the reason, he looks out for me and I listen attentively to the stories of his adventures.

Ryan is an adrenaline junky. He is an entrepreneur by occupation, but a daredevil at heart. He will find a potential money-making opportunity, help it blossom for a year or so and then he will move on to the next venture, while his bank account continues to grow.

So, it seems I will lose him, too, after a while. In the meantime, he is loads of fun to hang with. He has taken me bungee jumping and surfing already and is talking about us parachuting from a plane. Eeek!

He is at my apartment this morning, waiting for Emma to tell him what boxes go to Raleigh and which ones stay here for her parents to pick up.

Emma and Graham got back from Paris two days ago. After sleeping for almost eighteen hours, she and I spent the entire day together yesterday doing our favorite things. We got mani-pedis, went shopping, and ate lunch at our favorite restaurant, one where the tables are little aquariums and they serve the food right on top. I'm sorry, but eating sushi while fish swim underneath your plate— that just never gets old.

Emma and I are packing her things into boxes and wardrobes. I'm amazed at how much stuff she fit into her room in our small apartment. She is, thankfully, leaving me all of the furniture and most of the housewares since Graham is pretty much fully stocked.

We are carrying some of her best clothes out to hang them on a rod in the back seat of her car. Because, God forbid, they might wrinkle in the less than four-hour drive.

I think I'm hallucinating because I could swear I see Nate pull up in a sleek Ford F-150.

I momentarily lose myself in a daydream about being a seventeen-year-old girl in the front seat of a pickup truck, losing my virginity to the most gorgeous baseball player at school. I squeeze my legs together at the thought of him making me come in my panties simply by putting his hands on me. *In me.* And that voice, that raspy, sexy voice when he whispered in my ear.

"Brooklyn . . ."

Yes, that one.

Oh! Oh my God. I snap out of it. Said boy is now standing right in front of me. Only he is ten years older. Ten years sexier. Ten years hotter. My heart is pounding and I'm sure he can see it beating through my thin t-shirt. When did I become this gooey ball of emotion when he is around?

"Um . . . Nate?" I look at Emma in confusion. "What are you doing here?" I'm not sure why I am so excited to see him and I have to bite my lip to suppress the smile that wants to come out.

"I came to help Graham move Emma out, of course," he says, staring at my mouth.

I look over at Emma and she looks up at the sky.

"Oh. Uh . . . there are a lot of boxes still up in the apartment. You can use the back stairs." I point at the entrance to the apartment that is separate from the one inside the bakery.

"Thanks, I'll just head up then." He winks at me.

I give Emma the look. That look that says I know what you are trying to do and you aren't pulling one over on me. "Okay, okay." She holds up her hands in surrender. "So I knew he was coming. But I didn't want you to get mad at me and ruin our last weekend together."

I continue to stare her down.

"But by the look on your face when he pulled up, I'd say you are most definitely *not* mad at me." She smiles. "In fact, I think you want to hug me right now for bringing that man-candy to help me move. You know, it's hot enough that they might have to remove their shirts." She elbows me.

I roll my eyes at her. It's not lost on me that I tend to roll my eyes a lot when around, talking about, or just plain thinking of Nathan Riley. So far so good, because despite my mother's warning, they have remained properly placed in their sockets.

Back in the apartment, it becomes clear to me that we have missed something. Nate looks pissed and he is having a stare down with Ryan.

Crap. I know Ryan doesn't like Nate. I did try to explain that he wasn't the bad guy I thought he was. I think Ryan is simply being protective of me again, acting like the older brother I never had.

I also got the distinct impression from the conversation at our 'intervention' that Nate thinks there is something going on between me and Ryan.

Not that I care.

Because I don't.

Except that I do.

I guess I don't want Nate to think that I'm dating Ryan after I told him I wouldn't date anyone. Even if I did date someone, it wouldn't be Nate because that would betray Michael. But if I were to date anyone, the only face I can put on 'anyone' is Nate's.

I'm confusing even myself now. This is why I won't get involved anymore.

Too much drama. Too much emotion. Too much loss.

Ryan easily picks up a box and lifts it to his shoulder. His muscles flex and his long dark hair falls over his eyes and he reaches up to push it out of the way. Nate eyes him like a predator and puffs out his chest.

"Down, boy," Emma whispers to Nate. "You know they are just friends, right?"

"Bullshit," Nate says, loud enough for everyone to hear. "He wants in her pants."

"Dude, if I wanted in her pants, believe me, I'd be in her pants," Ryan asserts. Ordinarily, I would take offense to a comment like this. But I know Ryan. He is only pushing back. He's not being cocky. But Nate doesn't know that.

Nate's face gets red and his fists ball up momentarily. Then he leans over and picks up two boxes. Two boxes that I know are really heavy because I had just packed some of Emma's design books in them. His muscles are bulging as he is obviously struggling to carry them, being that they are probably heavier than he expected. It is almost comical watching him try to balance them. But he won't put one down. He nods at Ryan to go down the stairs. Probably so that he can drop a box or two on his head.

He follows Ryan and yells, "Hey man, don't put anything in my truck."

"What was that?" I question Emma.

"That was a pissing match." She laughs.

"No, not that. Why can't we put anything in Nate's truck?"

Emma's eyes go wide and she looks over at Graham.

"Um . . . he is staying back to visit his niece over in Richmond Hill tonight," Graham tells me. "You remember Candy the porn star, right?" He laughs.

"Oh." I blush at the memory of their wedding night and how jealous I was over what turned out to be an adorable little girl. *Jealous?* I shake my head at the ridiculous thought.

Emma says, "We want to unpack right away and not have to wait for him to come back. So that's why we can't put stuff in his truck. Plus, he is a terrible driver and I don't want my things spilled all over the Interstate." She rambles on, "And maybe my insurance wouldn't cover it if he m—"

"Emma, I'm sure Lyn doesn't care about all that," he interrupts, pulling her into the hallway. Probably to kiss her again. Their PDAs are reaching epic proportions. I grab a lamp and head downstairs so I don't have to witness it.

Two hours later we have Graham's large SUV and Emma's BMW loaded up with boxes. I walk past Nate's truck and see some boxes in the back so I guess they did decide to use it after all.

Graham gets pizza and beer for all of us and these poor guys have to sit around and listen to Emma and me as we laugh and cry at stories we tell about high school.

"Oh God, remember Homecoming? What was the guy's name that you went with?" Emma asks.

"Jeremy Bender," I say.

I notice how Nate perks up and leans closer to catch our conversation. I wonder if he knew Jeremy. I try to remember if they were friends.

"Right," she says. "Fender Bender—that's what everyone called him." She starts laughing loudly. "Nobody would get in a car with him because he had totaled like four cars by the time he was a senior. But he insisted on driving to Homecoming. So Lyn had to ride with me and my date to dinner and the dance."

We are practically rolling on the floor. My eyes are watering as we try to tell the story of Jeremy's dancing. It was worse than his driving.

All of a sudden there is a loud *crack!* We all turn to see that Nate has crushed a beer can with his hands. Why do I get the feeling that the beer can is a representation of poor Jeremy Bender? "Uh . . . sorry," Nate mumbles, when he sees us all staring at him. "Anyone want another beer?" He gets up and goes to the kitchen without waiting for a response.

It wasn't a real date. I only went to the dance to keep Emma company. Jeremy just happened to be the friend of her date. I didn't go out with anyone after Nate. Until Michael, that is. But Nate doesn't have to know that.

Later, after everyone is gone, I have a thought and text Ryan.

Me: **What happened between you and Nate when he first got here today?**

Ryan: **He was surprised to see me there. Thinks we have something going on. I know how you feel about him so I told him to back off.**

Me: **Oh, hell. What did he say?**

Ryan: **He didn't say anything. But I'm not afraid to tell you I feared for my life for a second before you and E showed up. Lyn, I kind of like the guy. Don't be too hard on him.**

Great, another one of my friends on his side. Well, at least Ryan told him to back off before he became his new BFF.

Maybe that is why Nate didn't push me today. I figured since we wouldn't be seeing each other anymore that he was really going to lay it on thick. But it was quite the opposite. He didn't make a big deal when he left. He shook my hand, of course, and once again, my whole body tingled in response to his strong fingers touching my skin. But it was almost like saying goodbye to someone you would see every day.

Chapter Twelve

This morning, Derek and I are on our way to a catering job. It's not a huge one, just a hundred or so pastries along with our mobile coffee and espresso bar.

Derek has been a life-saver now that we are catering. I was able to hire him with the extra funds Ryan invested. He is the perfect addition to Brooklyn's. He loves to bake and he is the brawn we needed for all of the heavy catering equipment. Yes, he is gay. But he is also strong, funny and the customers love him.

We are going to some ground-breaking ceremony for a new building. The company that hired us, R.A.D., has us laughing in the van. We are trying to guess what it stands for. So far all I've come up with is that they are a skateboarding or surfing business. Derek thinks it is a marijuana manufacturer. Really Awesome Dope.

We quickly set up the banquet table and coffee bar in the corner of a large tent that is right next to a roped-off construction site. We stand to the side, adorned in our Brooklyn's Bakery aprons, ready to help novices with the espresso machine.

"Brooklyn," someone says behind me.

I close my eyes. I know that voice. It is in my dreams. That low, raspy, sexy voice that makes my heart beat fast and my legs turn to Jell-O. I whirl around quickly and come eye-to-eye with Nate. Instantly, several emotions wash over me. Happy, relieved, confused.

"Nate! What are you doing here?"

Then I eye his shirt. There is a logo of a building with the letters R.A.D. just above it.

"You?" I say, surprised. "*You* hired me?"

"Well, not exactly. My company, or rather my dad's company, hired you."

I'm still staring at his shirt. I point to the logo, almost touching him. I want to touch him. I want to feel the muscles that I know are underneath the shirt he is wearing. But I don't, because . . . well, it would be weird. I am at work after all. And more importantly, he is off limits. All men are off limits.

"Riley . . . ?" I trail off and raise my eyebrows, looking from his shirt up to his face and into his deep blue eyes.

"Architectural Designs," he finishes.

"Oh. Right." I giggle, thinking of the silly names we came up with in the van. "So, what are you doing here?" I ask. "I mean, you didn't say anything yesterday."

"I wasn't sure how you were going to feel about this." He looks around nervously and says, "Brooklyn, I'm going to be in town for a while. My dad put me on this project and I'm here to oversee it."

In town for a while. My heart leaps for joy.

Joy? Wait, what?

My better judgment pops her head in. No, this is not a good thing. I'm weak around him. I need to stay the hell away from him for my own good. "How long will you be here?" Days . . . weeks . . . *oh, yes, please, weeks.*

"Probably a few months. It takes a while to get these projects up and going. We basically have to babysit the engineers every step of the way to make sure it will all work as planned."

Months! I didn't even hear a word he said after that.

Derek walks up and clears his throat. "Lyn, can you please help me with the espresso machine? That lever is sticking again."

"Oh, yes, sorry." I quickly introduce Nate to Derek and then get back to work.

It takes me twice as long as usual to get the machine working again. I'm well aware that Nate is staring at me. However, I'm not at all sure that what I'm feeling is uncomfortable, more like I'm hoping my butt looks good in these pants. I think back to this morning and wonder if I put enough mascara on to make my eyes look pretty. I even run my tongue over my teeth and am relieved when I taste the remnants of mouthwash, given he was standing so close to me just moments ago.

"I'll see you later, Brooklyn," Nate whispers in my ear on his way by.

I forget what I'm doing. I actually stop moving and can't form a cognitive thought in my head after feeling his hot breath on my neck.

$\sim$ $\sim$ $\sim$

Back at the bakery this afternoon, I can't stop thinking about what transpired this morning. Nate will be around for months. Will I see him? *Of course you will, stupid, he will probably make sure of that.*

I remember the stolen glances we made at each other this morning. I can still feel the heat of his touch when he brushed up against my arm as he walked by me, and the glare of his eyes when he watched me from across the tent. He was busy and I was busy, but somehow we always knew where the other was.

What am I doing? I have to stop thinking of him this way. He is a crush, an infatuation even, a schoolgirl fantasy I will never again experience. I have to strengthen my resolve. I have to make sure we aren't alone together. How hard can that be? It's not like I'll be seeing him every day. I can do this. Can't I?

Yes.

No.

I don't know.

Crap. I'm toast.

~ ~ ~

The benefit of living where you work is that when I work late, as I am today, I can just go right up to my apartment and relax. No commute, no waiting in traffic. It's one of the reasons I love this place.

It's not too late, only about six-ish, but it is late for me as ordinarily I cut out around three o'clock since I show up early in the mornings. I'm spent. My hands are raw after the thorough cleaning of the catering equipment. I'm dragging my feet up the stairs. I don't even think I have the energy to make dinner. I can't wait to dive into some ice cream and watch a couple of programs I've recorded.

I head straight to the kitchen and open the freezer. *Did I buy this much ice cream?* There are two gallons of mint chocolate chip ice cream staring me in the face. A going away present from Emma, perhaps. I grab one along with a spoon, bypassing a bowl completely and head to the couch.

That's when it hits me. Something is different. I can't quite put my finger on it. It even smells different in here. I look around and see some boxes piled behind the couch. *I thought they got all of them.*

I put the ice cream down on the coffee table and go over to my room. Everything looks okay in here. Now I head to Emma's room . . . er, the spare bedroom. My eyes widen and confusion sets in when I see several more boxes on her bed and some suitcases by the closet. "Emma?" I ask to no one in particular because there isn't anyone else here.

What's going on? I peek my head back out into the living room and look around. Then I stride across the room to the suitcases and find an ID tag hanging off one of them. I open it up, pulling the little leather flap away from the viewing window and take in a sharp breath when I read the name.

Nathan Riley.

"What. The. Hell?" I say out loud.

I run out to the kitchen and get my phone.

Crap. I deleted his number years ago. I tap my screen a few times and pull up a different number. It rings only once. "Lyn, sweetie, how are you?" she says about an octave too high.

Oh God. She knows about this. "Seriously, Emma?" I yell. "What are you thinking? There is no way in hell that I'm letting Nate Riley live with me for a few months. I do not want that man in the same town, let alone the same apartment. You call him right now. This minute. You tell him to come pick up his stuff and go to a hotel, or his sister's house . . . or anywhere but here."

Then it dawns on me. "How long did you have this planned? The whole seeing his sister thing, was that all a lie so that you could stonewall me into this?"

"Calm down, Lyn." I can hear her smiling and it pisses me off even more.

"Calm down?" I yell. "Calm down? Since when do you get to make decisions about my life without consulting me?"

"Because I know you," she says. "Because I knew you wouldn't go along with it. But also because I know that it's the best thing for you. You are alone now and I hate that. He is alone in a city that he despises. You guys need each other whether you know it now or not."

"Plus," she adds, "I do kind of own the building."

"Oh, you did not just play the landlord card with me." I stomp my foot like she can see it.

"Sorry, Lyn. I shouldn't have said that. But please, just give it some time. He really needed a place to stay. Nobody does short term leases anymore." I hear the pleading in her voice.

"I have to get out of here before he gets home." I quickly throw the ice cream in the freezer. Then I grab my keys and fly out the door and down the stairs. "I'll talk to you later, Emma."

"Wait—" is all I hear before I cut her off.

Then I turn off my phone.

I try to fill my parents in as best I can, but it is all kinds of uncomfortable telling them about losing my virginity at age seventeen. They knew I had a crush on him. They saw how broken I was after he left. But this is probably something they never wanted to know, not really.

They let me talk until my throat gets sore, then Mom leads me to my old room.

My room. My sanctuary growing up. They never changed a thing. It looks exactly the same way it did when I moved out four years ago. Right down to the picture of Nate tucked into the side of the mirror. It is wrinkled and weathered from the years it spent under my pillow, but Emma never let me throw it out. She said one day I'd be glad I kept it. I'm still waiting for that day.

My mom tucks me into bed, just like she did when I was little. "I want to tell you something that happened at Emma's wedding," she says. "I probably should have told you weeks ago but I didn't think you would see Nate again."

She is rubbing my hair and it is as soothing and comforting as ever. "I ran into Nate's father."

I turn my head around to see her face and I raise my eyebrows at her.

"He wanted to apologize to us for hurting you all those years ago," she tells me.

"What? Why would he do that? It wasn't his fault."

"Oh, but he thinks it was. Something about saying all the wrong things to his kids and making them believe their friends wouldn't associate with them anymore."

"I still think that if Nate wanted to get in touch with me, he would have." I frown. "It was his choice. He could have found a way even if his dad didn't want him to."

"Perhaps that is true," she says. "But why not give him the benefit of the doubt. Or at least talk to him about it before you condemn him. He was young back then, just like you were and, as we found out just tonight, you didn't always make the wisest decisions." She raises her eyebrows at me and gives me that look that only a mother can give that has my figurative tail going between my legs.

"Still, Mom, that doesn't change the fact that I don't want to live with him. I don't want to live with any man. Ever."

She smiles sweetly at me. "Sleep on it dear. It will be better in the morning. You've had a long day." She kisses my forehead and goes to the door. "Never say never, Brooklyn."

Chapter Thirteen

I can't help but stare out the front window of the shop. There he is, again, like he has been every morning this week. Nate is stretching out in the park across the street, getting ready for a run. He is without a shirt so I can see the ripples of his stomach, the outlines of his muscles, the hardness of his body. I can almost smell his scent. That mixture of clean freshness and Nate with a touch of man sweat. A heady combination.

I take a deep breath, knowing that I will get to enjoy his scent first-hand when in about forty-five minutes he will come in the shop and order a coffee, black, and a blueberry muffin. Same thing. Every. Day.

Then he will walk out the front door of the bakery and around the back to the private entrance of our apartment. When did it become *our* apartment?

I know he does this on purpose. Well, I think he does it on purpose. He never looks over this way to see if I've noticed him, so maybe it is just his routine. Oh, I've noticed. Along with every other red-blooded woman in the bakery at seven in the morning. And a few men, too.

"He's good for business," a cute redhead says, pulling me from my trance.

I look around and realize that the shop *is* more crowded than usual. People are hanging around instead of popping in for coffee and then leaving for work.

I roll my eyes and put on a fake smile. "What can I get you?" I try to complete her order without looking outside again. Instead, I look at all of the women eyeing my new roommate. Then I turn to see Kaitlyn all wide-eyed and frozen in place as she was cleaning the coffee filter.

"Et tu, Brute?" I use a napkin to dab the invisible drool from her chin.

"Lyn." She breaks the stare and looks at me. "If you don't get your head out of your ass soon and jump on that masterpiece of a man, someone else will."

Someone else. I abhor the thought of anyone else with him. Touching him, smelling him. Then I chastise myself. I am such a hypocrite. How can I be mad at other women for wanting him? He isn't mine. He will never be mine.

I get back to work and try to concentrate on anything but the man who I know will walk into my shop in—I check the clock—thirty minutes.

I think back to earlier this week when I made the decision to try and live with this situation. Make the best of it. Lemonade from lemons and all that.

When Emma went away to college she was placed with the roommate from hell her first year. She couldn't get her dorm assignment changed so instead, she rearranged her class schedule so that she was gone when her roommate was home. I decided to take a page from the Emma chronicles and go with avoidance as well.

I have moved my usual crack-of-dawn runs to the late afternoon so that I'm out when Nate gets home from work. I have caught up on loads of bookkeeping at the shop by coming down here after my shower and eating dinner while I reconcile the books. Then when I go back upstairs, I read in bed for hours, avoiding him out in the living room watching television.

It is working. I have barely said two words to him all week. In fact, I think I talk to him more when he is placing his order here at the bakery, than when in our apartment.

I only wish he would go out more. He sits at home every night watching movies or working at the drafting table he has set up in his bedroom.

I'm coming out of the back with a tray of fresh muffins when he walks in. I watch him make his way to the counter. He is walking towards me and all I can see is that sweaty body, muscles all shining and rippled. His eyes are on me, devouring me like the muffin I know he is about to order.

Women are practically lined up on either side of him as he walks by them, like a football player passes the cheerleaders lining the way out to the field. Their collective chins are hitting the floor as he reaches the counter and pulls out a few napkins to wipe off his face.

He doesn't look at any of them. He doesn't break eye contact with me. I think there must be twenty women in here that would like me dead on the spot. *I* would wish me dead on the spot if I were one of them, watching the way he looks at me like he is the moth to my flame.

Only I fear I will be the one who gets burned.

"Morning, Brooklyn." He smiles that white, toothy smile that gets my internal juices flowing.

"Good morning. The usual?" I ask.

"Yes. Thank you." He pulls a ten out of the pocket in his running shorts and hands it to me. It's moist with sweat and I resist the urge to put it to my nose. That would be wrong on so many levels. I put it in the register and give him his change which he dumps in the tips bucket.

"Thanks, Brooklyn. You look lovely today." It is the same thing he has said every morning this week. This is the same dance we do every day. He turns to walk out the front door, past the dozen or so eyes that are looking at him like a piece of meat and they are the lionesses waiting to attack.

Today, however, before I can even think twice and keep the words from leaping out of my mouth, I say, "Nate, why don't you just come through and use the back entrance?" He stops in his tracks. I can see the reflection of his huge smile in the window. He turns and walks past the women again, then past the counter and into the back room.

Ha! I think to myself as the lionesses stare at me in disbelief.

After work, I'm getting ready for my run. I grab a bottle of water from the kitchen. As I'm putting the bottle to my lips, I see that he has unpacked the last of his boxes and his rather large movie collection spans the shelves of the entertainment center.

I browse through his collection. I knew we shared an interest in movies; it is one of the things we talked about at the party all those years ago. I think he must have every slasher movie ever made. I'm not sure he will be able to get through all of these in a few months. I absentmindedly pick up my favorite, 'Scream'—the first one—it never gets old.

I hear his key in the door so I quickly put down the DVD and go to the kitchen to finish my water. He watches me without saying a word as I pass him by on my way out. Yes, I'm wearing my favorite red running shorts. The ones that make my butt look really nice. I think it is the extra spandex.

Later, after my shower, I head to the kitchen and make a sandwich to take downstairs when I hear the beginning lines of my favorite movie. I stand in the doorway of the kitchen, eyes glued to the TV, getting lost in the show.

"You know, I won't bite if you come sit on the couch," he says, patting the spot next to him. I turn away, finish making my dinner and then make my way out—to the other end of the couch. It is my favorite movie, after all.

We both laugh at the same parts. The parts that make most people jump, scream and hide their eyes. But we laugh. And then we look at each other out of the corners of our eyes and smile, because we know we are idiots.

I've never found another person who can watch a slasher movie like it is a comedy. Until now. Michael and I used to watch them, but he would squeeze my leg whenever he got scared, even though he would never admit he was spooked. He even asked me to leave the kitchen light on one night. God, it was funny.

I giggle out loud. But not at the movie, so Nate asks, "What's so funny?"

"Nothing. I was just remembering something." And it dawns on me. I just had a happy memory of Michael. I think I smiled the whole rest of the movie.

The following few nights we do more of the same. 'Freddy vs. Jason' and then 'Halloween H20'. We have established a routine. We don't talk about it, we just do it. I come in from my run, shower, fix myself something to eat and then we sit down to watch whatever movie he has picked out. Last night he even had something made for dinner before I came back. I think he did it on purpose, but he casually mentioned that he made too much for him to eat so I could finish it if I wanted to.

Nate never goes out. He did go to his sister's one night for dinner but other than that, it is only work or home for him. I, on the other hand, am trying to jump-start my social life sans Emma, so I went out tonight for a Girls' Night with Kaitlyn and Derek. Technically, I can still call it that since we could all drool over cute guys, right?

I arrive back home after midnight to find Nate asleep on the couch. I can't draw my eyes away from him. He looks so peaceful, childlike even. His hair is even more messy than usual because his arm is tossed over his head.

Oh, there is the tattoo, in full-blown glory for me to see. I shouldn't look. He says it is nobody's business. I tiptoe my way over to the backside of the couch, eyeing him the whole way. I look at his chest to make sure his breathing is still steady and deep. Why do I feel like a cat burglar?

When I'm a few feet away, I can make out the tattoo clearly and my breath hitches. I've never seen anything like it. Well, not that I'm a tattoo connoisseur or anything, but this one is outright morbid. On the underside of his arm is the black outline of a heart with a knife sticking out of it. The only color on the entire tattoo is the drops of red blood coming from the knife. And when I say heart, I mean the anatomical representation of an actual heart—with valves and vessels. It's awful. I mean, it is a great work of art, but it's awful.

There are words over it, the words that you can also see wrapping around the front of his arm. They go all the way around and over the heart. They are in script and of course, since they are in French, I have no idea what they say. 'Mourir Pour' is the part of the phrase that I etch into my memory so that I can Google it later.

"Like what you see?" I look at his face and see that he is grinning at me.

How long have I been standing here staring at his tattoo? I search my mind for an excuse to be so close to him. I grab the pillow off the chair to my right and say, "Um . . . you looked uncomfortable so I thought you might want this." I throw it at him and then I walk out of the room. Only to hear his muffled laughter behind me.

In my room, I open my laptop and Google the French to English translation of the few words I saw on his tattoo.

'To die for.'

Chapter Fourteen

I jerk awake and it takes a minute to remember where I am. I'm hearing music from 'The Shining' play over and over as the DVD is stuck on the menu screen. I look at the clock and see it is after eleven. The events of the day flash through my mind and I remember how exhausted I was when I came up from my monthly inventory.

Oh, we fell asleep on the couch. Together. My head is on his shoulder and my hand is on his leg. *Crap*. I jump over on the couch about two feet and that wakes Nate up. He has a smirk on his face.

"Okay, so exactly how long was I sleeping like that?" I feel a blush creep up my face.

"Not long," he says. "I couldn't bear to push you off me, you smell just like a cupcake."

"What?" I look at him like he is crazy. "I did shower after work you know."

"I know. I can smell your shampoo. Flowers?" he asks.

"Mmmm," I mumble.

"Anyway, you always smell like cupcakes. Vanilla, I think. You spend so much time baking that it probably oozes from your pores." He laughs.

I hit him with a pillow. Then I smell my arm.

"Brooklyn, it's a compliment. It smells nice. I will never be able to eat sweets again without thinking of you."

"Oh. Well . . . thanks, I guess." I decide to ask him what has been bugging me for weeks. "Nate, how come you never go out? I mean, it must be a bore hanging out and watching movies with me."

He puts his arm up on the back of the couch so that his hand is mere inches from me. "First, it is never a bore to hang out with you. Second, I don't really want to go out and risk running into a lot of people from high school." He shrugs and looks embarrassed and uncomfortable so I don't press him on the issue. He gets up and walks to the kitchen. I can hear him open the refrigerator.

When he returns, he places two beers on the table in front of us then proceeds to twist off the tops, handing me a bottle. Oh, I guess we're talking.

He tells me about his job and how exciting it is watching a building come up from nothing. He actually gets a gleam in his eyes when he talks about it. He is very passionate in his explanation of what it takes to design a new structure, and even though he has lost me with all of the technical terms, I'm in awe of how smart he is on the subject.

I tell him about starting up the bakery four years ago and he seems genuinely interested. He asks about any plans to expand the bakery or maybe franchise it out.

"No way." I take a drink then shake my head vehemently. "I would never disclose my secrets to virtual strangers. Besides, it was always my dream as a little girl to run a mom-and-pop bakery that was all my own." I look over and see his confusion. "I know, I know

. . . I brought in a partner. But that's mainly so I could branch out into catering." I pick at a fuzz ball on the couch. "I suppose I would consider a second location, but I would have to have a hand in everything. It's practically written in my mission statement."

He laughs and puts his arm up on the back of the couch so that his sleeve is riding up his bicep, showing off his tattoo. I stare at it. I wonder what the words say. *To die for.* What does that mean? Claudia is the one he would die for? Why the knife and the blood?

"It's just a tattoo, Brooklyn," he says. I can only imagine what an idiot I must look like staring at it.

"What does it say?" I bite my lip. "I mean, if you don't mind me asking. Did you get it for her? Your wife?"

"Ex-wife," he says the words harshly. "And no, I didn't get it for her. I'm not even sure I got it *because* of her." He doesn't explain further. "It is a Moroccan proverb. It says 'He who has nothing to die for has nothing to live for'."

I'm stunned. That is deep. Really deep. I'm not sure what to say. Am I ready to have this kind of conversation with him?

"Don't read too much into it, Brooklyn." He sighs. "I was in a bad way when I got it. I'm fine now."

He's fine now. Did he think he had nothing to live for? A knife in the heart. She must have really broken him. The way I am broken. Only I don't wear it on my sleeve.

He gets up and goes to his movie collection. "In keeping with the Steven King theme, how about 'Children of the Corn'?"

I look at the clock. Eleven-thirty. It's late and I should go to bed.

"Okay." I grab the blanket next to me and pull it over my legs.

~ ~ ~

I scrunch my eyes tight to try and keep the light out. I'm not ready to get up yet. My neck hurts so I move it around a bit on my very lumpy pillow. As I start to wake up more, I reach up to fluff my pillow and find myself poking around on Nate's lap.

Oh my God.

In horror, I realize that I've been touching the erection that is pressing against the fly of his jeans. I roll over and fall off the couch, hitting my head on the side of the coffee table. "Ouch!" I say, waking Nate in the process of scrambling off his lap. Then I hit my shin on the side of the couch and I can't limp away fast enough. I'm rubbing my head and holding my shin when I turn back to see Nate laughing hysterically on the couch. I think I must turn beet red. I can't put two thoughts together. I can't even keep myself upright so I fall back on the couch and cover my face with my hands.

He comes over and brings my leg up onto the couch and rubs the red bump that is forming. "Are you okay?" he asks in all seriousness, now that he sees I am injured.

"I'm fine," I say without looking at him. I look anywhere but at him. I know if I look over, my eyes will go directly to his lap and that will mortify me even further.

I pull my leg away and he says, "Brooklyn, it's okay. There is nothing to be embarrassed about. We fell asleep watching the movie. It happens." He laughs and looks at his lap. "Um . . . I'm sorry about that. That just happens, too." He shrugs.

I look over at him now, begging my eyes to keep above his neck.

"If you want to be embarrassed about something, be embarrassed about the dream you had last night," he says.

"What?"

"The dream. You know, the one where you moaned and called out my name?" He chuckles.

"I did not have any such dream," I pout.

He gets up off the couch and heads to his room. "Okay, whatever you say." He walks away. "So I guess I'll try not to take offense that I smell like—what was it—fresh laundry?" He shuts his door.

Shit.

Shit. Shit. Shit.

What did I say in my sleep? Michael used to tell me that I would sometimes talk in my sleep but he could never understand what I said. I rack my brain trying to remember any dreams I had last night.

I make sure I don't run into Nate again before work. I'm so embarrassed. I can't imagine what he must think of me. The last thing I need is him knowing that I dream of him.

$$\sim \quad \sim \quad \sim$$

Today turns out to be one of those days you wish you would have stayed in bed all day. I lost a big catering bid. They said I didn't have enough experience with major events. It's true, I know. But how can we get experience with big events if nobody ever hires us for big events? I was really counting on this to put my name out there. Ryan will be upset. Before he left for Costa Rica, he thought we all but had this in the bag.

I run an extra few miles tonight to help me calm down. Nothing clears my head more than pounding the pavement while listening to music.

I almost trip on the sidewalk when a song comes on my iPod. A song that's not on my playlist. A song I haven't heard in over two years. *'Be My Reason'*. It was the last text he sent to me after Raleigh. Nate! *He* put this on my playlist—the sneaky bastard. Yet, I don't turn it off. I listen to every word.

> *Something inside me*
> *Can't rest until I find*
> *The way to make it up to you*
> *The way to make you mine*
>
> *I know I messed up good*
> *And that you should walk away*
> *I have no right to ask*
> *But I'm begging you to stay*

Was he trying to say he was sorry for leaving me in high school? That he wanted to change his philandering ways after Claudia broke him? What I don't understand is why he would go through all this trouble for me. Why me?

As I listen to the chorus, I think about what a friend he has been to me lately. He has done so much to ease the pain of Emma not being around. He comforts me repeatedly all while living in a city that he hates. Everything he has done has been for me.

> *Be my reason . . .*
> *My cause, my light*
> *Be my reason . . .*
> *My purpose, my life*
> *'Cause baby it was always you*
> *You're my reason*
> *You've pulled me through*

And because I'm a glutton for punishment, I put it on repeat.

Chapter Fifteen

Nate must have noticed my bad mood when I came home. "You need to go out for a drink," he says, when I emerge from my bedroom after my shower.

"Yeah, I do. It was a crappy day. But I don't think anyone is available."

He looks down at himself and shakes his head. "What am I, chopped liver?"

"I thought you didn't go out."

"Well, for you I would make an exception." He smiles.

"Oh, no." I hold up my hand for him to stay where he is. "I'm not falling into that trap. We agreed, no pressure, no dating." I think back on the conversation we had after the first night of movie watching. I laid down the ground rules. He accepted my boundaries. This would push the barriers.

"No, not a date. Just a drink. With a friend." He blows a breath out of his mouth. "It looks like you could really use one of those right now."

Yes. Yes I could. I miss Emma.

I think of how he has been these few weeks. He has stayed true to his word. He hasn't asked me out. He hasn't so much as touched me. Well, if you don't count the times I've fallen asleep on him. But, technically, you could argue that was my fault. He has been nothing but a friend. A good friend. So I say yes. Of course I say yes.

We pick a nice little bar a few blocks down from the shop. I like to walk when I can in case I drink too much. But that won't be a problem tonight. I don't trust myself around Nate when I've had a few drinks. I will limit myself to two Cosmos.

Nate really is fun to hang out with. We even start to talk about high school, but only the early years, not about my junior year or what happened with us or his mom.

He is great at people-watching, just like I am, and we sit around and make up stories about people in the bar. We see a couple fighting and Nate says that she has informed the man that she is pregnant; only she is not his wife . . . his wife is the lady sitting at the next table eyeing them with spitfire.

We laugh and get along like we've been friends forever. It is an easy, comfortable night and my work worries eventually fade away.

He excuses himself to go to the bathroom and not a minute after he is gone, a large man who smells like a greasy hamburger sits down on Nate's barstool. He motions to the bartender to bring me another drink. "Name's Ben and yer about the prettiest thing here," he slurs.

The bartender puts another Cosmopolitan next to my unfinished one and I turn to the man and say, "Thanks, but I'm here with a friend."

"Don't mean ya can't talk to me, does it?" He leans a little too close and his breath reeks of whiskey and cigarettes. When he pulls back, Nate is standing behind him. His face is red and he is staring at the back of the man's head.

Oh, gods of drunken barflies, please let the man get up and leave us alone.

"What's going on here?" He eyes the man. "Brooklyn, are you okay?"

"I wuz jus buyin' the pretty lady a drink." He doesn't even turn around to look at Nate.

Nate reaches into his pocket, pulls out a twenty and throws it at the guy. "Thanks, man, but I've got it covered."

"The lady here—Brooke wuz it?" He motions to me. "She says she ain't got no boyfriend. Says she's just here with a friend. So why don't you piss off."

Oh, no. "Please mister, just leave," I plead with him.

"You heard her," Nate growls, "get the fuck out of here!"

The guy turns to me and says, "Now's that any way to treat a nice guy who got ya a drink?"

Nate reaches in and grabs the guy's arm and pulls him off the bar stool. "Leave," he says as he nudges him away from us.

The next thing I see is the guy taking a swing at Nate and then I hear *crack!* and the guy goes down. Nate drops to the floor holding his hand. "Son of a bitch!" he yells. He kicks the barstool several times until it falls over and hits the floor, drawing even more attention to the situation.

The bartender comes around the bar with a golf club and directs all of us to the door. "Sorry, man," he says to Nate. "I know it wasn't your fault, but you gotta leave or my boss will have it in for me. Rules of the bar."

Ben's friends gather him off the floor and apologize to us for his behavior.

On our way back to the bakery, I can see that Nate is clearly in a lot of pain. He is trying to hide it but the veins in his neck are bulging out, he is breathing rapidly and his eyes are watering.

"You need to see a doctor," I say.

"Yeah, I know." He looks down at his hand. The same hand that has all of those little scars. "Will you go with me to the hospital, Brooklyn?"

My heart drops into my stomach and I'm instantly pulled back into a small room with white walls and beeping machines. The room where I last saw Michael, lifeless and broken. The room that haunts my dreams when the walls close in on me, suffocating me while I frantically lash around to find a door that will allow me to escape the nightmare.

I close my eyes. "I . . . I can't." I look away, ashamed that I'm so weak.

"Oh, okay." He looks hurt, and not just from the pain in his hand.

"No. It's not that I don't want to go with you. I, uh . . . well, I don't go to hospitals anymore. After Michael . . ."

"God, Brooklyn. I'm sorry. I didn't think." He looks sad. Then he bites his lip and asks, "Would you consider an urgent care facility?"

I take a deep breath and look at the man I have come to call my friend. He has been nothing but nice and supportive of me. How can I deny him? Plus, his hand is starting to swell so he can't drive himself anywhere. "Yes. I can do that." I direct him to stand over by my car when we get home. "I'll run up and get my car keys."

"Thank you." He watches me go in the side door to the apartment.

Luckily, the urgent care center is not that busy and we only have a short wait. They take him back for X-rays while I text Emma to tell her and Graham what is going on. It takes ten or twenty texts and one phone call to get it through her thick skull that we weren't on a date. She won't listen. I think she is hell-bent on marrying me off so that I can be as happy as she and Graham are. What she doesn't understand is the pain she will feel when Graham is taken away. Or leaves.

The nurse comes out to get me. "You can go back now, he is asking for you." I follow her down the hall to a private room. A room with a railed bed and medical machines and pictures of diseases on the wall. A hospital room. I take a deep breath and cross the threshold.

"This must be hard for you," Nate says. "I'm sorry. I shouldn't have asked you to come."

He's worried about me. He has probably broken his hand, is in a world of pain and he is thinking of my feelings. God, I'm a terrible person for even saying anything. "Nate. It's okay, really. This is nothing like a hospital anyway," I lie. "How are you doing?"

"They gave me a pain injection while we wait for the doctor to read the X-rays."

"Good. I talked to Emma. She said Graham wants you to call him when you get home later."

He nods.

The door opens and a young doctor walks in and puts the X-rays up on that light-machine thing. He turns around and looks at Nate, then looks at me. "Oh, wow!" he says. "Nate Riley."

"John Morgan?" Nate says back to him. "It's been a long time. You're a doctor now—that's incredible! I'd shake your hand but . . ." He shrugs and holds up his swollen hand.

John starts to ask Nate about baseball since they were on the high school team together but Nate cuts him off. "John, man, is it broken?"

He takes a good long look at the X-rays. "Jesus, Nate, you have more pins in your wrist than a damn bowling alley." He looks over at him. "What happened?"

Nate looks at me and then back at him. "Baseball bat."

"Wow, sorry man. Is that why you're not in the MLB? I always thought you'd make it to the majors, brother."

"Yeah, listen . . . about the hand . . . broken?" Nate seems irritated. He must still be in a lot of pain.

"No. You are lucky. It's probably stronger because of the all the pins. You'll have some swelling for a few days. Make sure to keep it elevated and put ice on it."

Nate looks relieved and lets out a long breath. "Good, thanks. Uh, do you remember Brooklyn Vaughn?" He nods his head to me.

"Nice to see you, Brooklyn."

Of course he doesn't remember me. Anyone that knew me then, knew me as Lyn. He is simply being nice. "You, too. Thanks for your help."

He hands Nate his card, along with a prescription for some pain medication, and tells him to call him to hang out sometime.

"I'm not in town long, but I'll try," Nate says.

He won't call him. He hates this town. I'm not even sure why he agreed to come here. Maybe his dad forced him to take this job. Why else would he torture himself in a town full of people he doesn't want to see?

For you. My goddess within speaks.

On the drive home, he just stares at his wrist. Baseball bat, what did that mean? He broke his wrist on a baseball bat and now he has a bionic arm? I'm itching to ask him about it, but like everything else in his past, he is very tight-lipped.

He told me about the tattoo. Maybe someday he will tell me about this. I eye the scar on my own right hand. Maybe someday I'll tell him about mine as well.

"Maybe we should stick with movies," he jokes, as we make our way up the stairs to the apartment.

"Okay, you pick tonight."

He smiles that gorgeous smile at me. Then he grabs my hand and leads me over to the couch. I am aware that he is crossing the line but I don't care. His hand feels like heaven on my skin. He sits me down and releases me and instantly I feel cold. I miss his hand. The hand that held mine for mere seconds. I want it back.

He puts in the movie and sits next to me on the couch. Closer than normal, but not too close. We fall into our routine of laughing and yelling at the characters. I've never had so much fun staying at home as I have with him these past weeks.

My hair is tickling my neck and I realize that he is playing with a lock of it behind my ear. He is twirling it, over and over. I'm not even sure if he is aware that he's doing it, but suddenly it's *all* I'm aware of. I close my eyes and steady my breathing and my head falls back against the couch. He is putting me into a trance with the rhythmic twisting of my hair. Then I feel his hand softly stroke my check. And I could swear I hear him inhale deeply through his nose. *Is he smelling me?*

Oh, God, he thinks I'm asleep. My heart races and I try to control my breathing. I don't want him to know I'm awake. Why is he doing this? He should stop. But I don't think I want him to stop. I think I want him to keep going. My goddess within and my conscience are busy arguing about what I want when he lifts me off the couch.

Effortlessly, he carries me. I can feel his heart beating through his shirt. I can smell his minty breath as it rolls over my face. I think that this must be killing his hand but he doesn't make a sound. I try, but fail, to control my own heartbeat so that he can't see how this is affecting me.

Where is he taking me?

Please don't take me to your room.

Yes, do.

No, don't.

He places me on a bed and I can tell by the smell that it's not his bed. I don't dare open my eyes yet. I can feel him in the room—staring at me. What is he doing? I should open my eyes. I should say something. I feel a blanket coming up over me. Then I feel his hot breath on my face. He is going to kiss me.

Yes, please, kiss me.

I know I shouldn't, but if he kissed me right here, right now, I don't think I could resist. I know what he tastes like, I remember his kisses. I know I shouldn't want him. I know that I can't have him. But in this moment, I need him. I need him to kiss me.

"Goodnight, Brooklyn," he whispers, his hot breath floating across my face. Then his soft, firm lips touch my cheek for a lingering, yet chaste kiss. He lets out a deep sigh and I hear him walk out of the room and gently close the door.

I open my eyes and a tear rolls down my face. I cry because in this moment, I realize that I want Nate Riley. I want him so badly that my skin is humming everywhere he has touched me. I reach up and touch the place on my cheek where his lips fell moments ago. I want him to the very core of my soul.

And that is exactly why I can't have him.

Chapter Sixteen

I love lazy Saturday mornings. When I was little, I used to crawl in bed with my parents and watch cartoons. Now that I'm older, I stay in my sleeping shorts and tank top and snuggle on the couch, watching reruns of stupid reality shows. The programs may have changed, but the feelings are still the same.

Nine o'clock rolls around and I figure I'd better get my run out of the way before I waste away the day, so I get up and throw on my running clothes. I pass by Nate's door on my way down the hall. He is on the phone but he looks up at me and gives me a smile and a wave.

On my way out the bakery door, I cut the corner too close and my shirt snags on the door hinge. I look at it. Darn, it tore a hole in one of my best running tops. Silently cursing my way back to the apartment, I head back in and hear two voices.

I walk towards Nate's room and realize it is Graham's voice that I hear and that Nate has him on speaker. I'm about to turn and go get a new shirt when I hear my name.

Huh?

I'm not a nosey person by nature. Live and let live and all that. But when the guy who penetrates my dreams is talking about me with his best friend, well, that clearly has dilemma written all over it. Do I listen? I know I shouldn't. He doesn't know I'm back in the apartment. He is having a private conversation.

Nothing good can come from this. I need to change my shirt and sneak out. So why are my feet firmly planted outside his door? I'm pressed against the wall trying not to breathe. I can't get my legs to move.

I am going to hell.

"I don't know what to do anymore, man. I made her this promise. A promise not to ask her out, not to touch her. Do you know how hard that is? It's like trying not to breathe. She is so goddamn beautiful and she doesn't even know it. She has no fucking idea."

"Nate, give it time. You said she seems to be coming around, acting like you are friends and having a good time with you. It's only a matter of time before she realizes she wants you."

"I don't know if I can wait that long. It's like baby steps with her. She makes me think that maybe, just maybe, I might be getting under her skin and then she makes some remark about never dating. She's messed up from Michael dying or something. All I do is think about her. Do you know how hard it is for me to get this project off the ground when all I can see is her face, every time I sit down to sketch?" He pauses to breathe. "Dammit, now I sound like a pussy. What is happening to me?"

"I think they call that love, brother." Graham laughs.

What? Love? No, no, no, no.

He doesn't love me. He simply wants to sleep with me. I walk away. I don't want to hear what Nate says next. I have to get out of here. I race down the stairs for my run, not even caring that I forgot to change my ripped shirt. I run until I almost throw up.

He can't love me.

I have to fix this. I have an idea about how to do that. On my way back, I stop in the bakery and talk to Kaitlyn, putting my plan in place.

I shower and try to avoid Nate for most of the afternoon but I'm going to have to face him eventually. He will wonder why I'm not up for movie night.

I take some deep breaths and meditate for a minute, working up the courage to do what I have to do. What I know will hurt him. But it's for his own good. If I can spare him the pain, I should do that.

I find him at his drafting table in his bedroom. He is drawing something and I catch a glimpse of it before he sees me and covers it up. It wasn't the usual sharp lines of a building. It looked more like a face.

"Hey," he says.

"Hi." I bite my lip. "Um, I wanted to let you know . . . uh, I wanted to tell you that I'm going on a date tonight."

I jump back as he startles me when he stands up so quickly that his chair falls over and smacks against the floor. "What?" He looks at me with intense eyes. "I thought you didn't date, Brooklyn."

"I don't. I didn't. But I thought maybe I should."

He stares into my eyes and I know he is hurt. He is trying to hold it together but he wants to tear my head off. He wants to yell and scream at me. What he doesn't understand is that I'm doing this for him. "Who is he?" he asks through clenched teeth.

"Nobody, just a friend of Kaitlyn's." I try to sound indifferent.

He grabs his keys off the desk, sending papers and pencils scattering around the floor. He blows by me. "Do whatever the hell you want. I'm finished." He walks down the hall and slams the door on his way out. Hard. I think he might have even cracked the frame.

I'm standing in the doorway to his room and I can't move. I'm staring at a drawing of me that landed on the floor at my feet. He is an incredible artist. He makes me look beautiful. An unbidden tear runs down my cheek. I'm doing this for him. I turn away and go get ready for my date.

$$\sim \quad \sim \quad \sim$$

I've never been to this club before and I'm glad it is halfway across town. The farther away I am from Nate, the better.

Kaitlyn's boyfriend, Carl, has brought a friend to be my date. Scott is thirty-ish with dark hair, a solid body and a great smile. He is a firefighter so I imagine under that tight green shirt he has muscles to die for. He is gorgeous. Every woman's dream date.

I stare at him and try to get all warm and tingly inside. I laugh at his jokes and make pleasant conversation. On the outside it seems that maybe we're hitting it off. On the inside all I can think about is how he doesn't have dirty-blonde hair that curls up at the ends. He doesn't have that smile that is reserved just for me. He doesn't have that smell.

I close my eyes and try to invoke that smell of fresh laundry and Nate. When I open them, I think that I must be some kind of witch who has conjured up the perfect man of her dreams, because when I look across the expansive bar, there he sits. I blink twice and look around. I must be hallucinating. I look back again and there he is. I know it is him but he is not looking at me. He is looking at the beautiful woman sitting next to him.

I look to my right and see that Kaitlyn has noticed Nate as well. I give her my 'what-the-hell' look and she beckons me closer with her finger. She whispers in my ear, "He came down to the bakery earlier to ask me where we were going tonight." She smiles at me and shrugs.

"And you told him?" I say a little too loudly and then look around to make sure Scott and Carl aren't paying attention.

"Sure, why not? I thought it would be fun and who doesn't want a little excitement in their Saturday night?"

I look her dead in the eye. "You are so fired."

She laughs at me and says to everyone, "Let's go dance."

Out on the dance floor we are all finding our rhythm, dancing as a foursome. Scott is a good dancer and he is starting to attract stares from hordes of women. I wonder if any of them will ask him to dance. It dawns on me that it wouldn't bother me in the least if they did.

I look over at Nate. He has a beer in one hand, and the woman in his other hand. His hand is around her waist and his thumb is rubbing little circles into her back. He whispers something in her ear and she throws her head back, laughing in a deep throaty, sexy laugh that I can hear across the room.

I know this shouldn't make me mad. After all, I'm the one who is out on a date. He should be able to do whatever he wants. So why do I feel compelled to go over there and rip her eyes out and pour acid into the sockets?

He finally looks over in my direction and tips his beer to me. Then he takes his hand and rubs it up her arm all the way to her neck and plays with her hair. The same way he played with my hair last night.

Hmmpf. Two can play at this game.

I look away, vowing to forget he is over there with Miss Throaty-laugh. I take a few steps towards Scott so that I'm right up against him and I start to move. I move slow and sexy. I close my eyes and attempt to forget about everything for just a minute and feel the music wash over me.

Scott responds immediately, grabbing my hips and moving along with me. "This is more like it," he says, in a deep voice that should have me begging for more. His hands are rubbing on my hips. His chest is touching my breasts. His breath is on my face. This gorgeous hunk of man is mine for the taking and I don't feel anything. Not one spark, not one twinge. Nothing.

But Nate doesn't have to know that. So I pretend. I put on a show for all to see.

Scott twirls me around and pulls my back to his chest. I'm dancing against him with my hands over my head. He runs his hands up and down my ribs. He puts his hand on my stomach and pulls me hard against him—so hard that I can feel his erection growing into my back. This shocks me and I open my eyes only to lock eyes with Nate, who is now on the dance floor doing similar things with his partner.

I try not to think that maybe he has his own erection from the grinding his partner is doing up against him. She throws her head back so that she can see him and her tongue comes out to lick a place under his ear. He looks at me and a slow smile creeps up his face. Not the smile he has for me. This one is different. This smile screams 'screw you'.

The walls are closing in on me. I can't breathe. I feel bile coming up and burning my throat. I have to get out of here. "I have to run to the ladies room," I say to Scott.

I bee-line to the bathroom so that I can splash water on my face and get myself together. Why am I falling apart over this? This is what I wanted to happen, for him leave to me alone and get on with his life. But every time I think about him moving on, my stomach ties in knots and my fists ball up. I want to stomp right back over there and tell his date to get out, that he is mine. Then I realize how ridiculous it is that I can even think of claiming him. It goes against everything I believe, everything I know to be true. Nobody can ever be mine again. Because I don't deserve the right to claim anyone, and if I did, they would surely be taken away.

But in the hallway, before I can get to the bathroom door, something catches my arm and pulls me back. I turn and am smashed up against Nate's chest. "What do you think you are doing?" I yell at him.

"Nothing that you aren't, Brooklyn."

"I'm leaving, that's what I'm doing." I turn to walk away.

He pulls me back to him and before I can protest, he takes my head in his hands and kisses me. He kisses me hard. He is claiming my mouth in a way that it has never been claimed. I'm instantly lost to the world. The music, the people around us, they all fade away and all I can feel is him and his hands on my face. He parts my lips with his tongue and when it enters my mouth and explores my own tongue, my body shivers. My insides melt like a snowflake in the summer sun.

He tastes just like I knew he would, just like I have remembered all these years. My mouth becomes angry with desire and I suck lightly on his tongue, drawing a moan from his throat that sends pulses straight to my core.

A door slams behind us, pulling me back into reality. What am I doing? This is wrong. We can't do this. This will only lead to heartache. I push him away. My heart is pumping, my adrenaline flowing. I do the only thing I can think of that will end this.

I slap him.

Then I turn around and go into the ladies room.

I sit on the closed toilet and try to come up with excuses to leave this place. I can't stay here. I can't watch him with another woman knowing I can't have him. I pull myself together and re-join my foursome who is now at the bar. I'm about to tell them I need to leave when the bartender brings a tray of shots. I contemplate them for a minute before I lift one to my lips. It burns when it goes down, numbing my throat along the way.

Numb. That will work. I grab another shot. Then I order more.

I don't dance with Scott again. I don't want to hurt Nate any more than I have. I only want him to get the picture and move on. Nate, however, doesn't seem to be on the same page—the page about not hurting me—because right now, he is kissing the woman with the throaty, sexy laugh. He is kissing her with the very same lips that minutes ago were on mine. And he is watching me while he does it.

Then, just to add insult to injury, he whispers in her ear. She smiles, turns to pick up her bag and then they get up and walk out of the bar. My heart flops out of my chest and hits the floor. I sit and watch it get kicked around by people walking past me. A tear slips down my face. I quickly wipe it away, but not before Kaitlyn notices.

"Bastard," she whispers in my ear. "Lyn, I'm sorry, I really didn't think it was going to happen like this. This is all my fault."

"Get me out of here," I beg her.

It takes a while to get home—something about Scott having to go check on his sister. I don't even care right now that I'm slumped against the car door, silently crying. Kaitlyn has explained what happened in the nicest possible way and the guys were both very understanding. Scott even asked me if he should go kick his ass.

By the time they drop me off, at least an hour has passed. I see Nate's truck in the lot behind the bakery. I look around for another car. I don't see one, but that just means she could have ridden with him. I contemplate sleeping in the bakery kitchen but I can't think of anything to use as a bed.

I'm shaking as I put the key into the lock of the apartment.

Please be alone.

Chapter Seventeen

I try to make a lot of noise as I enter the apartment. What if they are having sex on the sofa? *Oh my God, please don't be having sex on the sofa.* Or in the bedroom. Or anywhere.

I'm the one that started this mess. It is my fault this happened. Why didn't I let things keep on going like they were? Why did I have to go and mess things up? We could have simply been friends. I'm such an idiot.

The apartment is fairly dark. Only the kitchen light is on, sending shadows down the hallway. I brace myself for what I will see when I come around the corner to the living room. But then I see that it is just Nate. I look around quickly to make sure nobody else is here. He is sitting there holding a beer. He hears me come in but he doesn't look at me. He looks behind me.

He thinks I've brought someone with me.

Relief washes over me. Relief washes over him.

He puts down the beer and leans forward so that his elbows are resting on his knees. Then he yells, "What the fuck was that all about, Brooklyn?"

"Me?" I yell back. "You are the one that kissed that skank and then left with her." I look around and wave my hand at the empty apartment. "What, are you already done with her?"

He stands up and looks pissed. "Unbelievable!" He runs his hand through his hair. "You are the one who went on a date. What do you care what I do and who the hell I do it with?"

"Oh, so you aren't denying that you brought her back here. I knew you didn't change. You go and sleep with the first girl you see at the bar."

"You slapped me, Brooklyn!" He kicks the couch with the heel of his foot. "I kissed you and you slapped me. You have no say in what I do if you don't want me."

He is right. I know he is right. But it doesn't change the way my heart hurts right now. He brought a woman back here, to our apartment. The one we share and laugh at movies in. The one where I sneak into his room and smell his pillow and the one in which he steals kisses when he thinks I'm asleep. Why did he have to bring her *here*?

"At least take your whores somewhere else," I say.

"I didn't bring her back here, Brooklyn!" he says in exasperation. "I didn't bring her anywhere. We said goodbye in the parking lot."

"But you kissed her. Right after you kissed me. Did you tell her that? Did you tell her that you kissed someone else two minutes before you put your lips on hers?"

"God, Brooklyn. Did you see the way you were dancing with that guy? You were practically having sex with him while everyone was watching. Don't you think you are kind of a hypocrite for calling me out on a kiss?"

"I was only dancing with him that way because you had your hands all over Skanky at the bar."

He laughs. "See? What is your problem? You want me. You were jealous. Why don't you admit it and go out with me?"

"What? You are crazy. I do *not* want you. You were the one who kissed me, remember?"

"Maybe it started out that way, but you didn't seem to mind shoving your tongue into my mouth now did you?"

I pace the floor behind the couch. "I had been drinking and you took advantage. As soon as I realized what was happening, I slapped you. Or did you forget that part?"

"As soon as you realized, my ass. Brooklyn, you were sucking off my tongue. You wanted me just as much as I wanted you. Why don't you stop hiding behind your dead fiancé and admit it already?"

Oh, he did not just say that.

"You asshole!" I yell. I pick up a pillow and throw it at him. "This has nothing to do with Michael."

"This has everything to do with him. He died. You loved him and he died." He takes a deep breath and looks at the ceiling. "But *you* didn't die. You are still here. Why don't you start acting like it?"

"You don't know anything about me." I point at him. "You think that a one-night stand ten years ago and a couple of weeks of watching movies together makes you an expert?"

"God, woman, you are driving me fucking crazy—"

"I'm not finished!" I walk up to him and put my finger in his chest. "*You* are the hypocrite, Nate. *You* are the one who got cheated on and then got a stupid tattoo because you were broken. You know what it's like to be broken and yet you sit here and tell me not to be."

We are both red in the face, breathing heavily and staring daggers at each other. And then, just like that, we lean forward and our lips crash together. We kiss so hard that I think my lips are going to bruise. He sucks on my lower lip, I lick his upper one. Then our tongues entwine as we explore each other's mouths. We kiss until we can no longer breathe without breaking apart.

He takes a breath, but he doesn't allow his lips to part with my skin. He trails kisses from the corner of my mouth down along my neck and up to that spot behind my ear. That same spot he found so long ago in the front seat of his pickup truck. He kisses me softly there. Then he licks me and blows a cool stream of air over it. "Brooklyn, you taste so good."

"Mmmm." My head falls back, giving him better access to my neck as he continues the trail of kisses until he covers every inch of skin from ear to ear. My skin tingles everywhere his lips have been. His hands are grabbing my hair, my hips, my shoulders, my back. They are wandering, touching, and squeezing like he can't get enough of me; like he needs to touch every part of me all at once.

I run my hands up his arms, around his broad shoulders, and over his back. I tug on his hair and a moan escapes him. He tries to pull away slightly, to look at me. But I don't let him. I am afraid if we break the spell, I will run away and at this moment I don't want to run. I want to take in every part of him, every touch, every feeling and I don't want to think. I don't want to think about what will happen after. What will happen next. I just want here and now.

He grabs my hips and lifts me up. I wrap my legs around him and he holds me up by my backside. My skirt rides up and my panties are all that stand between me and the fly of his jeans. The friction that results from us rubbing together is about enough to make me come.

It has been so long. This feels so good. I can feel his erection growing large and pressing into me through the material of his pants. He leans down and dips his tongue into my cleavage, licking his way back up to my neck, sending sparks shooting down to my center. He runs his mouth over my breast and takes my nipple into his mouth, right through the fabric of my thin top and lace bra. I instantly pebble up beneath his touch.

Since his hands are still busy holding me up, I reach down and grab the hem of my shirt and lift it over my head. Then I quickly undo the clasp of my bra and let it fall down my arms onto the floor. He looks at my breasts and then back up at my face. "Brooklyn, you are so beautiful." He leans down and takes my nipple into his mouth, sucking on it gently then swirling his tongue around and around. Then he does the same thing to the other one.

"That feels so good," I whisper into his hair.

He walks me over to the counter and sets me down on it, all the while kissing and sucking my lips. He swipes my lip with his tongue and again, I open for him. I take his tongue in my mouth and suck on it drawing more moans from his throat.

He pushes my panties aside. I know they are drenched. I can feel how wet they are. He slides a finger inside me with a hitch of his breath. "Brooklyn, you are so wet."

Oh, that feels good. I almost forgot what it's like to have a man's hands on me—in me. He puts another finger inside and yet another on my clit. He rubs it in circles and I can feel the tingling start in my belly. He is kissing my neck, working his way down to my breasts again and I feel like I will explode if I don't come soon. He lowers himself to his knees and puts his mouth on me. "Oh, God," I say, gasping for air.

His fingers are slowly working in and out of me as his tongue circles my sweet spot, licking and gently sucking, pushing me towards the edge of a cliff I so desperately want to fall over. "Oh, Nate . . . oh, yes . . . please," I whimper. Everything tightens and I clench my thighs around his face as waves cascade through me. I cry out in agonizing pleasure when my orgasm takes over my body. As I ride out the lingering pulses, I'm thankful that he is still holding my legs, or I'd fall right off the counter.

Nate stands up, looks at me and says, "God, Brooklyn, you taste incredible. I've dreamed for years about doing that to you." A blush sweeps across my face as he lifts me up and carries me to his bedroom. I am still riding in the afterglow and yet my body is screaming for more. Before he has me on the bed I am pulling at the hem of his shirt.

He sets me down and lifts his shirt over his head. I instantly have my hands on him, wandering them over his pecs, his strong shoulders and his toned arms. I reach for the button on his jeans and watch his face as I slowly zip down the fly. He closes his eyes and takes in a deep breath.

He quickly removes his jeans and boxer briefs in one movement and then he is standing gloriously naked in front of me. I stare, shamelessly, at his manhood. I can't believe my boldness. I admire his six-pack abs and that happy trail that leads to the very thing I want to have in my hands.

I reach out to touch him. He moans and I close my eyes at the heady feeling I get holding his velvety steel rod in my hands, knowing that I can elicit this sound from him. I start to move my hand up and down, but after a few strokes, he moves it away and says, "Brooklyn, you better stop that or this will be over very quickly."

He slides me back on the bed and removes my skirt. He smiles at me, then he bites his lip and rips my panties from my body. Actually rips them in two. "Oh!" I exclaim. *That was hot.*

"I've always wanted to do that," he says, kissing his way up my body.

I giggle.

"That is a wonderful sound," he whispers in my ear.

He kisses me again, softer this time; not so hurried; not so demanding. Slowly and deliberately, he kisses across my lips, down my neck and over my breasts. He takes turns with each nipple, sucking them gently. His hand occupies the nipple that is not in his mouth. He is tugging, twisting and pulling until the sensation starts building again.

"Nate, please . . . ," I beg, aching to be filled by him.

He opens the drawer in his nightstand and pulls out a condom. I try to take it from him but he stops me. "It's been a while, Brooklyn. If you put this on me, I might come on the spot."

Oh. Just how long, I wonder. I mean, it's been over two years for me and that seems like forever. With everything I know about guys—and Nate in particular—*a while* is more than likely a few weeks; maybe even a few months.

"Define a while," I ask through panted breaths.

"Well . . . how long has it been since I saw you at the convention?"

What?

Before I can get a word out, he thrusts into me, hard and deep. He buries himself in me completely and stills. "God, you are so tight, Brooklyn. You feel amazing." He starts to move. Slowly at first, then he increases the pace. My hips lift off the bed and I meet him thrust for thrust. We are moving together, a passionate dance of tangled legs and wandering hands. I reach around and stroke his sculpted ass, making him moan. Then he grabs my hands in his and places them on either side of my head, holding me down, captive to his heavy body.

He shifts position putting himself at an angle and, *oh God*, he hits a spot inside me that has white-hot pleasure shooting through my body. I start to tremble, the sensation building quickly. He is breathing harder, more erratic and I can tell he is getting close. "You feel so good . . . oh, baby," he says, panting.

His words are my undoing. "Oh yes . . . Nate . . . yes!" I yell, as my world spins and my insides tighten and spasm around his hard length. He buries himself fully inside my quivering sex. He stills and then a deep, growling sound escapes him as he shakes with his own release.

We lie, still tangled up and breathing heavily into each other as we come down from our high. I have never experienced such an intense, mind-blowing orgasm as the one he just gave me. "That was incredible," he says.

I lift my head and smile up at him. "Mmm hmm." It's all I can manage to say.

Once I have my breathing back under control, I remember what he said about not being with anyone since he saw me at the convention. "Why haven't you slept with anyone in two years?"

"I told you I was going to change." He props up on an elbow and plays with a piece of my hair. "I didn't plan on remaining celibate all that time. I knew you were engaged and that I should move on. But every time I dated a woman, I realized I didn't want to sleep with her." He tucks the piece of hair behind my ear and plants a gentle kiss on the tip of my nose. "None of them were you. Not even close. And this whole time, I assumed you were only engaged and I guess I thought that until I knew you were married, there still might be hope."

Hope . . . I contemplate the word that has become so foreign to me while he rubs those little circles on my hips until I fall asleep.

When I wake up, I'm beside him in his bed, still draped over his chest. I watch him sleep. He is gorgeous. I can't believe I am waking up next to him. I trace my eyes over his still-naked body and take him in. Last night was amazing. I never thought making love could be so . . . profound.

I look at this man, this man who I loved when I was a child, this man who has been to hell and back and yet he is still willing to risk everything. He never stopped being the man of my dreams, even when I was with another. He was the one I was supposed to be with, end up with, grow old with. It is his voice I hear in my head when I'm sad. It is his hands that I want on my body. And it is his heart I want beating with mine. My own heart skips a beat.

I love him.

My eyes grow wide. I gently untangle myself from him and then give him a kiss on the cheek. One last kiss. I want to remember him like this forever. I quietly pad out of the room.

Quickly, I gather up some clothes and get my purse. Then I write him a note before I leave.

I turn back once to look at his door before I place the note on the table. The note that has only two words on it, along with some of my tears.

I'm sorry.

Chapter Eighteen

I've been driving around for hours and the sun has started to rise. I wonder if he woke up yet to find me gone. I wonder how much he will hate me when he does.

I can't drive forever so I go to the one place that has always provided me comfort and unconditional love. Home.

My mother already knows something is wrong as I called her to cover for me at the bakery this morning. That is the first place he would look for me and I'm not about to have a confrontation there. That is, if he even still cares. Maybe last night was just another one-night stand for him. Maybe he needed to get me out of his system so that he could move on.

Thankfully, my dad is gone and will not be home until much later. I need some time alone without everyone trying to help me or fix this. I made my decision. It is for the best. I wish everyone could understand that.

I'm lying in my old bed, staring up at the ceiling. The ceiling with glow-in-the-dark stars and planets that my dad affixed to it when I was young. Back when there was no drama, no hurt, no pain. Maybe if I stay here long enough, I can become that carefree little girl again.

I lie here trying not to remember every kiss, every touch, every orgasm from last night, when music startles me. It takes me a second to realize it is my phone. I don't even have to guess who is calling me. He must have changed my ring tone for him. The ring tone that is now begging me to be his reason . . . his cause . . . his light. That song he won't let me get away from.

I cannot bear to hear it anymore so I reach into my purse and turn off my phone. Then I fall asleep, physically exhausted from last night, mentally exhausted from this morning . . . twisting my hair and counting to five, over and over.

I awake to pounding at the front door. I ignore it of course, thinking that eventually he will go away. Then I hear Emma screaming up at my window at the top of her lungs. "Lyn!" she howls. "Lyn, open the damn door. I'm not leaving until you let me in."

Crap! I know she means it.

I quickly look in the mirror and wipe away yesterday's smeared mascara from under my eyes. Then I check the time and see I've been sleeping for hours.

I go downstairs and look through the window by the front door. She is alone. Thank God. I open the door and Emma barrels through it, almost pushing me to the floor. "What the hell is wrong with you, Lyn?" She screams at me.

"Well, hello to you, too," I snark at her.

"Don't give me that, sister." She points her finger at me. "Do you know why I'm here? Why I've driven the four hour drive from Raleigh in about three hours?" She lifts her eyebrows. "Well, do you?"

"To return my JLo CD you borrowed twelve years ago?" I deadpan.

"Not funny." She pulls me into the living room and sits me on the couch. "Listen to me, Lyn, and listen good. I'm here because Nate called his dad this morning and asked him to take him off the job and give it to Graham."

I just stare at her.

"As in, Nate is leaving. He is packing his stuff as we speak and is going back to Raleigh." She hits the pillow next to me with a balled up fist. "Forever."

"Good. That is exactly what I want," I say to her. "He needs to get on with his life. The quicker he realizes that we can't be together, the better. He is right to leave here." Even as I say the words that I know are true, I have to fight off the tears that threaten to fall.

"Why is it that everyone else can see that you belong together? Everyone but you, Lyn."

"Maybe that was true once, a long time ago. But not anymore, a lot has happened and we can't be together," I say.

"What? Tell me *what* has happened? What is it that is making you so stubborn that you refuse to do the one thing that everyone else knows will make you happy?"

"Michael!" I yell at her. "Michael happened." A tear rolls down my cheek.

Emma takes a deep breath and puts her hand on mine. "Lyn, I know you loved Michael. He was a great guy. But you are ready for this and he would want you to be happy. I know you are ready to move on. I realized it six months ago, when you finally got rid of that old toothbrush of his." She smiles at me.

I remember that day, too. The day I tried to put him behind me. But it wasn't so that I could find another man. It was the day I accepted the fact that I could be alone and be okay with it. I didn't need someone else to make me happy. I had my shop, my parents, some close friends and that was going to be good enough for me. So, yes, I threw away that old toothbrush. The one I had still used every once in a while, just to feel close to him again. Then I took off my engagement ring and tucked it far back in my jewelry box.

I shake my head at her. "No."

"Why?" She is getting frustrated with me. "Why can't you allow yourself to be happy?"

I close my eyes and remain silent. She doesn't know. She couldn't possibly understand the burden of betrayal that I carry with me. My betrayal of a man who was quite possibly the most perfect person ever to touch my life. He didn't deserve what happened to him. He didn't deserve to be with a woman whose heart was fractured and couldn't ever be fully repaired. He was so much more than I ever could have lived up to.

"Brooklyn Anne Vaughn!" she yells at me. "What the hell is your problem?" She throws my hand back down onto my leg.

Tears are pushing through my closed eyelids and I can't take it anymore. "I don't deserve to be happy!" I yell back at her. "I killed him."

"What?" She looks at me with brows drawn together. "Who?"

"I killed Michael," I say softly and look at the floor, "and I don't deserve to be happy, especially with Nate." There, I said it. I finally let out what I've been feeling these past few years. It feels good to get it off my chest and tell someone, but it doesn't change the facts.

She shakes her head at me. "Michael died in a car accident when you were taking your exams. How can that possibly make you responsible?"

"Because I was with Nate, in Raleigh. I had feelings for him. I'm a terrible person."

"That is crazy, Lyn." She takes my hand once again. "Of course you had feelings for him. He was your first love. The boy you lost your virginity to. That doesn't make you a bad person. And nothing happened. You have nothing to feel guilty about."

"There was a kiss. Well, there would have been, anyway. That night in the rain." I tell her the whole story about what she and Graham unknowingly interrupted that night.

"Lyn, even if you would have kissed him, that still doesn't make you responsible for Michael's death. In the end, you did the right thing, you were loyal to Michael. You would be married to Michael right now if he were still alive. You have nothing to feel guilty about." She rubs my back to comfort me.

"No, you don't understand, Emma. I *am* responsible." I take a deep breath and say what I've never even admitted to myself until now. "I thought . . . just for a second back then I thought . . . what if Michael wasn't around. That I could be with Nate if Michael wasn't around." I drop my head to her shoulder and sob. I cry until my tears dry up and there is nothing left but heaves and hiccups.

Emma holds me to her as she continues to rub my back. "Oh, Lyn. We have all thought things like that at one time or another. Even now, as much as I love Graham and would never leave him, I can see a really hot guy and wonder what it would be like if I were single." She pulls my face up and places her hands on either side of it, looking me directly in the eyes. "We can't control our thoughts and feelings. But what we can control are our actions. You have nothing to feel guilty about. You did nothing wrong. You loved Michael and you were loyal to him. Please, Lyn, you have to accept that."

I nod weakly at her. I hear what she is saying and I want to believe her. But I know deep down that I am partly to blame. "Thanks for coming all this way Emma, but it doesn't change anything." I get up from the couch and head upstairs for my purse. "I need to get away for a while. Please don't follow me."

"You are making a mistake, Lyn," she says when I return to the room. "One day you will realize that and then it will be too late. He says he is done. He is not waiting for you anymore. If you let him leave, you won't get him back."

"I know," I say, as I go out the front door and close it, leaving Emma behind.

Hours later, after driving and trying to clear my head, I am sitting on a hard, cold concrete bench, talking to the person I've hurt more than anyone in this life. "I'm so sorry I did this to you. I'm sorry I had feelings for him. I hope you can forgive me someday, Michael."

I stare at his grave.

I close my eyes and remember the good times we had together. I think about the time he gave me eighty-six roses just because we had been together that many days. Then there was the rare weekend getaway we had to the beach, making love on the sand at dawn. He was such a romantic.

I jump slightly off the bench when I feel small, but gentle hands come around me from behind. "Aunt Lyn!"

I turn around to find my almost-niece, Amanda, smiling at me. She is a pretty twelve-year-old who has Michael's red hair and the most adorable freckles I've ever seen. And I love the way she calls me Aunt Lyn even though we are not related.

I hug her back and then ask Janie, Michael's older sister and her mom, "What are you doing here?"

Oh God, I'm stupid. Duh!

Janie motions to Amanda. "She had a dream about Michael so she made me bring her here. It's so nice to see you, Lyn." She smiles and we hug.

"Uncle Michael told me I should come visit him," Amanda says. I look at Janie and she shrugs.

Amanda continues, "He told me I needed to come here and that when I did, I would see my reason."

I instantly start shaking. "Amanda, what did you just say?"

She looks at me funny, rolls her eyes and repeats, "Uncle Michael told me that I should come here and that if I did I would find my reason."

My feet are frozen to the spot, my eyes locked on Amanda. Then I slowly look over at Michael's headstone. I shake my head at it in wonder as song lyrics flash in my mind.

Be my reason . . .
My cause, my light
Be my reason . . .
My purpose, my life
'Cause baby it was always you
You're my reason
You've pulled me through

Michael didn't know this song, did he? This is Nate's song.

I look back at Amanda and find her looking all around. She looks at the ground, then up at the bench. She walks around his headstone with curious eyes. Then she looks at Janie and says, "I don't understand it Mom, he told me to come here . . . but the only thing here is Lyn."

I look at Michael's grave. Tears are flowing from my eyes, blurring the perfectly etched dates that define his twenty-eight years on this Earth. I have never been a very spiritual person. I believe things are very black and white. But this—what is happening right now—could this really be . . . ?

I close my eyes and peace washes over me, through me. Everything I thought I knew to be true is replaced with the realization of what could be. What my life could be if I let the one person in that stole my heart all those years ago. I know it now. I know it for sure. I love Nate. I want him. I want him forever. Even if it means my heart will break one day. Even if he is not perfect. Because I know he isn't perfect . . . he isn't a perfect man. But he is the perfect man for me.

I whirl around and hug Amanda. This child has no idea why I'm crying, smiling, hugging and laughing. She must think I'm crazy. Janie laughs with me and says to Amanda, "Honey, I think you found exactly the reason." She gives me a wink and whispers in my ear, "One day you'll tell me what happened here, right?"

I nod at her. I have to go. I have to find Nate. I quickly say goodbye and turn back to Michael's grave. I close my eyes and silently thank him. Then I laugh again because this was such a Michael thing . . . always looking out for others. I will always love him.

As I get into the car, I fish my phone out of my purse. Nine missed calls. There were two from Nate, one early this morning and another a few hours after. The rest were from Emma, my mom and Kaitlyn. I don't have time to listen to them all. But there are two I have to listen to. I press in my code and listen . . .

"Brooklyn, where are you? What the hell do you mean you're sorry? Sorry for what, sleeping with me, sorry for leaving? I just want to talk. Last night was incredible. I know you are scared. Please let me talk to you. Call me back. Please call me back." He sounded frantic and worried and sad.

I am such a bitch.

His second call was hours later. "Brooklyn, I can only assume that since you haven't called and you didn't show up for work today that you want nothing more to do with me. Fine. I get it now. Graham will take my place on the job, so I guess you have finally gotten what you wanted. I'm leaving Savannah. I'm getting out of your life. Once and for all." He pauses for a long time. "But, Brooklyn, when you change your mind. Don't bother calling me. I'm done."

Worried and sad went out the window. He was flat-out pissed. I have ruined everything. My shaking fingers dial Nate. It goes straight to his voice mail—a sure sign he has his phone off. He doesn't want to hear from me.

In the car, driving way too fast back to the apartment, I dial Emma. "Lyn," is all she says and then she is quiet.

"Emma. I was wrong. So wrong. I can't explain now, I have to find Nate but he has his phone off. Are you with him? Can you ask him to please get on the phone?" I beg.

"Lyn." She blows out a deep breath into the phone. "It's too late, he is gone."

Chapter Nineteen

"He left about fifteen minutes ago," Emma says. "I told you he was leaving. And what do you mean you were wrong?"

"I don't have time to talk. Is he going back to Raleigh? Did he head for the Interstate?" I ask frantically.

"I guess. Where else would he—"

I cut her off and throw the phone down. No time for that, I have to concentrate on driving. I'll apologize to Emma later.

My phone rings but it is Emma, not Nate. I can tell from the ringtone, so I let it go to voice mail. For the first time, I *want* to hear that song. *Our song*. I'm willing it to start playing on my phone.

If he only left a short while ago, I may be able to catch up to him because I'm closer to the Interstate than he was.

I make it there in five minutes but I figure he is already ahead of me so I drive much faster than is safe; faster than I've ever driven before. I pray that the police are not out this afternoon because that would put a definite stop to my plans to chase him down. His truck will be easy to spot. What am I going to do when I find him, run him off the road? I guess I will if I have to. I have to get his attention. He has to stop and talk to me. I will make him listen.

Shit. I eye my gas gauge.

Shit, shit, shit.

The warning light is on. I look up to the sky. Why did this have to happen now? There is an exit just ahead. I will only stop long enough for a few gallons. He can't be that far ahead of me.

I pull up to the pump and there is a 'cash only' sign. I turn to look in the store and see a long line of people waiting to pay. *Oh my God. What else can go wrong?*

I quickly pump in five gallons and fish through my purse for some money while running into the store. I try to think of some reason that could get me to the front of the line. When I'm about to yell 'fire', I look out the front window.

My heart stops. There he is. Nate is pumping gas into his truck right outside the store.

Thank you, God.

I get bumped into from behind for holding up the line. I peel my eyes away from Nate just long enough to put my twenty on the counter and tell the clerk to keep the change.

My legs are trembling so badly that I'm not sure I will be able to walk. I slowly open the door and start to make my way over to him. He hasn't seen me yet. He is leaning against his truck looking the other way. I see his chest expand while he closes his eyes and tilts his head up, and then he releases a long, slow breath. He is shaking his head back and forth. His left hand comes up momentarily rubbing on his tattoo and I wonder if he realizes when he does that. His body language tells the story. He is defeated, broken once again by a woman.

He finishes pumping, replaces the nozzle and is going for his wallet when our eyes meet. He blinks a few times and then stares at me. "Brooklyn." He runs his hand through his hair and leans back against his truck, waiting for me to say something.

I walk the last few steps and position myself right next to him, leaning on the truck as well. I take a deep breath and try to muster up the courage to tell him everything I am thinking. "Nate. I'm sorry—"

"Yeah, I know, you already said that in your note," he cuts me off with a sharp bite to his words.

"Nate, please. Just let me talk. I need to tell you some things." I close my eyes and reach down deep and then I tell him everything that happened today. I tell him every detail. Right down to what I can only believe was a divine intervention at the cemetery. Well, maybe not every detail. I certainly don't intend on confessing my love for him here in the middle of a gas station.

I open my eyes and look over at him. He's still not talking, but at least he doesn't look pissed anymore so I continue. "Nate, I'm so sorry I freaked out and left. I know I've been difficult. I've been a bitch. I've not been fair to you at all. You were right about everything. About Michael." Tears are running down my face and I'm sure I look hideous but I don't care. "But I'm ready now. I want to be with you. On some level, I've always wanted to be with you. Will you please come back home with me?" I reach over and take his hand in mine. "Please?" I beg.

He looks conflicted. I can tell there is a battle going on inside his head. I only hope that in this war over his heart, I come out the winner. Any other outcome isn't an option. He doesn't pull away and he rhythmically rubs his thumb over the back of my hand shooting sparks up my arm. He turns towards me so that we are face to face. "Okay," he says as a slow smile creeps up his face. "But there will be ground rules."

And then he kisses me.

His hands are holding my neck and he kisses me gently, taking my top lip into his mouth and then running his tongue across my bottom lip asking for entrance. I open up to him. Of course I do. I want to kiss him like this forever. His lips taste salty and I realize that I must still be crying; only now they are happy tears.

He is feathering a trail of kisses up to my ear. Right here, in the middle of the gas pumps, he is kissing my neck.

"Such as?" I breathe out in a whisper.

I feel him smile against my neck. "Sex," he whispers in my ear. "Lots and lots of sex."

$$\sim \ \sim \ \sim$$

When we walk back into the apartment, Emma jumps off the couch. "Answer your damn phone once in a while, Lyn!" she yells at me. Then her mouth drops open when Nate walks in behind me. "Oh," she says, smiling at us.

My face hurts from the smile I've worn for the past thirty minutes. She looks between Nate and me. "What now? I mean, are you together-together?" She looks at me and adds, "Is this for real?" She looks at Nate. "Are you staying on the job? Are you moving into her room so that Graham and I have a place to stay when we are here?"

Nate starts laughing. "Emma, we've been together for all of two-point-five seconds. When we figure this all out, we'll send you a memo."

"Whatever," she grumbles. Then she points at me. "You better call me tomorrow and spill." She picks up her purse and heads for the door.

"You're driving back tonight?" I ask her.

"You don't think I'm staying here do you? I don't need to hear you two 'making up', " she air quotes. "Ick. I'll go stay at my parents' place and head back to Raleigh tomorrow." Then she addresses Nate, clearly trying to extract more information. "What should I tell Graham?"

"I already talked to him on the way here. It's all good." He smiles.

On her way out, she gives me a hug and whispers in my ear, "I'm so happy for you."

I turn around and look at Nate. He is standing there looking all delicious, with eyes that look like they want to eat me alive. *Oh, yes please!* "Sex or talking first?" he asks me.

My heart pounds at the memory of last night. "Sex, please," I say in the lowest, most sultry voice I'm capable of producing.

"I knew there was a reason I liked you." He smiles as he walks over to me and throws me over his shoulder like a caveman. "My place or yours?"

"Aaaaah," I squeal as I swat his behind. "Better make it mine unless you left your bed made while making your escape."

"Right, yours it is." He carries me into my bedroom and throws me down on the bed. He stares at me and I start to get self-conscious. He shakes his head. "Sorry," he says. "I just can't believe that you are here. I really thought that was it for us."

My eyes close and I shudder at the thought that I almost lost him. I almost pushed him so far away that I would never again have this feeling. This feeling that everything is bright and shiny new, that the world is at my fingertips. And, maybe, just maybe, I was wrong and I might deserve another chance at happiness.

I reach forward, grab his belt and pull him towards me. "No, that wasn't it for us. That wasn't nearly it for us."

He climbs on the bed and crawls up my body, putting his hands on either side of my head. "Thank God, Brooklyn," he says, right before his lips crash into mine. He kisses me gently, leaving his lips lingering on mine before he presses on with more determination. My hands weave into his hair, gently grabbing onto the locks of messy-blonde heaven that I have coveted in my dreams. His hands find the skin between my jeans and shirt and he makes his way under my top, caressing a trail around to my back. It is evident that we are both getting incredibly aroused by the fervor of our kisses. I can feel the hardness of his erection where it is pressing into my thigh.

He breaks our kisses only long enough to remove his shirt and mine. Then his mouth is on me again. He cascades soft kisses down my neck and over to my shoulders. When he runs his tongue over my breasts, I quiver with pleasure. I reach down to undo his pants and slip my hand between the cotton boxers and his bare skin. I close my hand around him and stroke him, causing him to moan into my cleavage.

"God, Brooklyn. I want you more than my next breath." He looks me in the eyes and kisses me with a passion I have never felt before. I don't ever want this feeling to end. I want to kick myself for thinking I could live without this, without him. He is like air to me. I need him to live. I will never walk away from him again as long as I'm on this Earth.

"Then take me," I whisper into his mouth.

We quickly do away with the rest of our clothing, throwing them into a messy pile on my floor. He runs his hands down my stomach, leaving a hot trail of sparks wherever he has touched my skin. His fingers find my wanting cleft and he draws the wetness into my silky folds. His fingers toy with me and I shudder under his expert touch. That familiar tingle starts to build up inside me. The world falls away and all I can think about is how much I want him inside me. How hungry I am for him.

"Please, Nate. I need you inside me," I beg.

"Not yet." He rubs circles on my sensitive nub, sending ripples of sensation to the essence of my being. "You first," he says. "Always, you first."

Then he leans down and licks my nipple, running his tongue all around the stiffened peak, gently pulling it inside his mouth and sucking. I am all feeling and wonder as his fingers slide in and out while his thumb works on my clit. My thighs tighten and white hot waves come crashing through my body as I pulsate around his fingers.

"Yes, baby . . . that's it. Come for me," he whispers, hot breath in my ear, while I ride out the quivering orgasm that is rolling through my body. His words, his endearment, draw out every last shudder, making me come harder and longer than I ever have.

Before I come down from my high, he climbs on top of me. He hesitates and I question him, breathlessly, "What are you waiting for?"

"Uh . . . I don't have a condom. I packed up my room and they are all down in the truck." He hits his fist into the mattress on the side of my head. He takes my head into his hands and kisses my eyelids. "Do you trust me, Brooklyn?" he asks.

"Yes, of course," I say.

"I promise you I'm clean."

"Nate if you say it's safe, then I believe you. Please, I want you so much."

His eyes lock with mine as he slowly slips his length into me. His eyes roll back into his head as he closes them and his breath hitches. He squeezes my neck and breathes into my hair. "Brooklyn, you feel so good. Baby, it's incredible. I . . . uh . . . God . . . it's so good," he moans as he quickens his pace.

He grabs me tight and rolls onto his back, taking me with him so that I'm on top. His hands are on my hips, guiding my movements up and down his long shaft. I rub my hands over his hard chest, feeling every rigid muscle. Then I place my hands alongside his head as I move myself up and down. I exert more force against him, finding that little place inside that about shatters me every time he rubs on it. Building up again, I feel so close.

"Nate, yes, don't stop." I start to tense up and I breathe heavy through my clenched teeth as he brings me to my second orgasm. I lean over through the waves of pleasure and bite down on his shoulder.

"Ahhh . . . Brooklyn . . ." He lets out a long groan and stills as he releases himself into me.

I collapse on his chest and we breathe, heavy and labored, until we come down from the best experience of my life. I can barely speak. I have no saliva left in my dry mouth. "Wow." I roll off to the side and he winces as he pulls out of me.

"Yeah, wow," he says. "That was . . . God Brooklyn, that was incredible. I mean, last night was too, but this—this was off the charts great. I mean bases loaded, grand slam home run great."

I giggle. Then I realize that was the first time he's made a reference to baseball since he's been back in my life.

He gets up on an elbow and looks at me. He runs his hand through his glorious messy-from-sex hair. "Brooklyn, I have never had sex without a condom before. That was my first time."

What? I think I must look at him like he is crazy. Did he forget about that little thing called a wife that he used to have?

"I know, I know. I was married." He reads my mind then hesitates. "God, Brooklyn, the last thing I want to talk about right now is my ex-wife."

"It's okay," I assure him. "But how . . . ?"

"She uh . . . she wouldn't let me go without one." He seems embarrassed to tell me this. "She was on the pill, too. She said she didn't want to ruin her body with a pregnancy."

I think about what a selfish person she must have been. I wonder how he ended up with her in the first place. But I think basking in the afterglow of our incredible love-making is not the time to ask. That is a conversation for another day.

The last thing I remember before I fall asleep is Nate rubbing little circles on my naked hip as I tuck myself between his neck and his strong arm to find a comfortable place to nuzzle.

Chapter Twenty

I stir awake, moonlight streaming through the open blinds of my window. I turn to find Nate's eyes heavy upon me. He brings a hand up to push the hair away from my eyes. "Are you still with me, Brooklyn?" he asks.

My mind flashes through what happened yesterday. I could have easily walked away. I was so incredibly naïve to think that I had any control over my feelings. I'm not sure I will ever fully understand the pull Nate has over me. He could have given up on me. Both of us have been through so much to get to this moment. Am I with him? Yes. Of course I'm going to say yes.

I put my hand on his chest and smile over at him. "Yes."

He lets out the breath he was holding. "Then let's go over those ground rules again."

I giggle. Then he proceeds to rock my world, once again, with two earth-shattering orgasms.

Afterwards, when I'm still breathing heavily, my head on his chest, he surprises me. "I didn't want to leave you back then," he reveals.

I raise my head off his chest to look at him. "Tell me."

"I had no idea. We—my dad and my sister and me—we had no idea that her spa was a front for . . . ," he hesitates and then winces when he says, "for a sex shop." He closes his eyes and his head falls back against the pillow. "That night, when I got home from dropping you off, the police were already at my house arresting her. We didn't get all the details until the next morning. My dad went berserk. He called a moving company and paid them double to come that same day and move us out of our house. He said we had to leave Savannah, that we would be the laughing stock of the city."

He plays with a lock of my hair as he goes on. "When I told him I had to see you first, he said nobody would want to associate with me—not even a girl who likes me. That my mother was a cheap whore and people would treat us like lepers. I wish now that we had phones that could text back then. I mean, I didn't even have a cell phone, but if I did and I could have texted you and found out that you didn't hate me . . ." he trails off.

"But I didn't have the courage to show up or to even call you. I was sure you wanted nothing to do with me just like my dad said." He pulls me tight against him. "I was seventeen and I was a stupid kid. God, Brooklyn, you'll never know how sorry I am for that."

I tear up and I kiss him. I kiss him with gentle, long strokes of my tongue so that he knows I forgive him. "It's okay," I whisper in his ear. "Thank you for telling me."

"I'll never forgive myself for that. That night with you, it was the best night of my life, until last night," he says sweetly into my hair.

Surely it wasn't better than his wedding night.

He pulls me close and locks eyes with me. "The *best* night, Brooklyn."

Okay then. My goddess within gives me a high five.

$$\sim \quad \sim \quad \sim$$

Five o'clock comes all too soon this morning. I kiss Nate on the cheek, careful not to wake him, quickly shower and then head downstairs. Derek is already there, taking out the fresh pastries for the morning. He studies me for a minute when I walk through the door.

"Didn't get much sleep, huh?" He draws his brows together, assessing me.

"Do I look that bad?"

"Honey, you look positively glowing . . . and thoroughly bedded," he adds.

"Derek!" I can feel heat creeping up my face.

"So I take it the crisis has passed and you've let that hunk of a man in your bed?"

I ignore him and head out front to start the coffee.

"Oh, hey." He catches me before I'm through the door. "I took a strange call this morning from someone looking for Ryan."

"Why weren't they calling his cell?" I ask, knowing he never takes calls at the shop.

"The guy said he'd been trying to reach him for weeks but that Ryan would never get back with him. Something about needing all the numbers if he still wants to move forward." He shrugs at me.

"I have no idea what that means, Derek. Just leave him a note I guess."

The morning flies by, and before long, it's noon and I realize that Nate never came in for his usual breakfast. Nor did he grace me and my customers with his sweaty presence after his morning run. He's not having second thoughts is he?

Just when I think I might drive myself crazy with wonder, my phone rings out with *'Be My Reason'*, which is now my favorite song. The song I have come to know and love, and I smile from ear to ear. I even hum along to it for a few seconds before I answer.

"Hey, you," he says when I pick up. "I wanted to make sure you were okay."

"I'm good," I tell him.

He laughs and says, "Yes, you say that but for all I know you could be south of the border right now."

"I'm so sorry I ran out yesterday. I'm not going to run again," I assure him.

"You might have to keep telling me that for a while." He sighs.

"Nate, I'm not running again. I'm here. I'm with you. I'm yours."

Oh, God . . . did I just say I'm yours? I'm such an idiot. He doesn't speak but I can hear him breathe into the phone. My mind goes wild with what he must be thinking. Probably that I'm turning into some stalker chick that will make him account for every minute of his day away from me. Maybe he doesn't want me to be his. Maybe I'm merely something to occupy his time when he is on the job down here in Savannah.

"Say it again, Brooklyn. Say you are mine."

Relief floods through me, my body relaxes and I am beaming when I declare, "I'm yours, Nate." I can practically hear him smiling into the phone.

"Hey, why didn't you go on your run this morning?" I ask him. "I had some very disappointed customers."

"Disappointed customers, huh?"

"Okay, so maybe I missed the Nate Riley show a little myself." I giggle.

He laughs. "I'll give you your own private show tonight."

Yes, please.

"Actually, I thought we could run together when I get home from work," he says.

If one's face can actually split in two from smiling too much, then mine would be divided right smack down the middle.

$$\sim \quad \sim \quad \sim$$

"Shower?" he asks, after our run, as we head back into our apartment.

"Duh." I roll my eyes and then head for my room. "See you after."

"Brooklyn." He follows me. "I meant . . . *shower*." His voice wraps around me seductively and desire clouds his eyes. A smile plays on my lips as my hunger for him ignites.

"Oh!" I giggle and hold my hand out to him. "Absolutely. Mine or yours?" But I'm already pulling him into my room.

He is ripping my sweaty top off before we even enter my bathroom. He kisses my salty shoulder and says, "You know, we could just take Emma's suggestion and do away with the whole my room/your room dilemma." He peels the rest of our clothing off and turns on the shower. "I mean, we already live together."

For now.

He pulls me under the warm stream of water and soaps up his hands before he runs them all over my body, making sure to clean every little bit. He takes special care with my breasts, running his hands over each of them, rhythmically squeezing them and tugging gently on my stiff nipples.

"What do you say, Brooklyn?" he asks, his hand creeping lower. "I want to wake up every day looking at your beautiful face." He runs his fingers through my small patch of hair, feeling his way to my slick opening.

"Ooookay . . ." I let out in a breathy groan and I feel his smile against my skin.

He abruptly turns me around and places my hands against the tile wall of the shower. "Hold on, baby." He rubs his erection on my behind. "I'm going to take you hard and fast." He easily slips his hard length into me. It feels divine. He pulls out and grips the flesh of my hips and then slams back into me hard, causing his balls to slap against me.

Wow!

"You are so tight like this. You feel so good." He reaches around to caress my breasts; pinching and tugging both nipples, making me moan and beg.

"Yes, Nate . . . don't stop," I implore him.

Keeping one hand on a breast, he moves the other down to find the apex of my thighs, rubbing slow, deliberate circles until I feel the familiar ache of pleasure in my belly.

"Tell me again," he groans. "Tell me you're mine." His voice causes me to shudder and tighten around him.

"Yes, Nate . . . oh God . . . yours . . . I'm yours!" I shout through my orgasm as I hear his own exaltations when he comes inside me, emptying himself completely.

~   ~   ~

Outside of work, we spent most of the last week holed up in the apartment existing on mint chocolate chip ice cream, sex, and the occasional take-out food.

Tonight, however, we are going out on our first official date. As I get ready for our night out, I wonder what it will be like to go on an actual date with him. We have become so comfortable with each other here at home. Sharing a bedroom even seems natural for us. We have been living in a bubble, our perfect little sex bubble. Will the bubble burst when we let the real world in?

I don't know where he is taking me, he wouldn't say. He simply told me to bring a jacket. When I emerge from the bathroom, he has a blanket and a large cooler ready to go.

In his truck, driving away from the apartment, he turns in the direction of my parents' house. I know he isn't taking me there. I can only think of one other place out this way. The Bend.

I stare over at him as we make the turn onto the gravel road. He says, "Have you been here? Since…"

I smile. He's not ready to burst the bubble either. I think about the last time I came here. It was the most incredible moment of my life. If I could have scripted the night I lost my virginity, the real thing was ten times better. Maybe it was because I had been in love with him since the seventh grade. Maybe it was because of his kind words and gentle hands. Maybe it was the shots of liquid courage Emma forced down my throat. Whatever the reason, it was the best night of my life. Until recently that is.

"No." I grab his hand. "There is only one person I would ever come back here with."

221

I never knew Nate could be so romantic. I lie on the blanket looking up at the stars and think back on tonight. He was so incredibly slow and gentle, almost like he was that seventeen-year-old boy deflowering a virgin again . . . only with food and wine this time.

I snuggle into him and lay my head on his chest. His heartbeat and rhythmic breathing are comforting. Our fingers are entwined and I absentmindedly trace the little scars on his right hand.

"I was twenty-two when it happened," he says. Then he lets out a long breath as I brace myself to hear his story. "I was a senior at Clemson. Claudia and I had been married about six months and we were out celebrating. I had gotten drafted by the Red Sox and even though I would start out on their AA team in Portland, it was about as good at is gets for a rookie ball player."

Boston? Portland? I never would have found him so far away.

I can feel his heart racing through his chest and I know what he is about to tell me is a painful memory for him.

"We were at a bar and had done some shots. She got up to use the bathroom and a few minutes after she returned, some guys came up to us and started talking trash. They said I had better put a leash on my bitch of a wife and who the hell did I think I was. I got up to defend her—defend us—when one of the guys took a swing at me."

Oh God, no. He lost his career in a bar brawl?

"Naturally, I swung back and took the guy down, all the while cursing at myself for hitting him with my pitching arm. Then, out of nowhere, his buddy comes up to me and swings a bat at my head. Instinctively, I put up my arm to protect myself. My right arm. My pitching arm."

I wince. "Oh God, Nate."

"I broke my wrist in six places, had ten pins put in. I couldn't play baseball again after that."

"I'm so sorry." I hug his chest tightly. Tears are welling up in my eyes.

"That's not the worst part." He hesitates. "Later on, I found out that Claudia was in the bathroom that night bragging about me to some of the other ladies, telling them that their boyfriends weren't good enough to get drafted and how much better I was than them."

He takes a deep breath. "It was her. She caused the fight." He sighs. "Then a few months later I found her in bed—our bed—with a ball player. Turns out it wasn't me she wanted. She just wanted the life of a ball player's wife."

Tears are flowing freely from my eyes, dripping onto his bare chest. He pulls my head up to see how wrecked I am. "Don't cry, baby," he says.

"But that was the one thing you wanted more than anything in life," I stutter.

"Not more than anything, Brooklyn." He takes me into his arms, kissing away my tears. "I've been thinking a lot about it this week. If I hadn't gotten in that fight, I wouldn't be here with you. I think that is why I can finally talk about it. I lost baseball. But I have you. I feel like I've won the goddamn lottery."

He crashes his lips into mine.

Chapter Twenty-one

Electric charges are shooting through my groin as I awake in the morning light. I rub the sleep from my eyes and I realize that I am not having a dream, but that the man of my dreams is busy assaulting my thighs with his unshaven jaw causing me to writhe beneath him.

I reach down and tangle my fingers in his hair, drawing him closer to my center as he draws me closer to my orgasm. I'm so close. *How long has he been at this?* My tension mounts, begging for release as I whimper, "Please . . . don't stop."

I feel his smile against my hot, swollen flesh. He reaches a hand up and rolls my nipple between his thumb and finger bringing that ache of pleasure that causes me to lose all sense of reality when my orgasm comes crashing down. My walls tighten and pulsate around his fingers.

He slowly climbs up my body, kissing my stomach, my breasts, my neck. Sensation overwhelms me. "God Nate, I love y—" I stiffen. "Uh . . . I l-love it when you do that," I stutter.

Oh God, oh God, oh God. Did I almost just say that? Does he know that I almost just said that?

"Mmmmm," he murmurs in my ear, unaware of my almost-declaration. "I love it when I do that, too. You taste like vanilla . . . always vanilla." He licks at my shoulder as he pushes his impressive length into me.

His hand comes around under my back and he raises my behind up to meet him. His lips possess mine as we moan panted whimpers into each other. Fire ignites in my belly once again as he twists himself to rub against that sweet spot at the front of my tight walls.

"You're mine, Brooklyn," he says, panting. "Say you'll always be mine."

"Yes, yours . . . forever," I mutter into the crook of his neck.

He reaches a hand down between us, sending ripples running through every nerve of my body as I rise up and then come crashing down, squeezing his hard shaft with the waves of my second orgasm. Seconds later he is crying out my name in the sweet agony of his own release.

He lays on me and we breathe each other in while we recover from another round of incredible, life-affirming sex. He kisses me tenderly as he pulls out of my body and moves to my side. We lie on our backs, holding hands in the most comfortable silence I've ever experienced. He squeezes my hand and I smile.

He brings my hand to his mouth and kisses every finger individually. Then he feathers kisses along my scar. "Quid pro quo?" He looks at my scar and then over at me with a raised brow.

It's only fair that I tell him about my scar; it wasn't nearly as traumatic as his own. But it was the day I met Michael which makes my heart hurt a little. I put my head on his chest. I'm not sure I want him to see my face as I tell him the story. I haven't told it to anyone since Michael died and I'm scared that it might take me back to darker places.

I surprise myself when I'm able to get through the entire story with not so much as a tear. I even find myself smiling and drawing laughs from Nate when I tell him about Dr. Cockblocker.

"So, that's why I never see you wearing bracelets. You are afraid they will catch on the oven again causing you another burn," he says, absentmindedly studying my wrist.

"Yes. It's a shame because I have a jewelry box full of them."

"Thank you for telling me." He kisses my wrist again and pulls me out of bed with him. "Shower," he demands.

"Really? Haven't you had enough yet?" I ask.

"Brooklyn, I waited over two years. I have a lot to make up for." He runs his eyes up and down my naked body. "And I will *never* get enough of you."

I can hardly contain my excitement, knowing my best friend will walk through the door to our apartment in just a few minutes. It's been weeks since I've seen her and the last time she was here, we didn't exactly get quality girl time.

Nate is psyched to see Graham as well. We moved all of Nate's things into my bedroom last week, leaving Emma's old room ready for them. The only thing Nate left in her room was his drafting table. He uses the room as an office so he doesn't bother me when he is working.

As if watching him work would ever be a bother. It's more like an aphrodisiac. He's always biting his lip and running his hand through his hair while sketching. It's sexy. Sometimes I stand in the doorway and watch him. Not surprisingly, we always manage to make love whenever he gets done working.

"Ahhhh!" I hear Emma scream as she pushes through the door, drops her bag on the floor and hurdles herself at me.

We share an embrace that can only be understood by tried and true BFFs. No matter how far away we are, we will always have this connection. A tear rolls down my cheek. I am both happy to see her and sad that we don't get to share our everyday lives anymore.

"This weekend is gonna rock!" she yells at the sky.

We have plans to go out clubbing with Ryan and his girlfriend, Laura. Ryan is back in town for a few weeks in between his thrill-seeking adventures. Our first official group date. I'm giddy like a schoolgirl knowing that Nate and I can be together in front of the world. There is no more guilt, no more bitterness, no more hurt. There is only love. *Well, for me anyway.*

Graham and Nate are catching up over a few beers when Ryan and Laura show up. Laura has never met Nate so I introduce them. "Nate, this is Laura. Laura, this is my . . . my . . . uh—"

"Boyfriend." Nate says extending his hand to her. "I'm her boyfriend." He rolls his eyes at me.

Boyfriend. Yes, I like the sound of that. I've just never said it before when referencing Nate. I dreamed of calling him that when I was young. I would even dance around the house with a large pillow, pretending it was my boyfriend, Nate. But I've never actually said the words out loud.

He pulls me close so that only I can hear him whisper his hot words in my ear, "And you're my girlfriend. Mine. Always." And once again, another piece of my heart gets chipped away, finding its way over to Nathan Riley.

The club Emma has chosen is a hip club with mostly top forty music—very easy for dancing. The six of us order drinks and chat for a while. Ryan has been regaling us with stories of his latest excursion. He was cave diving in Costa Rica. I am amazed at all of the incredible things that he has experienced.

Laura, on the other hand, looks bored and rolls her eyes at his stories. She must have heard them a thousand times before.

Ryan elbows me and starts to tell the story of when he taught me how to surf. He has everyone cracking up at his tale of trying to get me to keep my balance. I tell them that although it looks easy from land, it is quite different when you are trying to stand up on a surfboard on a moving, pitching, surge of water. That you must simultaneously leap from a prone position while shifting your weight left, right, front, and back to keep from diving face forward. The 'pop-up' as surfers call it.

"When you lost your top, I about died laughing," Ryan says. "I remember you trying to use the seven-foot surfboard to cover yourself up, in fifteen-foot-deep water with waves crashing all around you. It was hilarious." His eyes start to water.

Nate stiffens and squeezes my thigh. I look over at him and he is no longer laughing with the rest of us. He is looking at Ryan like he wants to punch him. I pull his hand up to my lips and softly kiss it. "Dance with me, babe?" I whisper, trying out the endearment on him.

He snaps his head towards me, seemingly forgetting all about Ryan and my lost bikini top and says, "Babe?" He smiles. "That sounded hot. Say it again."

I clear my throat and then I whisper in his ear in a low, sultry voice, "Babe, I want you. On the dance floor. Now."

He squirms in his seat, readjusting himself. Can I really affect him that much merely with my words? It is a heady thought. He pulls me up from the table and says, "Baby, you can have whatever the hell you want when you talk to me like that."

We lose ourselves in each other on the dance floor. Thank goodness it is dark and there are a lot of other people dancing. It doesn't matter if the song is fast or slow, our bodies are pressed against each other practically from head to toe.

He slips his hand in-between my skirt and blouse and runs his fingers around the sliver of skin all the way to my back, sending jolts of electricity through my body. My hands can't decide if they want to fist his hair, grab his biceps or trace the muscles of his back, so I do each in turn. I can't get enough of his skin under my trembling fingers.

He spins me around so that my back is to his front. He grabs my hips, moving me with him so that we dance as one to the blaring music. I can feel his growing erection pressing into my back. I close my eyes and drop my head back against his shoulder. He licks at my neck. "Mmmm, salty and sweet. My favorite combination," he says against my skin.

We dance like this all night. Who needs drugs? Who needs alcohol? Although now I understand the draw; Nate is an addiction I must satisfy. It's like I'm building up a tolerance and need more and more of him to get my fix. I will never get tired of this, of him. I can only hope he feels the same way.

Since our couple's night out turned into a grind-fest for Nate and me, Emma and I decide on the way home that tomorrow we are having a Girls' Day. But tonight . . . tonight Nate and I will finish what we started on that dance floor.

Two hours and three orgasms later, Nate and I lie in bed together, tracing our fingers across the bare skin of each other's bodies. He starts drawing something on my stomach. It tickles but I don't want him to stop. "What are you drawing?" I ask.

"My favorite thing. You," he says, kissing me where his fingers are touching my skin.

This reminds me of that sketch I saw fall to the floor the night he stormed out of his room because I was going on a date. "I saw the sketch you did of me that first night," I confess.

"Which one?" He raises his eyebrows.

"There's more than one?" I say excitedly.

"Um . . . you could say that." He sounds embarrassed. I wonder if it weren't so dark in here if I would see a blush creep up his face. "I could show you if you want."

I sit up and declare, "I want. I want."

He laughs and rolls over to turn on the light. He reaches into the bottom drawer of his nightstand and pulls out a sketch book. He looks at me, lets out a long breath and hands it over.

I open it slowly and can't believe what I see. The book contains page after page of *me*. Some sketches are of me close up. There is one drawing of me in the bakery; another of me lying on my stomach on the bed with my head propped up on my steepled hands.

The most shocking of all are the ones of me as a girl, back in high school. There is a sketch of me stretching on the track after a run. Another with the flute to my mouth. I check the date in the corner. It is dated the year we hooked up. The year he disappeared.

Oh my God.

"Nate, my God, these are incredible," I gush appreciatively.

"That's only because you are my muse." He leans over to kiss my cheek.

"It's amazing the way you see me. You make me look so beautiful." I blush.

"Brooklyn, you are beautiful. You just don't see yourself that way. That's one of the things I love about you."

"One of the things?" I blurt out without filtering my thoughts.

Oh, crap.

"Yes, baby, one of the things." He takes the sketch book out of my hands and places it on the nightstand. He pushes an errant hair behind my ear and cups my face. He looks into my eyes, his deep blue irises dancing with passion and purpose. "There are too many to list . . . because I love everything about you."

My heart jumps and I stop breathing.

"I love you, Brooklyn." He rubs him thumb across my bottom lip. "I think I've loved you in some way since high school. I know I've loved you since Raleigh."

I close my eyes and let the words sink in. *He loves me.* I think that this must be the most perfect moment of my life. I've had other note-worthy moments, but this one I want to remember when I'm a hundred years old.

I take in a deep breath. I smell Nate, with his manly scent mixed with fresh laundry and sex. I can hear his baited breath while he waits for me to speak. I can hear my heart pounding as it removes itself from my body and collides with his. I can feel the tingles of his touch as he glides his thumb over my lip. I etch the conglomeration of all five senses into a memory that will last a lifetime.

I open my eyes to see the man I have longed for since my youth. The man who waited for me even when he thought I was lost to another. The man that I hope to spend the rest of my life with.

"I love you, too, Nathan Riley."

Chapter Twenty-two

Morning light starts to peek through my blinds. I try not to wake up Nate. He's not used to getting up as early as I am. Our bodies are still entwined. His leg draped over my leg, my head on his chest, his arm over my waist. I go over last night's events in my head, replaying them over and over, making sure I wasn't dreaming. He said he loves me—everything about me. I never thought I would hear those words from a man again.

I was so sure that I was right about ending up alone and never taking a chance. He wore me down and I can't even begin to tell him how grateful I am that he was so persistent. I'm still scared as hell about what the future will hold for us. I don't know if I could stand it if he were to leave. And if he were taken from me, like Michael? I shake my head at the thought. Surely fate wouldn't be that cruel.

His right arm is resting out to his side leaving his tattoo in full view for me to look at. As I wonder about the true meaning of his tattoo, I start to realize that I would feel the same way if Nate ever left me. I would feel like my heart was shredded and surely I would want to die. Is that what he was thinking when he got it?

I lean over to place a gentle kiss on his tattoo when I feel his other hand running up my spine, leaving a line of sparks tracing up my body. I quickly pull away from his arm.

"Morning, beautiful." He leans up to kiss me, shaking his head because he caught me staring. Again.

"Morning yourself." I smile down at him, guiltily wrinkling my nose.

"What is it, baby?" he asks, taking a piece of my hair and twisting it in his fingers.

"I was wondering about your tattoo," I say sheepishly. "When you got it, did you . . . um . . . did you want to die?"

He takes a deep breath and lets it out while his eyes burn into mine. His hand comes up to run through his already messy morning hair and he bites down on his lip in contemplation. "No, Brooklyn. I didn't want to die." He turns us so that he is spooning me from behind. He is running his hand up and down my arm. "I was not in a very good place. I had just lost baseball and of course I had found out my marriage was a farce. Add all that to what happened with my mom and I was majorly screwed up."

He kisses my hair before he continues. "I never should have married her. In the beginning, when we first met, she seemed to be the perfect girl. She liked what I liked. She went out of her way to make me happy. She was full of kindness and compassion. All of that changed in the months after we got married. It was all an act to reel me in. Hell, I didn't even know that she didn't want kids until after we were married."

He wants kids? So many questions are running through my head but I try to remain still and quiet as this seems to be the best tack to take when he is in the mood to share information.

"My mom . . . she also went out of her way to make me happy. On the outside, she was the perfect mother. It was all an act as well." I can feel him shake his head and sigh into my back. "Fucked up by two women. Apparently that is why I went rogue."

I decide to chime in on his revelations. "You have quite the rare insight into yourself."

"I should," he admits. "I pay a goddamn fortune to my shrink."

Oh, this is news. On the one hand, it surprises me that Nate would see a therapist. He seems like the kind of guy who would never go to another person with his problems. But then again, I'm relieved to know that he did. I wonder if that is why he stopped sleeping around. It explains why he seems so different than he was a few years ago in Raleigh. He doesn't have as much anger in his eyes.

"Surprised?" he asks me.

I nod my head. "How long have you been seeing a therapist?"

"On and off for a couple of years. I knew after you came to Raleigh that I had to do something to get my head straight." He laughs silently. "The thing is, I went to try to get you out of my head, but all it did was make me want you more."

"Why?" I stretch a look over my shoulder at him.

"Because once I got Claudia out of my system, and out of my mind, I realized that there couldn't be anyone else for me but you. No matter how much I tried to find someone else, I couldn't. And my shrink wouldn't let me break my promise not to contact you. You know what they say about absence, right?" He kisses my forehead.

"Well, I guess I need to meet him and thank him," I tease.

"I already have." He laughs. "Thanked him, I mean. I called him last week and told him the news."

"Oh? And what did he say?"

"The usual. Do you make me happy? How do I feel about it? You know, shrink crap." He sighs. "Then he went off on me about my mom again."

"Why would he do that?" I ask.

His body tenses up behind me. "Because she still lives here and he thinks I should see her."

I whip my body around and sit up. "She lives here . . . in Savannah?"

He nods his head. "She still sends me birthday and Christmas cards every year and the return address is here in Savannah."

"What does she say? In the cards she sends you." I let out a breath I didn't know I was holding.

"I don't know." He looks down at his hands. "I throw them away without reading them."

"Don't you think she might be trying to apologize to you? To let you know she still loves you?" I ask.

"Of course that is what they say." He moves away from me, looking pissed. "My sister eats that stuff up, but I don't. I don't want to ever talk to that woman again."

"But she is still your mom. No matter what she did, I'm sure she still loves you," I plead with him.

"Don't go there, Brooklyn," he warns me. "I already have my sister and my shrink on my back. I don't need you there, too."

I decide to drop it, not wanting to ruin what we shared last night by having an argument this morning. I scoot myself over to him and straddle his hips. "Okay, how about if I'm on your front then?" I tease.

I see the tension drain from his face as he stares at my naked body. "God, I love you." He runs his hands up my rib cage to my breasts and puts one in each hand, studying them with his head cocked to the side. Then he frowns and gets a bitter look on his face. "I hate the fact that Ryan has seen your tits."

I smile sweetly and put my hands on top of his. "What does it matter, babe? They belong to you now," I say, hoping the use of the endearment will pull him out of his funk.

He smiles half-heartedly. "I know what you're doing . . . *babe*." He winks at me and runs his fingers over my nipples, making me shudder as shock waves dance through my body.

"And I *love* what *you're* doing." I watch him play with my breasts like a kid plays with a favorite toy.

"Tell me about your business relationship with him." His look is all serious and hardened.

Okay, so no morning sex then. My goddess within frowns.

I explain to him that I needed an investor to build my business. That, with the funds Ryan invested, I was able to purchase a second industrial oven, a catering van and hire additional help. I say that we've been able to expand our offerings at the bakery and take on larger catering jobs. I tell him that Ryan doesn't have any creative control over the business, that he only has a say in the business end and that I still retain over half of the overall business in my name.

I see the cogs working in his head as he processes the information I'm telling him. "So he controls when, where and how but not the what?"

"I guess if you look at it that way. But it's more detailed than that. He can't close the bakery in the current location, if that is what you are asking. Emma owns the building and I lease directly from her. Our contract states that he can't mess with my location. But he does have the authority to dictate other major business decisions should they arise."

"Hmmm." He narrows his eyes at me and I realize that he still has his hands firmly on my breasts as if claiming them from Ryan.

A knock on the bedroom door followed by a shriek of, "Girls' Day!" brings our discussion to an end.

"But I'm not done yet." Nate kisses my breasts and then trails a line up my jaw to the sensitive place behind my ear. Then he whispers in my ear, "I'll never be done with you."

My heart goes all gooey and soft hearing his words and feeling his hot breath brush over my ear. I want nothing more than to stay in bed and worship his body. Let him worship my body. I want to feel him inside me every minute of every day. I'm no longer a complete person without him. When I get up from this bed, part of me will stay with him and I can't reclaim that bit of me until we are together again. I now understand what it means when people refer to their 'other half'. He is, in fact, a part of me and I am a part of him. We fit together like a perfect puzzle that we can only solve together.

"Are you okay?" He looks at with me concern as he wipes a tear that has fallen down my cheek.

"I'm more than okay. I love you." I lean down to kiss him.

When we part, he simply says, "Me too, baby. Me too."

Chapter Twenty-three

We are in Graham's SUV, driving over to the River Street Seafood Fest on the other side of Savannah. I am so excited that I can share this little piece of the city with Nate. Although I know he is still worried that he might run into someone from high school. He is very quiet in the car, just staring out the window. I reach over and squeeze his hand and he gives me a small smile before turning away.

I'm looking at the back of his messy-yet-perfect hair as I think about what Emma said yesterday.

"Lyn, you know I've wanted the two of you together for years. But watch it with him. I think he has a huge issue with jealousy. Maybe it stems from his ex-wife cheating on him. He looked like he wanted to tackle Ryan every time the man was simply talking to you. And when Ryan put his arm around you to give you a hug, I thought Nate might have a freaking conniption."

She went on to remind me that he landed in urgent care after punching a guy who was talking to me at a bar. Well, that's not exactly how it happened. The guy swung at Nate first. I assured her that Nate is fine and that he is only being territorial about our new

239

relationship. The fact is, I do think he is a bit jealous of Ryan because of our business relationship. I would probably be jealous, too, if Nate had a gorgeous female partner.

I scoot over so that I'm pressed up against Nate and I whisper in his ear, "Thank you so much for coming along." I kiss his neck and lick his earlobe. "I will definitely show you my appreciation later."

I see the reflection of his slow smile in the car window. He turns towards me and pulls my face to his, our lips almost touching and he breathes into my mouth, "You better watch it or I might take you in the back of Graham's SUV." Then he pulls me into a kiss that has way too much tongue for public decency.

"I heard that. Get a room before you ruin my custom upholstery." Graham shakes his head laughing.

"We're here!" Emma squeals while bouncing in her seat.

We exit the car and are bombarded with the sights, sounds and smells of the festival. People are everywhere, laughing, eating, drinking and dancing in the streets that are closed off with barricades. Tent stations are set up for each food vendor and the smell of seafood grilling and frying floats in the air.

An hour into our afternoon, the sky turns dark and many patrons head for their vehicles. We, however, are troopers and are going to try to wait it out. As it starts raining, we all cram together under the small vendor tents. Bodies are mashing together all wet from rain and sweaty from heat. The music is still blaring over the huge speakers and I wonder how long it will be before they shut the whole festival down.

Then I hear it—the song that played on the radio in Nate's truck so long ago, right after I lost my virginity. Right before he left me. The Nickelback song, *'Someday'*, that had me refusing to listen to their songs for the past ten years.

Nate stiffens behind me. He knows the significance of the song. He told me so after Raleigh. "Brooklyn . . ." he whispers in my ear. Then he grabs my hand, pulling me out into the rain in the middle of the abandoned street. We are getting soaked from head to toe.

I look at him like he is crazy. I try to resist him pulling me. "Nate, what are you doing?" I yell over the sound of the music and the rain.

"I'm dancing with my girlfriend!" he shouts, smiling at me while rivets of rain pour off his head. "I recall another time in the rain with you that didn't work out so well. So I thought we could make a better memory for you." He twirls me around him. "Plus, I really like Nickelback," he says, winking at me.

So while everyone else is huddling together under the tents, Nate and I are dancing in the rain. We dance to the entire song, our bodies pressed together, moving as one, never losing eye contact. We must look like idiots. But I don't care. Right now, in this minute, it is only Nate and me. I am floored by the unexpected romanticism of this. How he keeps managing to reach into my chest and grab more pieces of my heart simply amazes me. This man, who longs to remain anonymous in this city, has publicly and quite conspicuously danced in front of half the population just to give me a good memory. I think tears are running down my face, but the rain masks them. I am overwhelmed by my love for this man.

The music stops. I think they shut it all down, but I don't care because Nate is kissing me in the rain. He is kissing me like I wanted him to that night in Raleigh. He is kissing me like it is our first and last kiss all wrapped into one. I'm lost in the sensation of his lips. It is the wettest, hottest, sexiest kiss I've ever experienced. I think we tell each other more with this one kiss than we did with our declarations of love the other night.

I jump at the sound of thunder. But as we pull apart, I realize it is not thunder, but applause. Everyone under the tents has eyes on us and they are all clapping and cheering. I look over and see Emma and Graham both shaking their heads at us while joining the applause.

Nate takes a bow. I hit him on the back of his very wet head which makes the crowd stop cheering and start laughing. He grabs my hand and motions for Graham and Emma to follow us and we all make a run for the car.

Back at the apartment, I'm grateful that Graham and Emma went to visit with her parents because we didn't even make it up the stairs without shedding some clothing. There is a trail of wet shorts, shirts and undergarments leading up the stairs and into our bedroom. Nate picks me up and my legs are wrapped around him as I feel his erection growing larger. We bump into random furniture trying to make our way to the bed when he gives up and sets me down on the dresser.

"I have to taste you." He stares into me, his blue eyes almost black with desire. "Now." He spreads my legs apart slowly, his hands burning my skin everywhere he touches me.

"Yes." It is the only word I'm capable of saying. I'm still reeling from our dance in the rain. Still high from the incredible kiss that we shared in front of hundreds of people. Still shaking from the intensity of my feelings for him.

He lowers to his knees and wraps my legs around his shoulders. I can't pull my eyes away from him. I watch as he kisses my belly and teases my thighs. I'm burning with desire. I want to push his mouth where my body is begging for it to be. I don't because I know that the anticipation will only heighten my sensation when he finally touches me there.

His eyes look up to find me watching him. A slow smile spreads across his face. "Watch me make you come, Brooklyn."

I can't help momentarily closing my eyes. That is the sexiest thing I've ever heard anyone say. I look down at him as he finds my clit, rolling his tongue over it in circles. The sight of him pleasuring me is pushing me higher and faster than ever before. I reach out to grab the sides of the dresser, sending everything on top of it flying to the floor as I lash out. "God, Nate . . . yes!"

He pushes a finger into my slick opening, and then adds another, crooking them upwards to find that spot that turns my body into liquid heat. Flashes of light cloud my vision as my insides tremble and quiver. Nate sucks my clit into his mouth and then flicks it with his tongue sending me crashing over the edge, pulsating around his fingers, my thighs squeezing his head as he draws every last wave out of me.

He lifts me off the dresser, my body still trembling with aftershocks, and he places me on the bed. "You are so incredibly hot when you come." He kisses around my neck, up to my ear and back to my lips. I can taste myself on him. It is strangely erotic. It reminds me of where he's been and I suddenly feel the need to return the favor.

I push him down on the bed and train my eyes on his hardness, absentmindedly licking my lips. I can see him smile. He knows what I'm about to do. His cock jumps in anticipation. I lean over and lick the head, swirling my tongue around the under, more sensitive side of his erection drawing out a deep, appreciative moan. I take his length into my mouth, running my hand up and down the base of him at the same time. My other hand reaches down to cup and stroke his balls.

The next thing I know, I'm thrown onto my back and Nate is driving into me. "Jesus . . . you were going to unman me before I could bury myself in you."

It is a heady feeling knowing that my mouth on him affects him just as much as when he has his mouth on me. He sets a steady pace and I lift my hips to meet him stroke for stroke. I'm slowly building again. But I want Nate to experience the earth-shattering pleasure that he gives me. "Nate, I want to be on top," I whisper in his ear.

"Yes," he murmurs as he flips us around, staying inside me the entire time.

I lean over him, dangling my breasts close to his face. He reaches out to grab them as I plant a slow, sensuous kiss on his lips. He works his tongue into my mouth and I suck on it, just as I was sucking on his manhood moments ago. He moans a hot breath into my mouth.

I push myself up and arch my back, causing his length to sink deep inside me. He reaches down and puts his thumb on my clit, rubbing circles and sending pulses of shock waves through my body. I lock eyes with him and reach my hands up to caress my breasts. His eyes grow wild with desire as his hips buck and shift under me. I pinch and tug at my nipples, extracting moans from each of us.

"Ahhhhhhhh," he draws out. "I'm gonna come, baby." He stills momentarily, grabbing my hips and holding me hard against him, all while reciting my name along with garbled declarations of love over and over. His voice pushes me over the edge and sensation overwhelms me as desire detonates inside my body and I explode around him.

I collapse onto his chest and we breathe each other in as we come down from our release. I can't move. I can't think. I am thoroughly obliterated. I have lost all sense of reality outside of what we are, right here, right now.

"Holy crap," he murmurs into my hair. And we both dissolve into a fit of laughter.

After I clean up, I come out of our bathroom to see Nate kneeling beside my dresser holding up some jewelry that had fallen out of my jewelry box when I sent it flying to the floor. He is trying to clean it up, but he doesn't have a clue about what goes where. He seems to be studying my bracelets. Then his breath hitches and he reaches out to grab something. I pad over to him and see him holding the engagement ring that Michael gave me.

"Is this . . . ?" He doesn't look up at me.

"Yes." And for the first time, I find myself looking at Michael's ring without being overwhelmed with sadness. The thought brings a smile to my lips.

He examines the ring, first holding it between his fingers, then laying it in the palm of his hand. He closes his eyes and runs his hand through his hair. It is the same pose I see when he sits at his drafting table. He closes his hand around the ring and looks over at me. "Can I have it?" he asks. "I mean . . . would you trust me with it?"

My brows furrow as I try to absorb the question he is asking me. Why on Earth would he want this ring? *Oh, no. Surely not.* My mind goes crazy with all kinds of off-the-wall thoughts.

Nate startles me back to reality when he touches my arm. He must see the confused expression on my face. He shakes his head and says, "Brooklyn, when I ask you to marry me, it sure as hell won't be with another man's ring."

Oh, thank God. I let out a long breath and my goddess within wipes her forehead. *Wait, what?* I think he just said *when. Oh, God, he just said when.* Am I ready to be someone's fiancée again? It didn't turn out so well last time. We are still in the bubble. The perfect boyfriend/girlfriend bubble. Everything is going so well. I want things to stay exactly as they are. Not rock the boat. Not tempt fate. Not piss off Karma.

Hot breath washes over my ear. "Hey, are you okay?"

"Huh?" I startle.

"You kind of zoned out for a minute. I was asking about the ring. Would you trust me with it?" He is begging me with his eyes. He is looking at me with nothing but love and caring. How could I not trust him with the ring when I would trust him with my life? Of course I'm going to say yes.

"Yes," I breathe. I turn to go take a shower. I want to wash away my fears, my doubts about our future . . . my worries from the past.

Chapter Twenty-four

I'm filling up the display cases with the morning pastries and I think about the ring. It's been over a week and I haven't asked him why he wanted it. I wonder if he thinks I still pull it out and look at it and dream of Michael. I don't. Not anymore. Not since I knew I was in love with Nate. Michael will always have a special place in my heart, but Nate is the man I have always wanted, even when I couldn't admit it to myself.

I frown when I look at the calendar on the wall behind the counter. I've started the countdown to Nate's departure. Two weeks. He will be gone in fourteen days and neither of us has uttered a single word about what will happen then. It's the bubble. We're still in it and neither of us wants it to pop.

Also on the calendar, circled in red marker, is an important meeting Ryan and I have been preparing for. If we can land this client, it will mean big business for Brooklyn's.

Ryan walks in from the back of the shop, looking like hell. He spends the next ten minutes telling me about his breakup with Laura.

When he goes to leave I walk him through the kitchen to the back door. I give him a hug. "It will all work out in the end, you'll see." I hold him tight and hope that my words are true, for him and for me.

"Want to get your hands off my girlfriend, man?"

Ryan releases me and puts his hands up in surrender. I spin around to see Nate glaring at us from the bottom step. I roll my eyes at him and say goodbye to Ryan. As he is walking through the back door, I remember our big meeting today. "Ryan, you look terrible, do you want me to reschedule our two o'clock?"

"No way, Lyn. I'll go get some sleep and be back later." He shuts the door after him.

"Well, isn't that cozy?" Nate narrows his eyes at me. "Did you enjoy your hug?"

I can't tell if he is joking or just being an ass so I try to ignore the attitude. "Laura broke up with him and he is having a hard time."

"How convenient that he is suddenly single right before I have to move back to Raleigh." His words bite me. Now I know he's being an ass. I can't believe that he picks now, right now, to talk about leaving. And why does he have to make it about Ryan? I start seething and I am about to lay into him when I realize that he is probably having a hard time dealing with the fact that he is leaving and so he is deflecting his emotions onto Ryan.

I reach out to Nate and pull him to me. I put my hands on his face and bring his lips down to meet mine. He is all fresh and minty and I kiss him softly with the hope that he understands that I am his. But like most men, they simply don't get it unless it is right in front of them, emblazoned on a flashing neon sign. I break the kiss and look him dead in the eye. "I'm yours, Nate. It doesn't matter where you live."

He lets out a breath and kisses my forehead. "I'm sorry, Brooklyn. I don't mean to be a dick. I don't trust him."

"But you should trust *me*, Nate." I sigh into his shoulder. "And if you won't take my word for it, go ask him yourself."

"I did," he says.

"You did?" This surprises me and I pull back from him to get a good look at his face. "When?"

"The other day, when you and Emma were out for your chicks' day."

I think back. That was right after our couple's date when he got all worked up because Ryan had seen my boobs courtesy of the bikini malfunction. "So then you should know that he isn't a threat to you."

"The hell he isn't." He possessively runs his hands up and down my arms. "In fact, I have more of a reason to hate the guy after what I found out. But I haven't had time to figure out what to do about it yet."

"Nate, you've lost me. Just spit it out."

"The bastard is going to franchise the bakery, Brooklyn." He shakes his head and his lips purse in anger.

"What?" I pull my arms from his. "That is crazy. I have no idea where you came up with that, but he knew good and well when I brought him on that I wanted to keep it small. He knows I would never franchise, that's not was Brooklyn's is all about."

"Well, you might want to remind him of that, based on the plans I saw on his kitchen table the other day."

"I don't need to ask him anything, because I know for sure that is not what the plan is. You didn't see what you think you saw. He has a lot of other business investments that he deals with, some that really are franchises. Those are what you saw." I go over to get him a cup of coffee to go. "I wish you would stop making Ryan the bad guy."

"I'm not *making* him anything, Brooklyn. He *is* the bad guy. He's going to take your business and do the very thing that you swore you'd never do."

I hand him his cup of coffee—my signal that I want to end this conversation. "Nate, you have asked me, on more than one occasion, to trust you. So, now, I'm asking you to trust me."

He groans in frustration and I can tell that he is trying to hold back so that he doesn't upset me by continuing the argument. I'm relieved when good wins out over evil in his mental battle and he kisses me goodbye. But while I'm watching him walk out the back door, I have to wonder if he is even capable of trusting a woman—of trusting me.

~ ~ ~

Nate decided to take me out in celebration of the big catering job we landed earlier today. If all goes as planned, the job will lead to more business in the near future. This is the kind of client I've been hoping for since I brought Ryan in. It will require a lot of work and planning but with Ryan on task, we will be able to handle it.

"To you, baby." Nate raises his glass of champagne.

"To Brooklyn's." I clink my glass to his and can't help the huge smile on my face.

We eat what is arguably the best lobster dinner that I've ever had. He has taken me to The Olde Pink House. I grew up always hearing about this place, but of course I could never afford to dine here. I still can't, but Nate wouldn't let me put up much of a fight. When the man sets his mind to something, he usually gets what he wants.

"I want to take you everywhere, experience everything with you," he tells me, while shoveling a forkful of decadent chocolate cake into my mouth. I roll my eyes and moan at the onslaught of chocolate flavors exploding on my taste buds and I wonder if they would give me the recipe.

"I don't need anything else as long as I have you." I look long and hard into his eyes and hope that he understands how much I mean the words. He stares back at me as desire blooms within me. I reach up and run my fingers along his unshaven jaw. He grabs my hand and lowers it to his lap where his arousal is evident, igniting the fire within me yet again.

"Oh, you have me. You definitely have me," he says. I give him a little squeeze down there. "By the balls, apparently," he adds, making me giggle.

He waives his hand at the waiter and quickly gives him his credit card. He nuzzles into my neck, then his lips linger to suck gently on my ear. "Mmmm . . . chocolate mixed with vanilla. Can it get any better than this?"

We practically run out the front door of the restaurant, tugging on each other to hurry. It's no wonder that we barely leave home, it's much easier there to throw down and have at it whenever the mood strikes us.

Suddenly, I'm jolted to a stop. Nate has stopped walking. I turn around to see why and find he has turned into a statue of a man. His face fallen, his expression blank, his mouth slightly open and his eyes wide. I look behind me to see what he is staring at. I see a thin, beautiful and incredibly stylish woman walking towards us. She looks to be in her forties, maybe fifty.

"Nathan, my sweet boy!" she cries out with a French accent as she nears us.

I feel all the blood drain from my face when I make the connection. I *see* all the blood drain from Nate's.

"No!" I hear him yell from behind me. He pulls me back to him and points a finger at the woman to keep her distance.

"Nathan. Please talk to me." Tears are falling down her face. "Please, will you just give me a minute?"

A distinguished looking man in a three-piece suit comes up beside her. "Sophia, honey, are you okay?" he asks with concern. Then he turns to Nate and spits out, "What have you done to upset my wife?"

I hear a strangled cry from deep in Nate's throat. He is squeezing my hand so hard I think my fingers have lost circulation. "Wife," he says with a crackle in his voice. He clears his throat and continues, "Wife?" He looks at the man. "Did you know that your *wife* is a two-bit whore, putting her tits on display and sucking off any man with fifty bucks?"

The man looks like he might storm forward and plow down Nate. But then he looks at his wife and back at Nate and he must realize what the rest of us already know, the woman is Nate's mother. "Nathan Riley?" he asks, looking over at us. All of the anger is gone and there is only compassion in his voice.

I look over at Nate and what I see is a broken seventeen-year-old boy. There is so much hurt in his eyes; so much rage. I see him struggle with his emotions. How confusing it must be to see your own mother after ten long years. He idolized her. She was June-freaking-Cleaver. Right up until she became the slut who ran the whorehouse out of her spa.

Without saying a word, Nate turns with me and walks us out to his car. His mom doesn't follow us but she calls out to him the whole time. Once we are inside the car he lets out a breath but he still doesn't look at me. I don't know what to say to this beautiful man who was trampled on by the actions of his mother. I reach over and put my hand on his leg.

"Don't," he says, closing his eyes. "Just don't."

"Nate, I—"

"Goddammit, Brooklyn, I don't need you telling me that I should talk to that woman. She is dead to me. She died the same night that I hurt you. She is the reason my life is so screwed up." He sits in silence for a minute before continuing. "If it weren't for her, I never would have left you, I never would have met Claudia and I sure as hell never would have lost baseball."

I look at his face and see the glistening of tears in the moonlight. "Nate, that's not what I—"

"Can we not talk about this?" he pleads. "Can you please shut the hell up about it?" He starts the car and peels out of the parking lot. Thank goodness we are only a few miles from home or I would genuinely worry about our safety with the way he is driving. I want to tell him I understand his reaction. That it is okay for him to feel this way. That I won't push him to do anything he doesn't want to do. But I don't think he would hear any of it so I remain quiet.

He pulls up to the curb and reaches across my lap to open my door. I look over at him with unspoken questions.

"Out," he says.

"But Nate—"

"Give me some goddamn space, Brooklyn." He doesn't look me in the eye.

I'm scared for him. Hell, right now I'm a little scared *of* him. So I do the only thing I can do, I get out of the car. "I love you!" I cry, as he pulls the door shut and squeals away.

What if he does something crazy? Is he leaving me? Oh, God, what if he gets into a car accident? I start to hyperventilate right here on the sidewalk when I hear, "What the hell happened, Lyn? I was going over this proposal when I heard a car peel out." Ryan is standing over me.

He takes me back into the office and quickly puts some papers away in his desk. After I explain it to him, he tells me that he thinks I'm overreacting because of what happened to Michael. He says that Nate needs space to process seeing his mom and her new husband. And that I should give it to him but let him know that I'm here if he needs me.

All very good advice but it doesn't keep me from thinking the worst. The bubble—it's been popped. It's had a razor blade jammed into its freaking heart. I feel so helpless. I wish he could talk to me instead of running away.

Running away. Just like I did. And Karma raises her ugly head once again.

Back in my apartment, I will my phone to ring with our song. I do this for hours until my eyes grow weary with sleep. When I can't take it anymore, I send him a text.

Me: **Nate. I'm here for you. I love you. B.**

Chapter Twenty-five

When I open my bedroom door, I can smell him—feel him even—before I see him. I walk right past where he is sitting on the couch without even a look in his direction. I get my cup of coffee and then I slam the door shut to my—our—room and then, because I'm so pissed at him, I lock it. I take longer than usual in the shower just to let him stew.

When I emerge from our room, Nate is sitting in exactly the same position as when I passed him almost an hour ago. I sit on the opposite end of the couch. When neither of us has spoken for what must be minutes, I finally say, "Is this how it's going to be? You shutting me out when things get tough?"

His eyes close and he blows out a breath in frustration. "I couldn't have you see me like that, Brooklyn."

"Like what? Pissed, sad, emotional?" I turn to him and add, "You need to let me know where we stand, Nate, because I was under the assumption that we were in a relationship."

"Oh, you mean like in a relationship where you believe your boyfriend when he tells you your business partner is going behind your back?"

I roll my eyes. "Nate, I'm so sick of talking about this. How did a situation with your mom turn into another argument about Ryan? If you aren't going to trust me then I don't know why we are even doing this."

"What does trusting you have anything to do with the fact that he wants to sell you out, Brooklyn? And it certainly has nothing to do with the fact that he wants to sleep with you."

"Oh yeah? Is that what he told you when you went to see him, that he wants to sleep with me?"

"He didn't have to tell me. A guy knows when another guy wants his girl."

"I'm not going to stand here and defend myself, defend my friend and partner to you." I get up to leave for work.

"Don't walk away, Brooklyn!" he shouts after me.

"I'm not walking away, Nate. You are pushing me away with all of your false accusations."

"False accusations?" He stands up and runs his hand through his hair. "Now who needs to go talk to Ryan?"

I throw up my hands in frustration. "I'm late for work," I say, as I walk toward the door.

"Yeah, you wouldn't want to be late and disappoint *him* would you?" he spits out.

I turn abruptly back to him. "You know what? Fuck you, Nate!" I spew at him.

Oh God, that felt so good, like I let the steam out of a pressure cooker. So I decide not to stop there. "I'm tired of you treating him like he is always doing something wrong. I'm tired of walking on eggshells around you because I'm afraid of injuring your fragile ego.

And I'm tired of feeling guilty every time I talk to another guy just because you had a cheating, bitch of a wife!"

I stomp down the hall, leaving him before he can respond. Leaving him in what I can only imagine is a state of shock because his normally quiet and obedient girlfriend dished him up a dose of reality.

I find it hard to concentrate on work not knowing what I will find when I get back upstairs. Will he be there? Maybe after seeing his mom and then hearing my diatribe, he will decide Savannah is too much for him. Maybe his going back to Raleigh in ten days is a good thing. I love him, but it is becoming increasingly difficult to live with the constant accusations. His jealousy was one thing, understandable even, given his past, but this thing with Ryan and my business—he is going too far.

By the time I leave work, I've decided to give myself some space. Space to think about our relationship. Time to figure out what I want and need in the long run. Distance away from the man I will cave to if he simply touches me.

I leave Nate a note on the breakfast bar.

Not running, just need some space.

I make sure Kaitlyn and Derek can cover for me for a few shifts before heading out. I pack a small bag with a couple of days' worth of clothing. I'm not even sure where I'm going. Mom's house is too close. Emma's too far. Plus, I really want to be alone.

My phone chirps.

Nate: **Who's shutting who out now?**

Me: **Nate, I don't want to shut you out but I can't deal with all of your allegations right now. Please give me some time.**

Nate: **In ten days you'll have all the time you need. Do you want me to leave now?**

His words punch me in the chest and take the air out of my lungs. No, I don't want him to leave now. I don't want him to leave ever. But at the same time, I don't want him with all his baggage. I'm so confused.

Me: **I don't know what I want. Please, give me a few days. I don't ask you for much.**

It takes a few minutes, but he finally responds.

Nate: **Okay. Listen to the song, Brooklyn.**

Before long, I find myself driving out to the coast to stay in a little hotel by the beach that Emma dragged me to after Michael died. I can still hear her words in my head.

"There is nothing like the beach, with the rhythmic sound of the waves and the hot sand under your toes, to make you feel better and bring clarity to your life."

Clarity . . . that is exactly what I need right now.

I get up early to catch the sunrise, searching for that clarity that Emma assured me was here. I'm sitting on the beach trying to remember what drew me to Nate in the first place. Sure, it was his looks; I mean I wouldn't be fooling anyone if I said otherwise. And it was his kind heart. I can still see that sometimes, like when he takes me dancing in the rain, but it was also his confidence. Maybe that is what's missing now. He is more than confident when it comes to his job and the rest of his life, but when it comes to me . . .

Why can't he be more like Michael? Hell, even when Michael *had* a reason to be jealous and lash out at me, he didn't. Then I shake my head and laugh at myself, remembering a time when I wished Michael could be more like Nate.

I call Emma. She will know what to do. She always does when it comes to men.

"Lyn," she says, after I've brought her up to speed, "these are two amazing men we're talking about. Jealousy aside—because we both know why Nate has those issues—do you really think he would lie to you to try and get Ryan out of your life? On the other hand, do you think Ryan is even capable of doing what Nate claims? I mean, he's like your new me."

Who do I trust more? That is what she is really asking me. I want to trust Nate, I really do, but with all of his past issues, can I? Then there is Ryan, who not only knew my wishes for the shop from the very beginning, but who has been nothing but supportive of me and my relationship with Nate.

I say goodbye to Emma and decide to run it out on the beach, hopefully giving me a double dose of clarity.

I listen to our song. The words implore me to let him in, help him get past his insecurities, be his reason for becoming a better person. I know he wants to say these things to me and can't. This song is his way of communicating with me when he feels defeated— just like when he texted it to me two years ago.

I want so badly to be his reason. I want to support and love him unconditionally. The fact that I can't, may be the clarity I'm looking for. The realization stops me dead in my tracks. I'm five miles up the beach, but I walk back the entire way, unable to run through my tears. The tears that are falling because in the battle between my head and my heart, my head is winning.

When I near the hotel, I see a familiar face sitting on the beach. Ryan.

I walk over to him. "How—"

"Emma called me." He looks down at the ground where his fingers have been digging up a hole in the sand.

Oh, no. Emma must have told him everything. "Ryan, I am so sorry. Nate has no business making such accusations. He is jealous of you and—"

"Lyn, listen to me," he interrupts. Then he closes his eyes and lets out a long, slow breath—a sure sign that he is about to tell me something difficult.

"Please don't hate me, Lyn." He looks up at me again with guilty eyes.

Oh, God. He does want me. No, no, no, no. How could I have missed this?

"Nate was right. I was going to sell franchises of the bakery." He winces and it looks like the words physically hurt coming out of his mouth.

"What?" I don't know if I'm relieved that he doesn't want me, or pissed that he was going to do the very thing that I told him I didn't want when I took him on as my partner.

"What are you talking about, Ryan? You knew I didn't want that from the beginning." I shake my head in confusion.

"I know you didn't. That's why I wrote the contract specifically excluding any clauses pertaining to franchising. I came into this with that very intent, before I got to know you, before you became like family to me, so I made sure I could legally franchise, knowing I would screw you over."

I can't believe what I'm hearing. He was going to sell me out. Nate was right. "So you were playing me the whole time?"

"At first, yes. But these last few months, after I really got to know you, I realized I couldn't mess with your dream. You are one of the most kind-hearted people I know, Lyn. So, I changed my mind and backed out of the deal I was negotiating."

Nate was right.

"I never wanted you to find out about this. I thought I could throw away all of the paperwork and you would never be the wiser. I didn't want to hurt you and I didn't know how to tell you." He looks ashamed. "I had no idea that when Nate came to my place a few weeks ago he saw the collection of contracts and negotiations laid out on my table that I was gathering up to throw away."

Nate was right.

"Lyn, can you please forgive me? I promise I'll stick to the contract. Hell, I'll let you kick me out, buy me out, be a silent partner—whatever you need to make you trust me again."

Nate was right. He was right all along. And I called him a liar. My chin falls against my chest as my eyes lower to the ground. "Ryan, all I can think about right now is that Nate was telling me the truth and I didn't believe him." I see him hurting so I add, "Honestly, I'm almost happy that this happened, because I was about to . . . I don't know what I was about to do, but right now I can only thank you for being a back-stabbing slime ball."

He laughs at me. "You're welcome?" he says.

"I have to go. I have to get back to Nate." I start to run back to the hotel.

"Um, so are we good?" he yells after me. "Do you want me out?"

I turn and yell back, "No, Ryan. You are a great partner and I do think you have a good heart—at least for those of us you call family. Just don't screw up again."

I leave him standing on the beach and go up to shower. But first I have to send a text to Nate.

Me: **I'm coming home, can we talk? Are you still there?**

My heart surges when almost immediately he responds.

Nate: **I never left, baby.**

Chapter Twenty-six

Driving back from the coast, I think about how to make my apology to Nate. This is new territory for me. Flowers seem too girly. A card seems too cheap. He has to know it is sincere and from my heart.

Thirty minutes later, I'm climbing the stairs to our apartment, my hands full of two chocolate shakes and a couple of orders of fries from the same place we went on our night in high school. I'm so nervous. I know, based on the tone of the last text he sent me, that he probably won't leave me or anything that drastic. But I'm terrified of his reaction and have come fully prepared to grovel.

Nate quietly watches me cross the room over to where he sits on the couch. I place my offering on the table before him and he eyes them with pursed lips and then raises his eyebrows at me.

I sit on the couch next to him and angle my body towards him, taking a calming breath. "Nate, I can't begin to tell you how terrible I feel for not trusting you. You were right the whole time. Not about Ryan's feelings for me—he doesn't want me—but about the bakery.

He was planning on selling franchises. He was planning it from the very beginning."

Nate cocks his head to the side, staring me down, inviting me to continue the apology.

"He even said that he orchestrated the contract so that he could legally get away with it even though he told me that wasn't his plan when I took him on. You should know that what you saw that day, on his kitchen table, those were the franchise negotiations that he was going to destroy. You see, he changed his mind. He changed it months ago when we became such good friends that he didn't want to screw me over."

Nate looks bored with my apology so I decide to throw in some more groveling. "I am so sorry I didn't trust you. I just thought because you don't like him, that you . . . well, it doesn't matter because I was wrong. I was so wrong and you were right and I promise to trust your instincts in the future. Well, not about him wanting me, but about other stuff . . . " I trail off feeling like I'm rambling on when I look up to see a smirk on Nate's face and I can tell he is trying to suppress a laugh.

"What?" I ask, confused about his reaction.

"Um . . ." He smiles up at me sheepishly. "Emma kind of called me and told me the whole story this morning. I guess she didn't want me to high-tail it out of here without talking to you first."

I throw a french fry at him. "You idiot." I smile. "You let me go on and on like that when you knew the whole time?"

"Well . . . yes." He shrugs. "It's such a rare occasion that *you* are apologizing to *me*, that I figure I should milk it for all it's worth." He reaches over to take my hand. "I still don't trust the guy. And, Brooklyn, you should make him sign a new contract."

"I know, and he said he will," I assure him.

He nods his head.

"But, Nate, we still need to work on some of our issues." I squeeze his hand. "I mean, first you shut me out and run away because you didn't trust me with your feelings and then I needed space because I didn't trust that you were being straight with me."

He reaches over and pulls my face around to his. "I know I screwed up, baby. I'm sorry I hurt you when I left. My head was messed up and I wasn't thinking about anything but myself."

Over shakes and fries, he talks to me about his mom and I realize that it was her, as much as it was Claudia, who screwed him up so badly. *Fucked up by two women*, he once told me. All this time, I thought the words of his tattoo were in French because of his ex-wife. Now I know they also bear the scars from his mother.

"So, is this okay? Are we okay?" he asks, pushing a piece of my hair behind my ear.

"Yes, we're okay." I reach out to run my fingers across his strong jaw.

He kisses the palm of my hand.

"But, there will be ground rules," I say.

His eyes go wide and he smiles up at me with a raised eyebrow.

I whack him in the back of the head. "Not *those* ground rules, you idiot. *My* ground rules."

"Anything. You name it." He pulls me onto his lap.

"No running. No matter what. We work our problems out together."

"Done," he says quickly.

"I'm not finished yet." I scold him.

"Sorry," he says with a boyish smile.

"Trust. We have to try to trust each other. I promise to take what you say into more consideration than maybe I have in the past. But, Nate, you have to trust me, despite your past, you have to place your trust in me until I give you reason to question it."

He closes his eyes and nods his head. "Okay, baby. For you . . . I will try."

I extricate myself from his lap and gather up the courage for the conversation I am about to initiate. I've done a lot of thinking the past few days. He is leaving soon and we have to deal with it. Plus, the bubble already burst so . . .

"Nate, what are we going to do when you leave in nine days?" I brace myself for his response.

He leans back against the couch cushion and pulls my legs over his lap. "Yeah, I thought you might want to talk about that."

"It's just that, these last few days apart, they were horrible. I'm not sure what I will do without you here." I reach up and brush my fingers over his three-day stubble that I have come to love so much. "I know the circumstances were different, but still . . ."

"I've thought a lot about this," he says. "Not only in the past few days, but since I moved in here. Even before we were together I was wondering how it was going to be when we couldn't see each other every day." He looks me straight in the eye. "Brooklyn, if you ask me to move down here, I will."

What?

Okay, this I did not expect. Him move down here? I thought he would ask me to go with him to Raleigh. I was sure of it. I was also sure that I couldn't do it. I couldn't leave Brooklyn's. But he is offering to move here—for me—it's the perfect solution.

"You can work from Savannah?" I ask, hopefully.

"Well, yes and no." He furrows his brow. "I won't be able to stay with R.A.D., but there are plenty of other firms that would probably make me a nice offer."

Okay, not a perfect solution then. He would have to quit his job as junior partner with his dad's company. The company that he hopes to run one day. Plus there is the fact that he hates it here. His mother is here. He avoids going out whenever possible. I remember when we were in Raleigh, how he had so much energy and excitement about the city. He couldn't wait to get out and show us his favorite spots.

No. I can't ask him to leave the city and the job that he loves. I love him too much to ask him to do that. "I can't ask you to move here." I close my eyes and sigh. "I can't ask you to give up all the things that you love."

"I love *you*, Brooklyn." He brings my hand up to his lips and kisses the back of it. "I love you more than those things."

If it is possible, my heart swells with even more love and adoration for this man. I feel a tear trickle down my cheek. "Oh, Nate. I love you, too. And that is why I won't ask you to move here." I sit up, turn towards him with my legs crisscrossed in front of me. "Emma and Graham lived apart for two years. *Two whole years*. And they ended up married." I feel the blush creep up my face. "Well, not that . . . um . . . "

Nate laughs. "I get it. I know. I lived with the other half, remember? I saw the late-night Skyping and endless phone calls and weekend visits."

"Do you think we could do that? Live without touching each other every day? Live for the weekends?" I ask him.

He watches himself trace a finger down the side of my arm, making goose bumps appear all over my body. "It'll be hard. I'm not gonna lie. Not touching you is going to practically kill me."

In a bold display of courage I say, "Well, when you can't touch me . . . we'll Skype and I'll do it for you." I scrunch my eyes shut and feel the heat come up my face.

He stills completely and says, "Brooklyn, you just made me get instantly hard." He takes my hand and directs it to his lap. "Do I really have to wait until I'm back in Raleigh to see that?"

"Yes. You have to wait." I give his hard length a squeeze. "I have to give you something to look forward to."

"Now I can't wait to move," he teases. Then he picks me up and carries me to our bedroom. "I guess I'd better show you what you'll be missing."

$$\sim \quad \sim \quad \sim$$

Needless to say, we did exactly that. I lie here in bed, on the morning of his departure and think back over the past week and a half. We put ourselves firmly back into our bubble. Nate really enjoyed my repeated 'apologies'. We had so much sex I ended up getting a UTI, 'honeymoon-itis' they called it. But it was worth it. We also worked out a schedule. Every weekend, we will alternate visiting each other. Nate even went out and bought us matching new laptops with the largest screens possible, for the 'ultimate Skype experience' he said. He is such an idiot.

But he's *my* idiot. And I love him more than words can express. I watch him sleep. I've been up since dawn watching him sleep. This is what I will miss the most. Waking up in his arms, our limbs tangled together, his hands running down my back. His breath in my ear. His mouth on my body.

"Are you objectifying me?" He slowly opens his eyes while his mouth spreads into a huge smile.

"Every chance I get," I say, leaning over to plant a soft kiss on his lips.

"Mmmm," he mumbles. Then he breaks the kiss and moves away slightly, reaching over to his nightstand to open the drawer. "Before we get into this—and believe me, we *will* get into this—there is something I want to give you." He runs his foot up the length of my leg making me quiver.

He presents me with a small box. It is larger than a ring box, thank goodness. I'm not sure my heart could take *that* today. I eye the pretty, velvety box and run my fingers along the edges. "A going away present?" I frown. "But, I didn't get you one."

"Brooklyn, you give me a present every day." He winks at me. "Sometimes two or three times."

I giggle while I examine the box.

"Not a going away present. I would have given this to you had I stayed," he says.

I look up at him before I open it. He is biting his lip and then he runs his fingers through his hair. He is nervous. *Oh, God.* What is in the box?

My now trembling fingers open the lid. What is lying on a bed of soft black velvet is a bracelet. There is a flat yet slightly-rounded platinum surface that looks almost like an ID band, and attached to each end are flat links of platinum chain that in total looks much too small to fit my wrist. And embedded right in the center of the platinum band is the unmistakable diamond from Michael's engagement ring. Then on each side of the center stone, there are a couple of smaller, embedded diamonds, each a little tinier than the previous stone, all the way to the edge of the band.

My breath hitches. It is the most beautiful thing I've ever seen. But I frown. I don't wear bracelets. I thought he knew this. I hesitate for a minute wondering if I should say anything.

"Nate, it's beautiful . . . breathtaking even. But I—"

"You don't wear bracelets," he interrupts me. "Trust me. Try it on." He unclasps it and holds it out to me.

He puts it on my wrist and pulls on a tiny piece of chain by the clasp which tightens it and makes the bracelet fit me like a second skin. "There. It's a perfect fit." He smiles down admiring my wrist. "It's so tight that it shouldn't get caught on anything, but if it does, I had the clasp designed to give way while still keeping the bracelet from falling off your wrist. That's what this little piece of chain is for."

"You had it designed?" I ask, tears welling in my eyes.

"Yes. And I had it inscribed, too." He takes it off my wrist and turns it over. "See?"

I read the tiny print. *To remember the past ~ To trust in the future.*

"Consider it a gift from both me and Michael." He brushes a stray hair behind my ear. "But if you don't like it, I can get you the ring back exactly as it was. I had them keep the setting just in case."

Tears are spilling over and running down my cheeks. I can't understand how this man keeps surprising me in ways I never thought possible. Who does this? Who takes another man's engagement ring and turns it into something wonderful that has me thinking of the two most important men in my life? It is the most incredible, romantic and selfless thing I can imagine him doing. I feel like the wind has been knocked out of me. My hands tremble and my breathing is shallow.

"God, Brooklyn. You don't like it." He lowers his head. "I'm sorry, I thought—"

I move my fingers up to his lips to stop him from talking. "Nate." I clear the frog in my throat. "This is undeniably the best gift I have ever gotten in my entire life." Another tear falls down my cheek and he reaches out to wipe it with his thumb. "Words can't describe how you have made me feel by giving this to me. 'Thank you' just doesn't seem enough. It—it's incredible. *You're* incredible. I'll wear it every day. I promise."

He lets out a breath and visibly relaxes with my revelation. "Thank God!" He shakes his head. "You scared me for a minute. I thought you hated it."

"I could never hate anything you give me. And after this . . . I mean, somehow it will be easier to let you go today, because I'll always have a piece of you with me."

He pushes the jewelry box aside and leans down to whisper through my hair into my ear, "I'm not going anywhere until I watch you come two or three more times."

And with that, all thoughts of jewelry and moving are gone. I can only think of what he is doing to me, where his hands, his fingers, and his mouth will go next. What sensation he will extract from my body. What love he will instill in my heart.

Chapter Twenty-seven

I've done a decent job of keeping myself busy with the bakery these past few weeks. I'm working a lot more than usual to help pass the time. My phone is practically overheating with all of the texting going on between Nate and me, and we have a nightly Skype date at precisely nine o'clock. I went up to Raleigh last weekend and he is coming back here tomorrow after work. It's all going exactly as planned. Our bubble has just expanded by a few hundred miles.

Brooklyn's has been very busy with new catering business and Ryan and I are in the process of hiring another employee. We came up to my apartment to go over all of the applications and decided to eat Chinese take-out while we work.

My computer dings at me and when I look at the clock, I realize that we have completely lost track of time and that my nightly Skype time with Nate is upon me. I excuse myself from Ryan and run to my room to say hello.

"Hey you," I say when his gorgeous face pops up on the screen.

"God, I love to hear your voice and see your beautiful face at the end of every day." He bites his lip seductively then continues, "And I can't wait to have you in person in—," he checks his watch, "—twenty-three hours."

I giggle and start to tell him I'll have to call him right back when he gets a stern look on his face. "Who the hell is that?" he asks, looking over my shoulder.

I turn around and see Ryan standing in the doorway behind me. "Hey man, how is Raleigh?" he asks Nate and then mouths 'sorry' to me as if Nate can't see him.

"Lonely," Nate says harshly. "Mind telling me what you are sorry about and why the hell you are in my girlfriend's bedroom at nine o'clock at night?"

I roll my eyes at my over-protective boyfriend and say, "Ryan was just leaving. We were going over job applications at dinner and we lost track of time."

"Were you going over a new contract as well? One that protects your interests?"

I shake my head. "No, not yet, but we will. Do you want me to Skype you back in a minute, after Ryan leaves?"

"No. I'll wait right here while you put him out." I can see him lean back in his chair and cross his arms.

"Fine," I huff. I get up and walk Ryan to the front door while whispering my apologies to him.

"Don't worry about it. I don't blame the guy for trying to mark his territory," he says. "You have told him he has nothing to worry about, right? I mean why would I want a girl with a face as ugly as yours?" he teases.

"Very funny," I say. "See you tomorrow, dork."

I head back into my room and am rewarded with, "Took you long enough, did he try to kiss you or something?"

I let out a long sigh as I sit in front of my computer. "Nate, you really need to be nicer to the guy. He likes you and you should remember that when I'm with him, he keeps the other guys at bay."

"Other guys?" His eyes open wide. "What other guys?" he asks. "And you had him to your apartment—*our* apartment—for dinner?"

Well, crap, now I've gone and pissed him off even more. I'm tired of the same old argument about Ryan. Almost every night we do some kind of dance around the Ryan issue. I spend a lot of time with him, yes. He's my partner. He's my friend. But my reasoning falls on deaf ears.

Rather than waste our precious Skype date on meaningless bickering, I do the one thing I know will get his mind off Ryan. I stand up and adjust the monitor. I take a few steps back and slowly remove my shirt. I smile as the shirt comes over my head because Nate has stopped talking mid-sentence. I've never done a striptease for anyone before. I haven't even been able to touch myself like I told Nate I would and bless him, he hasn't pushed me.

But the Cosmo I had earlier is making me brave and I commit myself to following through. He is still sitting close to his screen so I can see the desire building in his eyes as I unclasp my bra and slide it down my arm, dangling it off of my finger before letting it fall to the floor. His mouth opens slightly and he bites his lip so I know he is enjoying this.

I continue my seduction by slowly and deliberately peeling my jeans off and away from my body. Then I hook my thumbs into my tiny pink panties and shimmy them down my thighs ever so slowly. I'm embarrassed and completely out of my element but when I look up and see Nate licking his lips and devouring every inch of my body with his eyes, I get the courage to continue.

When I skim my hands up the sides of my body and cup each of my breasts, I hear him moan. Then I hear, "Wait! Give me a sec."

I see him moving the laptop and realize he is carrying it back to his bedroom. I can tell he has placed it on his bed and I long to crawl under the sheets with him and be wrapped up in his warmth. He angles the laptop so we can see each other. I follow suit and put my machine alongside me on the bed. Once we are both in position, Nate removes his clothes. Not quite as seductively as I did. In fact, I think he's just set a record for the quickest striptease in history.

I laugh at him and he says, "Please continue," in a very businesslike manner.

"Yes, sir." I resume the placement of my hands on my breasts, squeezing them and pushing them together, giving him a close up view of my cleavage.

I soon realize that my actions are not only affecting him, but I feel my own build-up, causing moisture to spread between my thighs. I pinch and roll my nipples, closing my eyes to imagine that it is Nate's hands on me. I throw back my head and moan.

"Good God, woman," he groans.

When I open my eyes, I take in a surprised breath as I see him running his hand up and down his hard length.

Oh. My. God. That is incredibly hot.

Liquid heat pools inside me. Watching him touch himself is the most erotic thing I've ever seen. The thought that he feels the same way about me gives me the courage to take the plunge. I remove a hand from my breast and run it down over my stomach and below my small patch of dark curls. I find my slick opening and use my finger to spread the moisture up to my clit.

"Sweet Jesus," I hear Nate breathe out. His strokes are getting faster and I see his eyes cloud over with desire.

As my wet finger rubs in little circles around my nub, I watch his hand stroke rhythmically up and down his shaft and I feel my orgasm building up deep inside. The quivering starts in my middle, spreading down to my thighs and I know I'm getting close.

"Baby, I'm gonna come," he grunts. "Come with me. Slip your fingers inside yourself and come with me," he commands.

I do what he says without a thought. I'm so turned on right now watching him and hearing him direct my actions that I instantly start falling into spasms and explosions as my climax takes me over and has me squirming under my own hands. My eyes are closed as I ride out the final waves when I hear him yelling out his own exaltations. I open my eyes just in time to see his forceful stream jet up and over his naked belly.

As I come down from the most illicit, erotic experience I've ever had, it dawns on me what I've just done and I feel my entire face heat up. I bring the bed sheet up to cover myself.

I see Nate reach for a tissue and wipe himself up. Then he looks over at the screen and finds my eyes. "Wow, Brooklyn!" He smiles. "You've been holding back on me. That was incredible."

My goddess within takes a bow and blows air kisses to the crowd.

Chapter Twenty-eight

"To us!" Ryan exclaims, handing me a glass of Cristal that he purchased right after our most successful client meeting ever.

I think about how nervous I was earlier today during our proposal with the suits of a local literary publishing house. But we pulled it off, thanks to Ryan, and all of a sudden, Brooklyn's Bakery is on the map.

I almost jump out of my skin when I hear the door to my apartment slam shut and see Nate storm in and glare at Ryan and me, eyeing the champagne glasses in our hands.

"Nate, you scared me!" I look at the clock and smile. "You're early."

"Apparently not early enough." I can see the hurt in his eyes. He turns to head back out.

I quickly hand off my glass to Ryan and run after him, catching him in the stairway. "Nate, I'm not sure what you think is going on here, but let me explain."

"It looked pretty damn clear to me what was going on." He peels my hand off his arm.

I squeeze around him in the small stairwell, blocking his exit and then I put my hands on his chest. "Hold on. We just landed a huge catering account. Bigger than I thought would ever happen—it will double my business. We are celebrating. Please come back and celebrate with us. With me." I stand on my toes and plant a kiss on his cheek and run my hand over the stubble on his jaw.

I can feel him relax under my touch. He leans back against the wall and closes his eyes and mutters something to himself about not being like her, but his words are garbled and I can't make out what he is saying. He grabs my hands, pulling me against the length of his body. "Of course I will celebrate with you. God, Brooklyn, I'm sorry. I thought . . . when I heard him say 'to us', I thought—"

"I know, Nate. It's okay." I wrap my arms around him. "I'm yours . . . always."

He picks me up to give me a proper kiss hello then he carries me back up the stairs into the apartment where a confused and slightly pissed off Ryan is packing up his papers to leave. "Ryan, don't leave," I beg. "You were the catalyst for this job. Please, stay and celebrate."

He looks at Nate and they must have some brief, silent, man conversation with their eyes because he shakes his head at Nate and says to me, "No, that's okay. You guys enjoy the rest of the champagne. I know how much you look forward to your time together."

I start to protest when Nate pipes in, "Thanks man, that means a lot. We'll see you around then."

The door closes after Ryan makes a quick exit. Nate walks over and grabs the two half-full glasses, tops them off and says, "You heard the man. Let's make good use of this."

My body is still high from the memory of last night and adrenaline is still coursing through my veins from my meeting. I don't want to ruin this night by fighting with Nate over Ryan. Eventually he will have to get used to my being around him.

So, I do what I do best, I fling myself at him and lose myself in him for the rest of the night.

$$\sim \quad \sim \quad \sim$$

Saturday mornings are like Christmas morning now. Waking up in Nate's arms after being apart for the entire week is a precious gift. We lie in bed exploring each other, regaling stories of our week and giggling under the covers. These are the moments I will cherish the most when he leaves again tomorrow. I try not to think about it, I simply want to live in the moment.

My phone chirps. So much for the moment.

"Really?" Nate stretches his head over me to glance at the clock. "It's only seven o'clock in the morning, what could possibly be so important?" he says, yawning.

I reach for my phone and see that Ryan has texted me. I read the text and sigh, knowing that this isn't going to bode well. "Nate," I say sweetly as I turn to him, "it seems that I have to go into work for a few hours. Ryan was able to set up some interviews for this morning."

"Of course he was." He gets up and pulls his boxer briefs out of the pile of clothes we left at the side of the bed last night. As he's walking away to the bathroom I hear him mumble, "Douchebag is getting me back for last night."

I shout at him through the door he just slammed, "I'll be quick. I promise. A few hours tops!"

"Whatever," he grumbles. Then I hear him turn on the shower.

Less than two hours later, Missy has become the newest addition to Brooklyn's Bakery. On my way back up to the apartment it dawns on me that I now have three employees and a partner. I've come a long way from a year ago when it was only Kaitlyn and me. I'm practically bouncing up the stairs. I can't wait to crawl back into bed with Nate.

But I come up to an empty apartment. Nate has left me a note on the counter telling me that he's gone for a run. I decide, instead of counting the minutes until his return, that I'll head down and give Kaitlyn a little break.

While restocking the cases after the morning rush, I look out front and see Nate stretching after his run. I'm getting ready to drool over his hot, sweaty body when I notice the woman standing next to him. She is also hot and sweaty. My eyes are glued to the front window as I watch her remove her headband, shaking her hair out seductively over her shoulders. They talk for a few minutes and when she puts her hand on his forearm and laughs, my entire body stiffens. He shakes her hand and allows his hand to remain in hers a little too long. Then I watch Miss Hair-flipper mentally undress my boyfriend as he walks away from her and into the bakery.

He smiles at me sweetly as he walks by but doesn't say a word. I follow him into the back. "Nate?" I say, silently asking him a thousand questions with that one word.

He turns back to me right before he reaches the stairs and says, "It sucks, doesn't it, being on the other side of things?" And then he walks away.

What just happened?

Kaitlyn relieves me after her break and I get up to the apartment as he is getting out of the shower. I throw my phone down on the bed just to emphasize how mad I am. I've had a few minutes to stew over this. I understand that he is jealous of Ryan, but I have never given him a reason to be. Ryan doesn't want me like Miss Sweaty-pants wanted Nate. I don't flirt with Ryan—he is a business partner and a friend. Huge difference.

"Listen, Nate." I sit down and cross my arms over my chest. "I know what you are doing. You are trying to make me jealous."

"Is it working?" He raises his eyebrows at me and I try to ignore the drops of water running down the lines of his torso.

"Of course it is, you idiot!" I yell at him. "That girl was pretty and she obviously wants you. And it didn't much look like you were discouraging her." I hesitate before asking him, "Do you want her?"

He quickly answers, "No, Brooklyn, I don't want her. But I wanted you to feel what it's like to have someone else want me."

I roll my eyes at him. I'm not ready for another fight about Ryan. "Nate, I don't know what else I can do to show you that I don't want Ryan and he doesn't want me. Why don't you go talk to him? Let *him* tell you."

He laughs. "Oh, and you think he will come right out and tell me he's after my girl? Yeah, right. Besides, I already tried that once before and if I recall, it resulted in you telling me to 'fuck off' before you had your little beach holiday," he provokes.

"Oh my God, Nate, you are so frustrating." I stomp my foot. "I love *you*. I want *you*. It doesn't matter if other men may want me—which they don't—I'm with you and nothing else matters."

"Apparently *he* matters." He looks at the floor and his lower lip comes out. He is pouting. I pull my lips into my mouth to stifle a smile that wants to creep up my face.

"Yes, of course he matters. As my partner and my friend. But I don't love him." I get up and walk over to him and take his face into my hands. "Nate, I love you. And you matter more. You matter the most," I say.

He grabs me hard, putting our bodies in perfect alignment so that I can feel every ridge and ripple of his tight abs. Then he whispers into my hair, "God, I love you."

"Not any more than I love you," I assure him.

And with that he lets his towel fall to the floor and we proceed to finish what we couldn't in bed this morning.

Nate and I spent the rest of the weekend in bed aside from the time we had sex on the couch. And in the kitchen. Oh, and the shower. We took a small break so that he could make dinner for us. By the time he left, our bubble was fully intact and we couldn't have been happier.

It is only Monday and he hasn't even been gone twenty-four hours but I miss him like crazy. It's a good thing Missy was able to start work so quickly because I can stay busy training her this week. I hope the time will fly by.

After work Ryan asks if I want to go rock climbing with him. "Of course, it's just at the climbing gym," he says, rolling his eyes, "not even close to the real thing, but I have to do something to get my blood pumping."

It sounds exciting and I could use something to pass the time until my Skype date with Nate. "Sure," I tell him, "as long as I'm back by nine." I grin sheepishly. He knows all about my nightly Skyping with Nate. Well, not *all* about it.

~ ~ ~

I can barely contain my excitement driving up the Interstate. In a few minutes, I will get to see Nate. I know it's only been five days since I've seen him. Well, actually only eighteen hours since I've seen him, but five days since I've *touched* him and that is what matters. His touch, his kiss, his scent. Those are the things I can't get through a computer. It's only been three weeks and sometimes I wonder how long we will be able to keep this up. I go crazy without him near me every day. He goes crazy knowing Ryan is around me even though I reassure him every chance I get.

My phone chirps.

Nate: **Can't wait to see you baby. Hurry up and get here. Be safe. But hurry. And don't text and drive.** xoxo

I laugh. I really want to text him back and say 'then quit texting me'. But I have the feeling he wouldn't find it so funny. When it comes to my safety, Nate is vigilant. He insisted on adding a security system to my building and had extra deadbolts installed on the apartment doors before he moved. My safety is definitely something that he and Michael have in common. Like Michael, he insists that I have provisions and my phone with me at all times while running.

I take a quick peek at my bracelet and think of the only two men I have loved. I shake my head, still not believing that he designed this for me. Michael's diamond sparkles brightly when the afternoon sun hits it and I think how much I love Nate for having it made for me.

Minutes later, I honk my horn as I pull up to Nate's building. The door to his apartment swings open and he runs down the stairs to meet me at my car before I can even turn the engine off. He opens the door for me and reaches down to pick me up out of the car. I grab my purse before he has me completely out. I'm laughing. He's kissing my neck. I'm locking the car from my key fob. "Guess we'll get my stuff later." I giggle.

"Damn right we will," he whispers in my ear. I lean into his chest and take a deep breath and bask in the scent that is fresh laundry and pure Nate. I've missed the smell. I even refused to launder his pillowcase this week because I didn't want his scent to wash off. But I will never admit that to anyone.

~ ~ ~

This morning I'm once again doing my favorite thing—enjoying being draped in Nathan Riley.

We stayed up late watching horror movies in the buff, eating anything we could find off each other's bodies—which pretty much consisted of chocolate and peanut butter. We became a messy, sticky, Reese's cup, but all the cleanup was worth the three orgasms he gave me.

I watch him as he sleeps. His breathing is deep and regular. His hair is spectacularly messy, especially since we went to bed wet from our late-night shower. How this man is able to look incredible twenty-four hours a day is beyond reason. I belatedly notice that he hasn't shaved in at least a few days. I know he's done this just for me. He knows I think he looks sexy this way.

My phone chirps out in his living room and I'm careful to untangle myself without waking him. I quietly throw on Nate's shirt from yesterday and take a second to smell the collar, and then I pad out to check my phone.

It's a text from Ryan. They are having trouble with the espresso machine again and nobody seems to be able to fix it except me. I call

Ryan, hoping to quickly walk them through it so I can get back and enjoy some precious lazy time with Nate, but they can't seem to explain to me the state the machine is in.

I exhale in frustration and tell them to hang up and Skype me so that I can see what they are doing. I put the phone down and grab my laptop off the floor where all of my stuff landed when we finally got back down to the car late last night. On the way back to the living room, I shut the door to Nate's room so that we don't wake him.

It doesn't take much time to walk them through the repair now that I can see what they are doing. Ten minutes later, it is working again and I hear the collective cheers from some customers. Ryan carries the laptop into the kitchen and sets in on the counter as we say goodbye.

"See you tomorrow night at the gym?" I ask.

"Absolutely, Lyn." He smiles at me. "You're the best and you know I love you, right?"

I laugh. "You, too," I respond and shut the lid to my computer.

Then I jump off the sofa when I hear something shatter behind me. I look over and see that Nate has thrown something onto the glass sofa table, shattering it completely. My eye catches a baseball rolling away, finally coming to a stop when it meets the baseboard.

"W-what happened?" I ask him in horror. "Why did you do that?"

His eyes fill with rage and his fists ball up. The only other time I've seen him like this is when that guy in the bar tried to hit on me. "Why do you think I did that, *Lyn?*"

It's not lost on me that he uses my nickname.

"You're meeting him at the gym tomorrow? Right after you leave me?" he yells. "*You're the best, Lyn . . . I love you, Lyn,*" he quotes Ryan's words back to me. He paces around the back of the couch not even caring that his bare feet walk right over some broken glass. "Are you fucking him?"

My jaw drops open and my eyes grow wide. I can't even believe he just asked me that, after the incredible night we shared; after the declarations of love and whispers of forever in the early hours of the dawn.

"No, of course not!" I shout at him. "Nate, I don't know what you heard, but Ryan called me from the shop, I had to help them fix the espresso machine again. There is nothing going on between us." I move to get up and go to him.

"No!" He points at me keeping me from moving. "Don't touch me. I know what you're doing. Don't think I haven't noticed that every time we talk about him, you distract me so that you don't have to fess up."

"Fess up?" I shake my head. "Nate, there is nothing to confess. Ryan is my friend and my partner. That's all."

"I'll bet he hasn't even signed a new contract yet, has he?" He shakes his head in anger.

"No, but—"

"I didn't think so," he interrupts. "What about the gym, and the *I love you*?" He closes his eyes on the words. "That doesn't sound like he's your friend. It sounds like he is your friend with goddamn benefits."

"Nate, that's not the way it is." I sigh. "You know me. I love you. I think that us being apart is causing you to have insecurities based on your past relationships," I try to reason.

"Do you deny that you use sex to deflect my questions about him?" He looks me hard in the eyes.

"It's not like that, Nate," I plead with him. "I would just rather make love with you than waste precious moments fighting about him. Especially when there is nothing to fight about."

He is pacing around the apartment, his hands frantically running through his hair. "I trusted you, Brooklyn. How could you do this to me?"

I throw my hands up in defeat. "I haven't *done* anything to you, Nate!" I huff.

His eyes cloud over and he has a wild look about him. "I can't believe this is happening again. I knew it wouldn't last. Nothing good ever does. You were right. We never should have done this." He reaches his left hand up and blindly rubs his tattoo over and over.

"Happening again?" I ask him. "What do you mean by that?" I rack my brain, watching the rhythmic motion of his hand across his bicep. Then it dawns on me. "You're not saying I'm like *them* are you? Claudia and your mom?"

"If the shoe fits," he says through clenched teeth. I don't think I've ever seen his eyes look so dark and distant.

"Nate, please calm down, you are scaring me. There is nothing going on." I pick up his phone and walk it over to him. "Call Ryan, he'll tell you."

He takes the phone but instead of making the call he sends it flying into the wall. It falls to the floor, crashing into pieces. I know how it feels. My heart is shattering right now as well.

I back away, shocked and hurt by his words and actions. Tears are streaming down my face. He stares at his broken phone. Then he glances over the shards of glass and finally he looks up at me, studying my face and following the trail of my tears as they fall off my chin. He visibly takes a deep breath, letting it out slowly and I think he is calming down. I think he must see how out of control he is. I say a silent prayer that he will snap out of this and realize that in his paranoia, he has conjured up this entire thing in his head.

I'm not prepared in the least for what comes out of his mouth next.

"Him or me," he says harshly, staring at me with cold, empty eyes.

"What?" I cry. "What are you saying?"

"Him or me," he repeats. "Your choice. Do you want him or do you want me?"

"You!" I yell at him. "I want you. It's always been you, Nate," I say, trying to get through the wall that has come up between us.

"Then leave him. Buy him out. Do whatever it takes to get him out of your life."

"Nate, that is crazy. He's my partner, we have a legal contract. Plus, he's my friend," I beg.

"Him or me, Brooklyn," he says flatly.

Oh my God. He is truly and honestly giving me an ultimatum. I close my eyes and my body slumps down into the couch. How can he expect me to choose between my business and him? Because that is what he is doing by asking me to choose him over Ryan. I would never ask that of him, it's why I couldn't ask him to stay with me in Savannah.

"If you love me," I plead with him, "if you really love me, you won't ask me to choose."

He remains silent. I watch him stare blankly out the window of his apartment. My broken man, maybe he can't be fixed. Maybe he is incapable of a relationship. Maybe I can't live my life with a man who can't trust me.

I turn and go to his bedroom and quickly put on last night's clothes. Then I grab my laptop and still-packed bag and head for the front door. I turn to look at him. He hasn't moved and he is still staring out the window. This is not the man I know. This is not the man I thought I loved.

As I reach out my hand to turn the handle of the front door he says, "So, you've made your choice then."

Sobs threaten to billow from my body, tears stream down my face faster than I can wipe them away. My heart is being ripped apart, just like the one that is carved into his arm.

"No," I choke out, "you have."

Then I walk through the door and close it behind me.

Chapter Twenty-nine

I'm not sure how I made the ten-minute drive to Emma's place. All I can remember is pulling over to lose the contents of my stomach into a ditch along the side of the road.

"Oh my God, Lyn!" Emma shrieks when she answers the door and sees my wrecked state. "What happened?"

I collapse in her arms and sink to the ground, my body shaking uncontrollably. I think Graham must have shown up at some point and carried me inside because I end up settled on the couch, covered by a blanket with a steaming cup of coffee in front of me. I look over at Emma who is patiently waiting for me to say something. She is rubbing her hand soothingly on my back.

I must look a complete and utter mess. I glance down at my wrinkled clothes that are dotted with wet tear stains. I reach up to wipe my eyes and see yesterday's mascara smudged all over my hands. I run my fingers through the tangles in my hair. God, I must be a sight.

"That slime ball better look a might worse than you or I'll kick his ass," she says when she finally speaks.

I look at her and break my own silence. "Graham?" I ask, looking around their apartment.

"He went to Nate's. I haven't heard from him yet." She places her hand on my arm to comfort me.

I spend the next few hours alternating between fits of body-wrecking sobs, telling her what happened and heaving over her toilet.

When Graham finally comes back, I see him shrug and slowly shake his head at Emma. The look in his eyes says it all. I can tell he feels sorry for me and I know what that means.

Nate is done with me.

I have to leave. I have to get out of here but Emma practically forces me into the shower. I guess I don't blame her, I must smell like vomit. She then drives me back to Savannah in my car with Graham following behind in his SUV. The entire way I try to make sense of what happened. I know he has trust issues but how am I supposed to be with someone who will accuse me of cheating with every man I come in contact with? I try to convince myself that I have done the right thing. I love him, but I won't let him or any man control me.

I wake up Sunday afternoon feeling well rested thanks to the sleeping pill Emma made me take. The first thing that hits me, other than re-living the horrible moments of yesterday morning, is the smell that comes from Nate's pillow. Tears once again well up in my eyes and I feel sick so I run to the bathroom. Nothing is left in my stomach. I haven't eaten in thirty-six hours so I just dry heave over the toilet.

I shower and throw on a tank and yoga pants before going in search of my phone. I find Emma and Graham sitting at the kitchen table drinking coffee and arguing. Emma tells him that he better keep his psycho friend away from me. Graham says that he isn't a psycho but has trust issues stemming back to his mom. She tells him that Nate better work his shit out if he ever wants to even talk to me again. He agrees with her that we need to stay apart but he admits he's not sure Nate will ever be able to have a normal relationship.

My heart sinks, yet again. Emma rises to fetch me some coffee and my hands tremble as I lift the mug to my lips. "Did he call?" I ask, eyeing my phone that is sitting on the table between them.

"No, sweetie, he didn't," she responds.

"Text?" I ask hopefully.

She shakes her head and lowers her eyes from mine. "I'm so sorry, Lyn." She moves to my side and guides me to sit down next to her. "But I really think you might have to walk away." She sighs. "He needs to figure out his life and you need to let him."

Graham and Emma stay the rest of the day. They comfort me, feed me—well, they try to anyway, I don't feel much like eating—and they talk me into letting go of Nate, for my own good. For *his* own good. Who knows how far he would go if he truly thinks I am cheating. Graham tells me what lengths he went to after Claudia cheated on him. He thought Nate might kill the bastard that slept with his ex-wife and Graham had to physically restrain him on several occasions until he was able to convince him that Claudia wasn't worth it. However, Graham does have a point. Maybe Nate thinks *I'm* worth it. Would he really come after Ryan? I like to think he wouldn't but if Nate and I aren't together, he would have no reason to.

I've stopped trying to keep the tears from falling, it is a futile effort. I realize that I have to let him go. I have to let him go to protect him from himself. Bile rises in my throat at the thought of never being with him again; never feeling the body that quivers under my touch; never having the heart that worked its way into my soul.

I finally send Emma and Graham on their way after convincing them I'm not suicidal. I take another sleeping pill and hope that it obliterates all thoughts from my mind and gives me temporary peace.

$$\sim \quad \sim \quad \sim$$

The past few weeks I have resembled a robot going through the same motions day after day. I do what it takes to get from morning until night. My head hurts from talking so much when people ask about Nate. I'm tired of telling the story, and although I leave out most of the details anyway, it exhausts me every time.

Exhausted. Yes, that is the one word that describes me. Everything about me is tired. And even though I no longer take sleeping pills, I still sleep at least twelve hours a day. I figure it is my body's way of getting over Nate. The more I sleep, the less I think of him.

But the thing is, I still think of him. I think of him every waking minute of every day. When I see something funny, I look around for him to see if he is laughing, too. When I run, my mind races with thoughts of his hot, sweaty body. Every morning when I wake up and realize that I'm not in Nate's arms, I run to the bathroom and get sick. And damn it, if I don't punish myself by listening to Nickelback's greatest hits and our song, 'Be My Reason', over and over again. I guess I wasn't really his reason to change. Maybe he wanted me to be, but his love for me wasn't strong enough.

I reach over and grab the pillow that still smells of Nate. I know I will have to wash it someday. But I'm not ready. Just as I'm not ready to take off the bracelet that has adorned my wrist since he placed it there. Now, it is only a reminder of the men I have loved and lost.

Every day, I fight the urge to contact him. I don't know how many times I've written an e-mail or text and deleted it at the last second. I have to remind myself that even if we could be great together, he will always have issues and could be a threat to Ryan or any other men in my life. I'm protecting Nate by keeping away. I recite this over and over. It has become my mantra.

I also remind myself that he has not contacted me once in the past two weeks. If he loved me—cared about me at all—he would have made contact. To apologize, to explain, to even see if I'm okay. But nothing.

Ryan has been my rock when Emma can't be here. He is constantly checking up on me. He fills in for me downstairs when I'm too tired to move. He even cancelled his trip to Australia to scuba dive the Great Barrier Reef.

He has come to make me dinner, yet again. "You ready yet?" he asks, as he comes through the front door.

"Not yet. Maybe tomorrow." It is the same exchange we have every night when he comes over. He wants me to get back to living, to go to the climbing gym and try to kick his butt on the rock wall again. And every day I give him the same answer. Every day I hope it is the truth, that tomorrow I will be ready.

He has made me lasagna tonight and it is heavenly. The man can cook. He is the perfect guy really. He has it all. Looks, money, charm. Maybe he is exactly what I need to get over Nate. Without thinking, I lean over the table and kiss him. I want to erase the past and the bad memory of that horrible day when Nate made me choose. I want to do something that will numb my body and my mind. I want to lose myself in something or someone.

I quickly realize that not only is Ryan not kissing me back, but he is pushing me away. He drops his napkin on the table, and pulls me up by my shoulders then he leads me over to the couch and gently pushes me to sit down. He sits next to me and takes a deep breath and then lets it out.

He looks me straight in the eyes. "Lyn, is this what you want?" he asks. "I mean, deep down, when you look at me, and when you kissed me just now, what do you feel for me?"

I lower my head in shame and look at my fingers as they fiddle with my bracelet. "I love you," I admit. "I love you like the brother I never had."

"And I love you like a little sister," he says.

"I thought . . . I mean since he thinks I'm cheating on him with you . . . that I might as well be." Now that I say it out loud, I realize how ridiculous it sounds. "Oh God, Ryan," I say, heat creeping across my face, "I'm sorry. I'm such an idiot. Can you ever forgive me?"

He laughs at me and shakes his head. "You don't even have to ask, Lyn. Of course I forgive you. And it's understandable that you want to do something radical to get yourself out of this funk you're in." He reaches out to grab my hand. "But how about something more constructive like kickboxing or skydiving? Maybe scuba diving? I can get us down there in a matter of days," he says hopefully.

I smile at him. "I don't doubt you would do that for me." We get up to go finish our dinner.

Ryan's phone rings and he is quick to answer it and step outside of my apartment to talk to whoever is on the other end. He is Mr.

Mysterious lately. He has done this a lot in the past couple of days, dropping whatever he is doing to give his full attention to a phone call. He must have a new girl in his life and he doesn't want me hearing his lovey-dovey conversation when I'm still a flat-out mess. I appreciate him for that. But when I ask him who he was talking to, he always says 'nobody'. I guess he doesn't want to burst the bubble yet.

The bubble. And my thoughts are instantly back on Nate.

Chapter Thirty

Every day gets infinitesimally better. Although I'm improving slightly emotionally, my body can't seem to catch up physically and I still feel like crap. So in an effort to kick my own butt back in gear and have a life—I have decided to seize the day. Make the leap. Take the plunge.

I have asked Kaitlyn to fix me up again. I know full well that Scott, the hard-body firefighter, probably won't touch me with a ten-foot pole after the emotional display I put on. But I thought maybe Carl might have another friend who would take a chance on me.

Ryan walks in the bakery kitchen as Kaitlyn is going down the list of Carl's friends that she thinks are good prospects. She is talking about great hair and tight asses when Ryan interrupts.

"Well, thanks, ladies. I think you are both quite attractive, too." He winks at us.

Kaitlyn barely misses him with the spatula she hurls across the room. "Not you, Ryan." She laughs. "We are going over a list of possible dates for Lyn. Apparently, this filly is ready to get back on the horse, so to speak." She elbows me and raises her eyebrows.

Okay, I didn't quite put it *that* way when I asked her. "I don't intend on getting on anyone's . . . um, horse," I say, getting all embarrassed. "I just think that after almost a month, it's time for me to think about moving on."

Ryan pales. He puts down whatever he was doing and walks over to me. "Lyn, are you sure you are ready? I mean, maybe you should wait. And have you talked to Emma about this yet? You really should talk to her before you do anything rash."

"Rash? You think going on a date is rash? I thought you wanted me to quit moping around." I furrow my brows at him.

"All I'm saying is that maybe you should talk it over with Emma. You know, *your best friend*," he emphasizes.

I guess I haven't really discussed this with her yet. She stopped her weekly sympathy visits down here after the first two weekends 'post Nate', when I told her to get back to her own life.

"Fine," I acquiesce.

He walks back to pick up some papers that fell off the counter. "You won't forget? You'll talk to her first."

"Yes. I'll talk to her. Geesh." He really is playing the part of a brother. Over-protective brother, I'd say.

I lean over to help him gather up his files and I see the original invoice from the company that made the 'Brooklyn's Bakery' marquee back when I first opened the shop. I didn't even know I still had records going back that far. "What are you doing with this, Ryan?" I question him.

He takes the invoice from me and places it, along with all the other strewn about papers, back in his file folder before he answers me. "Uh, well I like the sign so much I thought I might want to use the same company for another business of mine."

I give him that stare. A cold, hard stare with a slight raise of my brow that says 'I'm not sure you are telling me the truth.'

"Brooklyn, I know you have every right to be paranoid given what I was going to do, but I promise you, this has nothing to do with franchising the bakery."

"Hmmm," I mumble.

"Hey, that reminds me," he says, turning back to me, "I have to leave town for a couple of days to check out another business opportunity."

"Oh? What kind of opportunity?" I'm curious and a little bummed about an opportunity that might pull him away from Savannah. Although I've known all along that he wouldn't stay around forever.

"I really don't want to say anything yet. I might jinx it."

I wonder if it really is another business opportunity. He's been so secretive with all the phone calls lately, I'd bet he's going away for a tryst with his new fling. But I keep my mouth shut.

"Okay. Well, good luck then," I tell him.

Later, when I'm taking the trash to the dumpster out back, I overhear Ryan outside the bakery on the phone. ". . . you heard me. No, of course I didn't . . . I know . . . just do something and fast . . . okay see you soon."

I head upstairs and make my daily phone call to Emma.

"Hey girl, how's it going?" she greets me.

"Fine, I guess." We exchange pleasantries and talk about our day as usual. "Hey, I wanted to get your opinion on something."

"Always. Hit me." She laughs.

"Well, I'm thinking about having Kaitlyn and Carl fix me up." The words feel strange as I force them out of my mouth for the second time today.

"No!" she shrieks and I have to pull the phone away from my ear.

"Okaaaaay, tell me how you *really* feel." I roll my eyes at the phone. "No, really, why not?"

"Lyn, it's only been a month. I think any guy you date is sure to be a rebound guy. That's not really fair to him now is it?"

Well, I didn't really think of that. I guess she has a good point.

"Tell me, why do you want to get out there again so soon?" she asks.

I decide truth is the best way to go with her. Anyway, she'll see right through me if I feed her a load of crap. "It's not that I really *want* to." My finger traces an invisible spot on the counter in front of me. "It's just that I feel awful. Like, every day. I'm tired and cranky and I'm sick of being physically sick over him." I sigh into the phone. "I think if I meet a guy and see that other great guys are out there, maybe it will give me hope for the future and—"

"Wait," she interrupts me. "Wait a goddamn second and go back."

I'm confused now. "Huh?"

"You said you are tired and bitchy and feeling sick. Like puking sick or generally feeling like crap sick?"

"Uh, well I have been throwing up a lot. But then I usually feel better. It's usually in the morning when I wake up and realize that Nate isn't here and he isn't coming back." I frown.

"What else? Is there anything else going on with you . . . physically?" she asks.

I think for a minute. "Headaches I guess. Oh, and I can't stand the smell of his blueberry muffins anymore. They make me sick." Nate's favorite, I think to myself.

"Lyn. Oh my God," she says with concern. "It sounds like you're pregnant. There is a girl in my office who recently found out she is knocked up and I swear she told me the same things you are saying. Tired, cranky, headaches, food aversions and morning sickness."

Morning sickness? Food Aversions? God, no. That is not what's going on. Emma is being dramatic. It's just my body trying to get over Nate.

"Have you had your period lately?" she quizzes me.

"Yes, of course. I had it a few weeks ago," I assure her. "Plus, I'm on the pill, you know that."

"Was it normal?" she asks. "You know the pill isn't one hundred percent effective, right?"

I think back. "I guess it was a little light, but Geez, Emma, I was in a really bad way. I still am. That's why I'm so sick."

"Not sick, Lyn. Pregnant," she says confidently. "I'd bet my life on it."

I think about what she has said. I think about the way I've been feeling lately. Sick every morning, tired all day. Could it be? Surely not. Fate wouldn't be this cruel.

"Oh God, Emma!" I cry out.

I hear her shuffling around and making all kinds of noise on her end. "Don't move," she says, almost out of breath. "Stay right where you are. I'll be there in four hours."

Lying on the exam table, my feet in stirrups, I still don't believe the home pregnancy test that Emma made me take last night. Yes, there was a faint line, and, yes, the directions said that any line, even a faint one was a positive result. But, even so, I don't believe it. I can't wrap my head around what this could possibly mean for me so I refuse to accept it without concrete proof.

Emma sits at my side, holding my hand while the doctor inserts a very uncomfortable wand thing up inside me, that, ironically, is covered with what looks to be a condom—the very thing that would have prevented predicaments such as this. The irony is not lost on me.

My eyes are closed as I say silent prayers over and over that the test was a fluke. That I really have just been sick over losing Nate. That my life is not about to be thrown into a tailspin.

"Here," the grinning doctor says, and I open my eyes and look at the monitor that he is pointing to. "This small sac right here, this little peanut, that's your baby. And that pulsing right there, that's the heartbeat." He smiles brightly at me. "Congratulations, Ms. Vaughn. You appear to be about eight weeks pregnant."

The look on my face must alert the doctor that this isn't exactly news for celebration. He quickly removes the instrument, wipes me off and says he will give us a minute as he leaves the room.

"Oh, Lyn." Emma pulls me into a hug. "Don't worry. Everything will be okay. Wait and see. Things will turn out for the best. I promise you."

Back at my apartment, I lie in bed trying to digest everything the doctor told me. Apparently, the antibiotics I took a while ago for my UTI probably interfered with the potency of my birth control pills. And that being on the pill caused breakthrough bleeding right around the time I would have expected my period.

Tears roll down my cheeks onto Nate's pillow as I stare at the small slip of black paper the doctor printed for me that has a picture of my little peanut. Nate's baby.

I swear Emma to secrecy. Of course I will have to tell Nate about this sooner or later. But I have to figure some things out for myself first. She says she will stay with me the next few days as she was planning to visit this weekend anyway.

Emma crawls in bed with me. After I cry my eyes out, yet again, I come up with some ideas that make this whole situation easier to swallow. I wipe my face and try to look confident. "I can do this." I nod my head at her. "I can be a single mom. Look at my business, it is perfect for a working mother, I can set up a play pen in the corner of the bakery kitchen. Heck, I can even put the baby to sleep up here and get one of those video monitor things to keep an eye on it."

She smiles sweetly at me. "I know you can. And you'll be the best mom, Lyn. Don't worry about anything. It will all work out, you'll see."

I fall asleep dreaming of precious blue-eyed girls with long, dark hair and adorable tow-headed boys with Nate's dimples.

Chapter Thirty-one

Two days after Dr. Happy dropped the bomb on me, I'm still walking around in disbelief but am slowly coming to accept what is happening. I've even thought about picking up the phone a few times to call Nate. I chicken out every time, of course. Maybe he will think that I'm trying to trap him. Or worse, he will say he doesn't want anything to do with the baby.

I'm sitting in the bakery office, tears rolling down my cheek for the umpteenth time—freaking hormones—as I stare at the bracelet still firmly attached to my wrist and contemplate being a single mother. I unclasp it for the first time since Nate put it on me. I slip it off, turn it over and rub my thumb over the inscription. *To remember the past ~ To trust in the future*

I close my eyes tight and try to envision a future without Nate. I have some close friends that I know will step up to help me out. I'm even quite certain Ryan will offer to be a surrogate dad . . . or at the very least, a favorite uncle. With my friends and family here, I know I can make the best of this. I have to make the best of this. For him or her—I rub my still-flat belly—I will do what I have to.

I open my eyes and think I must have fallen asleep and slipped into a dream when I see none other than Nate Riley standing in front of me holding a dozen roses in one hand and a thick folder in the other. God, he is a sight for sore eyes. He is wearing worn jeans and a tight black shirt that shows off his impressive physique. His hair has grown out, making it curl up even more at the ends and he has what looks to be several days of stubble on his jaw. He is gorgeous.

For a split second, my heart leaps and I get so excited that I almost bolt out of my chair and crash into him. But then I realize what has most likely happened and my excitement turns to anger. Emma must have told him about the baby. That is the reason he is here. Not for me.

"What are *you* doing here?" I spit out at him.

He looks guiltily at the floor, and then he raises his eyes back to meet mine. He gives me a smile that makes my body betray me, almost melting me on the spot. He takes a few steps towards my desk and places the vase full of beautiful red roses on it. Then he puts the folder down and retrieves a sketch book out of it.

"I have so much to tell you, Brooklyn." He runs a hand through his hair. "I don't know where to start so I guess I'll just show you."

He opens the book for me and stands back. I thumb through the many pages of drawings he's made of the bakery. Sketches of the outside of the building, the counter area, even the kitchen and office. They are incredible, but I'm surprised that they lack the copious detail that he usually brings to his drawings. The placement of the display cases are all wrong, the office is a much larger scale than it really is and the outside of the building looks like part of a strip mall or something. The outside picture looks nothing like my stand-alone building, although the marquee above the doors is a dead-on replication.

Confused, I look up at him with a million unanswered questions.

"Just let me talk for a minute." He motions to the chair opposite mine. "May I?"

"Fine." I blow out a long breath.

"Brooklyn," he says, holding my gaze, "I love you."

I shake my head at him. "Nate, I—"

"Baby, please will you let me speak? I have so much to tell you," he begs.

I stay silent and cross my arms over my chest. Maybe as a subconscious measure to protect my heart.

"Like I was saying . . ." He raises an eyebrow at me. "I love you. I love you so much it hurts to even look at you right now, not knowing if I can ever have you again. I know I completely screwed up. It was unfair of me to ask you to choose between me and him— me and your business. But I swear to you I'm better now. I won't ever do that again. I will make it up to you if you give me the chance."

He stops talking for a second and I take that as a sign that I'm allowed to speak. I momentarily wonder why he hasn't mentioned the baby. "Nate, I believe that you are sorry. But I've thought a lot about it over the past five weeks and I don't think it will work with us. I understand why, and I don't fault you for the women that have caused you to have trust issues, but I don't think I can live life with a man who is always wondering if and when I will cheat on him."

"No." He leaves his chair and gets on his knees next to my chair and touches my leg gently, sending familiar sparks up to my tight chest. "No, Brooklyn, I need you to understand that I've addressed my trust issues. I've been seeing my therapist and he has given me coping mechanisms. I know you aren't sleeping with Ryan. I knew even back then that you weren't. It wasn't you I didn't trust, it was him."

"Still, how do I know you won't have these same issues with him again, or with any other man in my life, for that matter?" I ask him.

"That's what I'm trying to tell you, Brooklyn." He looks up at me from his place on the floor. He takes my hand in his. "Dr. Bloom, my therapist, he told me that one of the things I can do to help with my trust issues is to make friends with all of the men in your life. And not just meet them either, really get to know them on a deeper level," he says, squeezing my hand, "and, it works. It's working."

"What do you mean it's working?"

"Well, weeks ago, only days after you left, after my first session with Dr. Bloom, I contacted Ryan and—"

"What?" I interrupt him. "He didn't say anything." I look at him and search his eyes for answers.

"I asked him not to. I wanted everything in place before I came down here to try to win you back. You see these sketches? This is what Ryan and I have been working on. You are looking at the newest location of Brooklyn's Bakery. Up in Raleigh. You will own a chain." His eyes light up.

My eyes widen with alarm.

He shakes his head. "Not a franchise, Brooklyn, a second location. One that you will have complete control over." He retrieves some papers from the file folder. "See, this is a new contract allowing you to buy out Ryan over the next few years."

"Buy him out? But that's not—"

"His idea, not mine," he assures me.

I am stunned silent. I try to process this information. *New bakery . . . he and Ryan are friends . . . he wants me back.*

He interrupts my thoughts when he says, "There is one more sketch I want you to see." Then he slowly lifts the sleeve of his left arm up to his shoulder, revealing a new tattoo. I can't quite believe what I'm seeing and I'm not sure if I'm going to laugh or cry. Right there on the outside of his arm, for the entire world to see is my name, 'Brooklyn' emblazoned over the outline of a cupcake that is identical to the one on my marquee. Underneath the picture are two small italicized words that read '*My Reason*'.

I trace the tattoo with my finger and notice goose bumps traveling down his arm. "When did you do this?" I ask him.

"About three weeks ago. It's fully healed, see?" He pokes his finger on it.

Three weeks ago? But I just found out about the baby three days ago. "Nate, I have to tell you something." I brace myself for his reaction.

"No, Brooklyn. You don't. I already know everything, he told me. Anyway, it doesn't matter what happened while we were apart. We are together now and I'm better and I will spend the rest of my life making it up to you if that is what it takes for you to forgive me."

He knows everything? Then why doesn't he talk about the baby? He has been here ten whole minutes and hasn't brought up the fact that we are going to be parents. Is he scared? Maybe he doesn't really want it. Plus he said '*he* told me everything'. Who told him? Graham? I asked Emma not to tell anyone. I'm so confused.

I look down at the sketches again. "So, I guess you expect me to just forgive you and move up to Raleigh to run the new shop?"

He angles his head to study my reaction. "No, not at all," he says, "but I certainly won't object to you spending lots of time up there. You do what you want. It is your choice."

He stands up and holds his hand out to me. "Will you come with me?" he asks, begging me with his eyes. "Please? Will you go on a drive with me?"

I want to say no. I should say no.

"Okay," I whisper.

He runs out to the kitchen and has a quick conversation with . . . Ryan? I didn't even know he was back. Then it dawns on me. New business venture . . . he was up in Raleigh with Nate and he probably came back down here with him.

He leads me out to his car and we ride in silence. As soon as he makes the turn, I know where he is taking me. As we pull up to The Bend, memories shuffle through my head. The first time we came here, he took my virginity. The second time we came here he stole my heart forever. I fear this third time will erase those memories if we end up fighting over where I'm going to live or who will raise the baby. "Nate, do we have to—"

"Yes, Brooklyn. We *have* to be here. This is the one place we absolutely have to be right now. There is no other place I could imagine being with you on this day."

He parks the car and runs around to open the door for me. He walks me over to a clearing that is already set up with a blanket and a cooler. He drops my hand then heads back to the car to retrieve something from the glove box.

He walks back slowly towards me, hand running through his hair. I see beads of sweat dot his forehead even though it is a mild day. He steps onto the blanket, taking me with him but we don't sit down. He takes a deep breath and blows it out slowly as he gathers my hands in his.

"Brooklyn, I love you so much. More than I ever thought possible. You are my reason." He gestures with his eyes towards his new tattoo. "You are the reason I changed, you are the reason I'm still changing because I want to become a better person for you." He gestures to his old tattoo and says, "You are my reason to live and I know for damn sure I would die for you."

He reaches into his pants pocket and pulls out a small velvet box while tears roll down my face. He starts to lower himself onto a knee.

Oh, God. He is going to propose. This is all happening too fast. I can't let him do this. Not for all the wrong reasons. I know that I will love this man until the day I die but I can't let him be forced into marrying me. He will end up resenting me and I love him too much for that.

I shake my head at him. "Nate, no. You can't do this just because of the baby."

His face pales and he takes a step back. "What did you say?"

"I know that Graham told you, you said back at the shop that he did," I say.

"Graham?" He looks confused. "What Graham told me?" He shakes his head. "Graham didn't tell me anything. *Ryan* told me that you made a pass at him. He told me that you were trying to get over me and that you kissed him. I told you back at the shop that it didn't matter, that none of that matters anymore."

Oh, God. He doesn't know. The new bakery, the tattoo, the flowers, the proposal . . . it was all to get me back. Not because he was forced into anything.

He stands before me, hands trembling, and blood draining from his face. "Brooklyn, what did you say about a baby?"

"I—I'm two months pregnant. I just found out a few days ago." My voice hitches as I try to get the words out. "I was going to tell you soon but I didn't know how. I didn't know if you would be mad or what. It was the antibiotics I took. I didn't do it on purpose, if that's what you're thinking."

As I keep talking, trying to explain how this happened, he falls to his knees, wraps his arms around me and puts his lips to my stomach. He holds me so tight that I fear he may squish little peanut right out of my belly.

He hears me grunt and loosens his grip. "Sorry." He looks up at me. "My God, Brooklyn. I'm going to be a dad?"

"Yes, Nate, you're going to be a daddy."

His eyes are brimming with tears and he blinks letting them roll down off his face and onto my shirt. "I didn't know until this very second," he says into my belly. "I didn't know that hearing those words would make me the happiest man alive."

He wipes his face off and looks around on the ground for the box that he dropped. He opens it up, still down on his knees, and looks up at me and says, "Brooklyn Anne Vaughn, just when I thought loving you more was impossible, you go and prove me wrong. My heart is yours. It will always belong to you, that is, if you'll have it . . . both of you." He rubs my tummy. Then he takes the ring from the box and holds it out to me. "Everything about you makes me a better man," he quotes a verse from our song, taking yet another piece of my heart and meshing it with his. "Will you please make all my dreams come true by becoming my wife?"

I look down at my not-so-broken man and think of what he has done for me. Not just today, but every day. I reflect back on all of the times he has shared his most private thoughts and fears about his mom, his ex-wife and baseball. I think about how he is always watching out for me and protecting me and I know he will extend that to our child and make a wonderful father.

Memories of dancing in the rain, bracelet inscriptions and his intricate sketches of me flood my thoughts. Of course I'm going to say yes. Any other answer was never an option.

"Yes," I squeak out through my joyful sobs. "Of course, yes!" I cry out as he slips the most beautiful diamond I've ever seen onto my finger.

Chapter Thirty-two

Nate pulls me down to the blanket and kisses me with the intensity of the thousands of kisses that we have missed over the past five weeks. He worships my lips with his lips and my body with his hands. He whispers in my ear that he is going to touch every inch of my body first with his hands, then with his tongue.

Moisture spreads between my thighs as I anticipate what he promises to do. My desire builds quicker than I thought possible, simply by the friction of his body rubbing on mine. Before I realize it, I'm being pulled under, my body a boneless fit of quivering mass as he is pinching and tugging my nipples through my shirt.

"Wow," I say to him, surprised as he is at what just happened.

"Damn." He looks at me with desire streaming from his eyes. "We should have ten kids if this is what pregnancy does to you."

I giggle at him but quickly find it is no longer funny, but so incredibly sexy, when he gets up and removes all of his clothing. I lie here and admire every curve and ridge of his gorgeous body that I have missed more than I can say. I practically drool when his erection springs free from his boxer briefs and stands at full attention before me.

He can see I'm already building up again so he wastes no time removing my clothing as well, only stopping when he unbuttons my jeans to place a gentle kiss onto my belly. When he has me stripped completely naked, he starts down at my feet and delivers on the promise he made to me moments ago. He touches, kisses and licks up each leg and each arm before he again claims my mouth.

"Nate, please," I beg. "It's been so long."

"I know, baby, and that is why I need to savor every beautiful part of your incredible body." He continues licking and sucking his way up to my ear and around my neck before he descends upon my breasts.

He takes them into his hands and moans in pleasure, "God, Brooklyn, your boobs got bigger. I mean they were perfect before, but the surprises keep coming." He smiles appreciatively and takes each of my nipples, in turn, into his mouth. He sucks and pulls and puts just enough pressure to make me writhe and moan beneath him. "I've missed that sound." He looks up at me. "I've missed everything about you so goddamn much."

A happy tear slips from my eye. "Me, too, Nate. I've missed you more than words can say."

He trails kisses along each of my ribs down to my belly, where he spends some extra time. He mumbles something about baby and I can't tell if he is speaking to me or the peanut. And at this moment, I don't care. He has me wound up so tight that I'm going to come crashing down around him as soon as he touches me down there.

He tickles his fingers around my thighs, kissing and sucking everywhere but the spot that he knows will detonate me. Finally, after what seems like hours of tortuous pleasure, he slips a finger into my slick opening. He lets out a groan. "Oh, you are so wet for me."

Then he leans down again and slowly, sensuously runs his tongue along my cleft sending waves of hot-white heat through my body. He assaults my clit with flicks and laves of his tongue while two fingers work their way in and out of me.

He reaches up to pinch my nipple and that's all it takes to push me over the edge and send me spiraling into pleasurable explosions of need and desire. I grip his hair as my thighs clench his head, holding him captive while I ride out the flood of sensation that overwhelms me.

As I come down from the phenomenal orgasm he has just given me, he crawls up my body and says, "Jesus, Brooklyn, that was the hottest thing I've ever seen." He positions himself over me. "I can't wait another second to be inside of you."

"Then don't," I beg, as I lift my hips up to him while he slides his hard length inside me. I close my eyes and try to feel every bit of him as he slowly makes my every nerve ripple with pleasure as he works himself in and out of me. "That feels incredible. I love you so much. I promise I'll be yours forever."

He stiffens and grips my flesh, panting whispers of love in my ear as he finds his release, shooting his hot stream deep inside me. His rough, sexy whispers bring me to my own third glorious climax.

I don't think I can move and I belatedly hope that nobody will pull up and see us in our full naked glory here in the bright mid-day sun. However, I'm not sure I would even care.

Nate reaches over to the cooler and pulls out a bottle of champagne and two glasses. He shrugs and says, "Sorry." He nods to my stomach. "I didn't know or I would have brought sparkling water."

"A sip won't hurt the peanut," I tell him. "We have to celebrate."

"The peanut?" He raises his eyebrows at me and I nod.

Thirty minutes later we are packing up to head back. Nate types out a text on his phone. "Work stuff," he tells me when I look at him sideways.

We hold hands and talk about the peanut the entire way back home and I feel like this is the most natural thing in the world. By the time we pull up behind the bakery, my face hurts from the grin I've had plastered on it for the last twenty minutes.

We enter through the bakery door and I turn to go upstairs when Nate says, "Come with me, I want to show you something." He has a huge smile on his face like a kid on Christmas morning.

I follow him to the front of the shop. When he pulls me through the swinging door, we hear, "Congratulations!" collectively from what looks to be everyone who matters to me in the whole world.

I look at the happy faces of my parents, my best friend, her husband, Ryan and the rest of my staff. Nate's dad and sister are here. Even Michael's sister, Janie, is here. She has tears rolling down her smiling face as she nods her head at me like she finally understands what happened at Michael's grave. Every single person that I could dream about sharing this moment with is right in this room.

I turn to Nate. "The text?"

He nods at me. "God, Brooklyn, I was so scared you would say no. I've been planning this for weeks. With lots of help, of course." He gestures to Ryan and Emma.

Ryan walks up and to my surprise, Nate shakes his hand and gives him one of those man hugs. "Thanks for all your help, buddy," Nate says to him.

I give Ryan a hug. "You don't have to do this," I say, referring to the new contract. "I won't sign it, you know."

"You will sign it, Lyn." He smiles. "I have a strict policy never to be in business with family."

We greet everyone in turn. I learn that Nate asked my dad for my hand in marriage. He also has Emma doing the interior design for the new bakery. The shop staff put this party together all without my knowledge.

Emma walks over and hugs me, tears streaming down both our faces. "You said yes! I'm so happy for you."

"Well, how could I say no to the guy who tattooed a cupcake on his body for me?" I say, earning laughs from everyone around me.

"Speaking of cupcakes, what's with only having red velvet?" Emma points over to a display table adorned with a beautiful setting of dozens of red velvet cupcakes.

Nate walks us over to the table and picks one up. "For luck," he says. "I have one before every game." I think back to that night in high school when he told me about his pre-game routine with the red velvet cupcakes. He holds me tight and kisses my cheek. "And this will be, by far, the biggest game of my life."

Nate takes me to the side, pulling me down onto his lap at a table in the corner. "You know, the game has changed now." He rubs a thumb over my belly. "I don't think I can live one day without you . . . without peanut." He takes a breath and runs his hand through his hair. "What do you say, Brooklyn. Will you two move to Raleigh with me?"

He bites his lip and entwines our fingers as he awaits my response.

I look at my larger-than-life man. He is not perfect. He may always have issues with trust. He may always have issues with his mother. But I can't imagine not having him in my life. I look around at the party and see how much everyone loves him. How they've all gone out of their way to help him win me back. They know we belong together. I know we belong together. The road may not always be easy. But then again, it's the bumps in the road that make us stronger. I rub a finger over my bracelet and remember another man I was engaged to. Then I look down at the ring that sits on my left ring finger.

I look into the alluring blue eyes of my new fiancé and realize that he is my home. I can't live without him, I can't breathe without him. Of course I'm going to say yes. Any other answer was never an option.

"Yes." I smile and raise an eyebrow at my strong, incredible man. "But there will be ground rules."

Acknowledgments

The writing of this book was the result of an epiphany. Maybe it was my age. Maybe it was the stay-at-home mom in me wondering if I would leave a legacy other than the four children I am raising. Maybe it took getting out that piece of paper to write my bucket list. But, whatever it was . . . it couldn't have come at a better time in my life.

The journey to create this novel was surreal. Twenty years ago, I wanted to become a writer. It was a pipe dream, a fantasy; something only other people could do. And now, here I sit writing acknowledgments that will appear in the back of my—*my*—published work.

I have to thank the endless support of my editors, Jeannie Hinkle and Ann Peters. If it weren't for the hours upon end that you corrected my grammar and punctuation, this novel would not have been worthy to be published. Thank you to my beta readers Stephanie Smith and Lisa Crawford, whose input and support carried me through when I was ready to set my manuscript on fire.

Most of all, I need to thank my family. My four children have grown up rather quickly during all of this. My younger ones have learned all the intricacies of microwave cooking due to the endless supply of frozen meals I've bestowed upon them over the past several months. My older children have baby-sat, carpooled and mediated adolescent arguments more than should be required of young adults.

My husband has intimate knowledge of every fast food place within twenty miles of our house. Honey, for you to work as hard as you do and come home to an empty kitchen, never to complain—I'll never be able to thank you enough. Having a husband who will allow me to follow any dream, no matter how ludicrous it seems, is the main reason I am who I am today. Bruce, you are and will always . . . be my reason.

About the Author

Samantha Christy's passion for writing started long before her first novel was published. Graduating from the University of Nebraska with a degree in Criminal Justice, she held the title of Computer Systems Analyst for The Supreme Court of Wisconsin and several major universities around the United States. Raised mainly in Indianapolis, she holds the Midwest and its homegrown values dear to her heart and upon the birth of her third child devoted herself to raising her family full time. While it took some time to get from there to here, writing has remained her utmost passion and being a stay-at-home mom facilitated her ability to follow that dream. When she is not writing, she keeps busy cruising to every Caribbean island where ships sail. Samantha Christy currently resides in St. Augustine, Florida with her husband and four children.

You can reach Samantha Christy through her website www.samanthachristy.com.